SACRAMENTO PUBLIC LIBRARY
828 "I" Street
Sacramento, CA 95814
06/18

D0466882

ANGRY BIRDS™

GAME PLAY

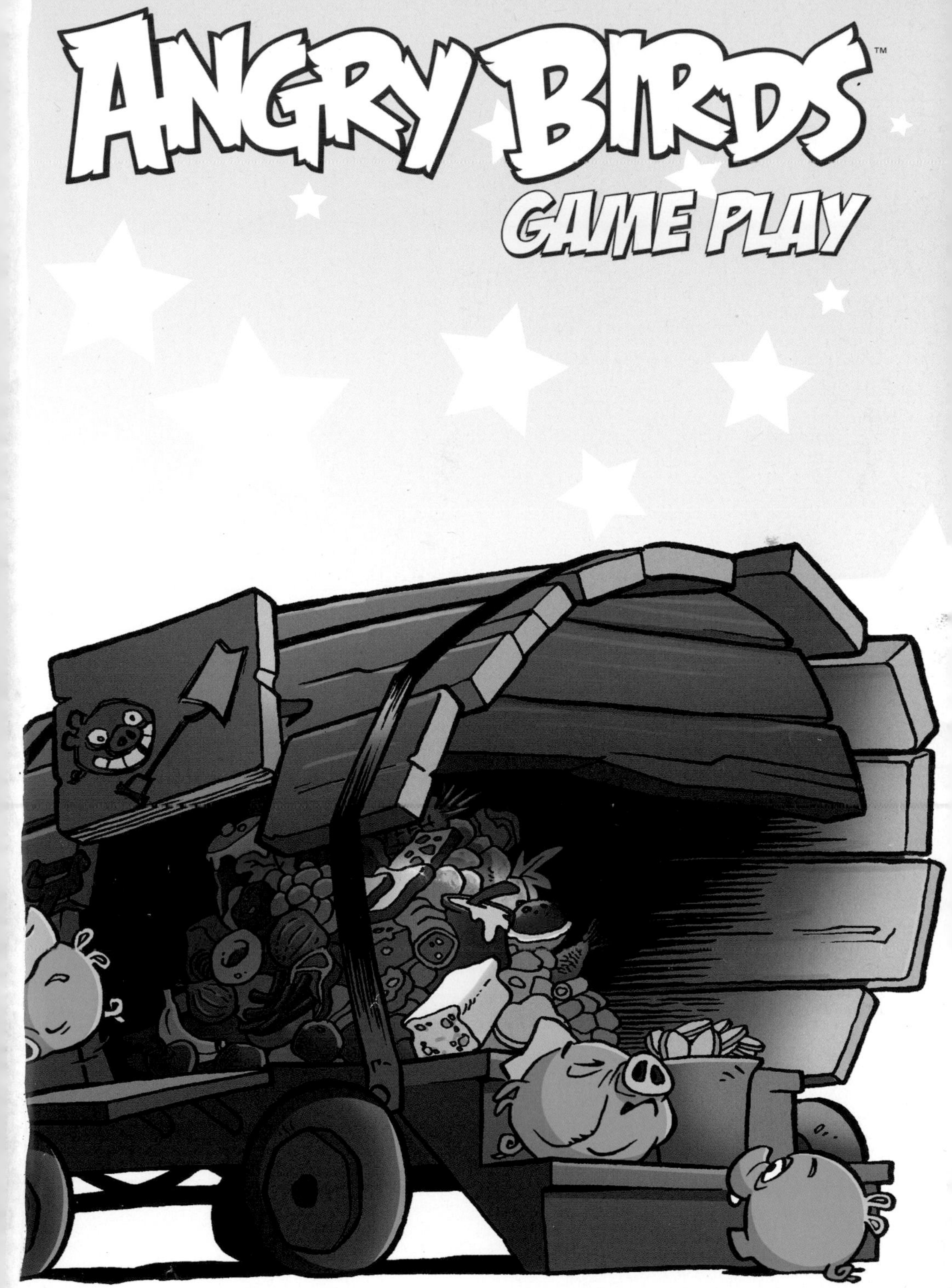

COVER ARTWORK BY: CIRO CANGIALOSI
EDITED FOR IDW BY: DAVID HEDGECOCK
EDITORIAL ASSISTANCE BY: DAVID MARIOTTE
COLLECTION EDITS BY: JUSTIN EISINGER & ALONZO SIMON
COLLECTION PRODUCTION BY: SHAWN LEE
PUBLISHER: TED ADAMS

KAIKEN
PUBLISHING LTD.

Mikael Hed, Chairman of the Board
Laura Nevanlinna, Publishing Director
Jukka Heiskanen, Editor-in-Chief, Comics
Juha Mäkinen, Editor, Comics
Terhi Haikonen, AD
Nathan Cosby, Freelance Editor

ROVIO

Thanks to Jukka Heiskanen, Juha Mäkinen and the Kaiken team for their hard work and invaluable assistance.

For international rights, contact licensing@idwpublishing.com

ISBN: 978-1-63140-973-8

20 19 18 17   1 2 3 4

www.IDWPUBLISHING.com

Ted Adams, CEO & Publisher • Greg Goldstein, President & COO • Robbie Robbins, EVP/Sr. Graphic Artist • Chris Ryall, Chief Creative Officer •
David Hedgecock, Editor-in-Chief • Laurie Windrow, Senior Vice President of Sales & Marketing • Matthew Ruzicka, CPA, Chief Financial Officer •
Lorelei Bunjes, VP of Digital Services • Jerry Bennington, VP of New Product Development

Facebook: facebook.com/idwpublishing • Twitter: @idwpublishing • YouTube: youtube.com/idwpublishing
Tumblr: tumblr.idwpublishing.com • Instagram: instagram.com/idwpublishing

ANGRY BIRDS COMICS: GAME PLAY. OCTOBER 2017. FIRST PRINTING. © 2009-2017 Rovio Entertainment Ltd. Rovio, Angry Birds, Bad Piggies, Mighty Eagle and all related titles, logos and characters are trademarks of Rovio
Entertainment Ltd. All Rights Reserved. © 2017 Idea and Design Works, LLC. The IDW logo is registered in the U.S. Patent and Trademark Office. IDW Publishing, a division of Idea and Design Works, LLC. Editorial offices: 2765 Truxtun
Road, San Diego, CA 92106. Any similarities to persons living or dead are purely coincidental. With the exception of artwork used for review purposes, none of the contents of this publication may be reprinted without the permission of
Idea and Design Works, LLC. Printed in Korea. IDW Publishing does not read or accept unsolicited submissions of ideas, stories, or artwork.

Originally published as ANGRY BIRDS GAME PLAY issues #1-3.

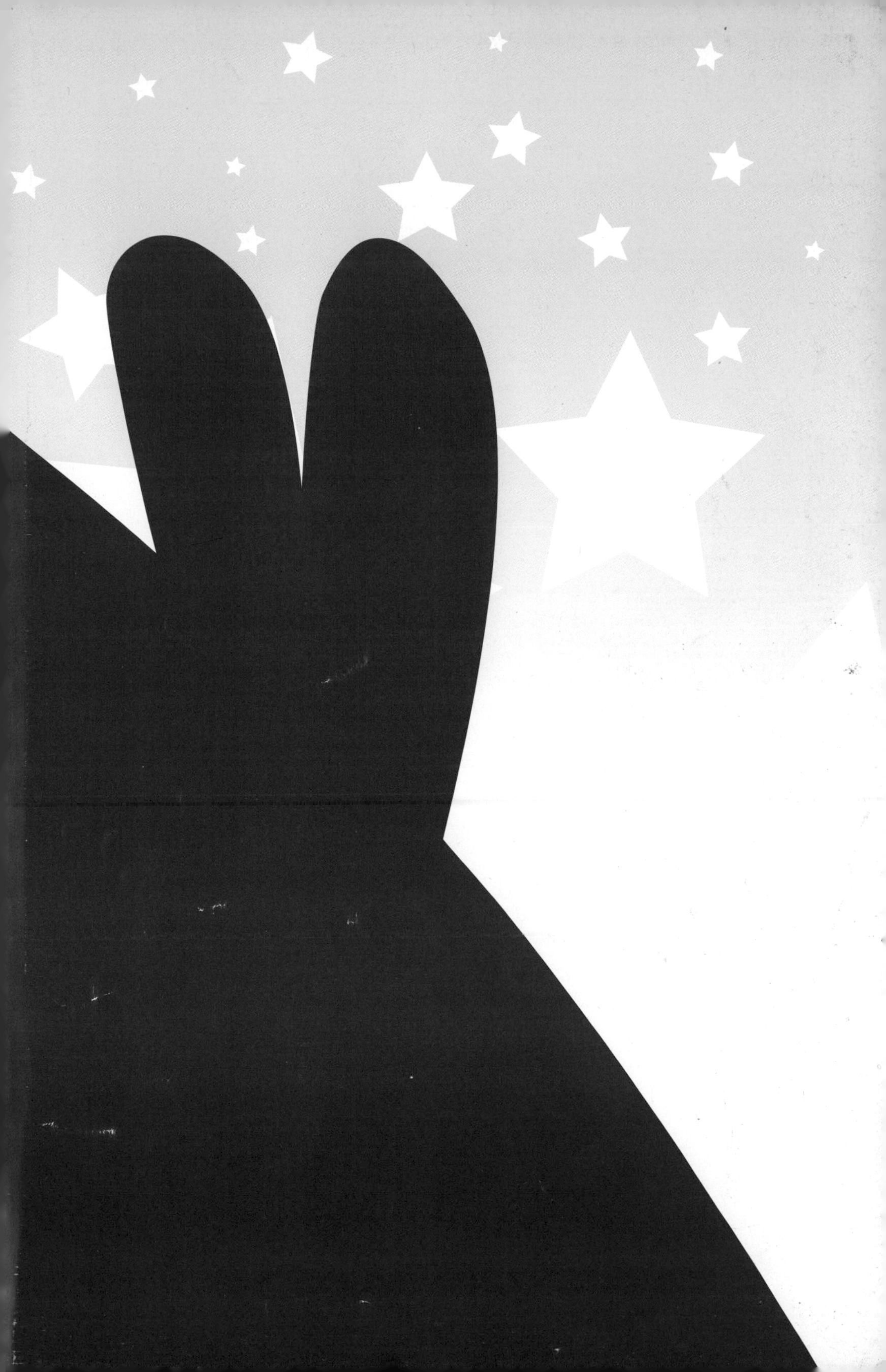

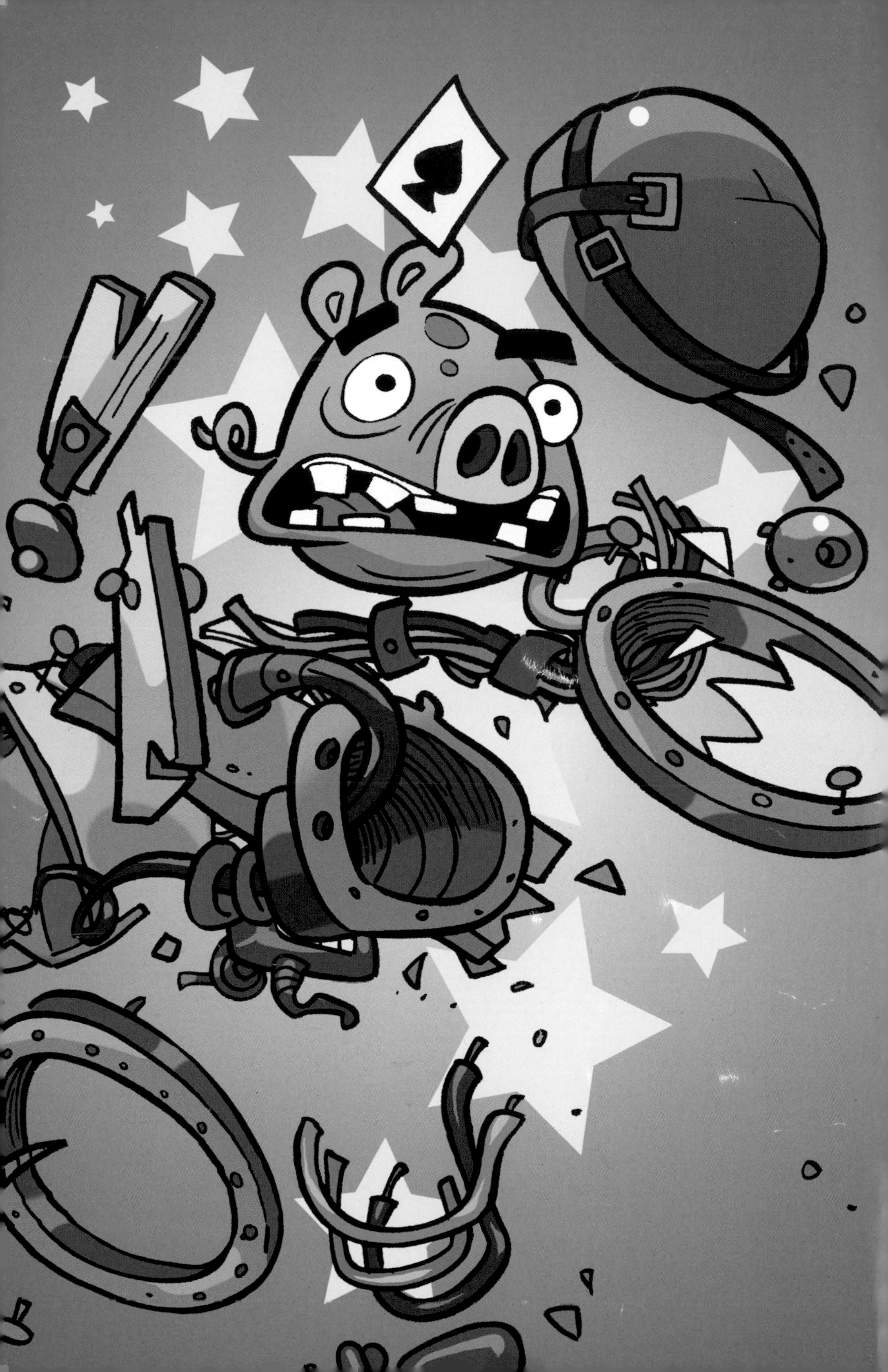

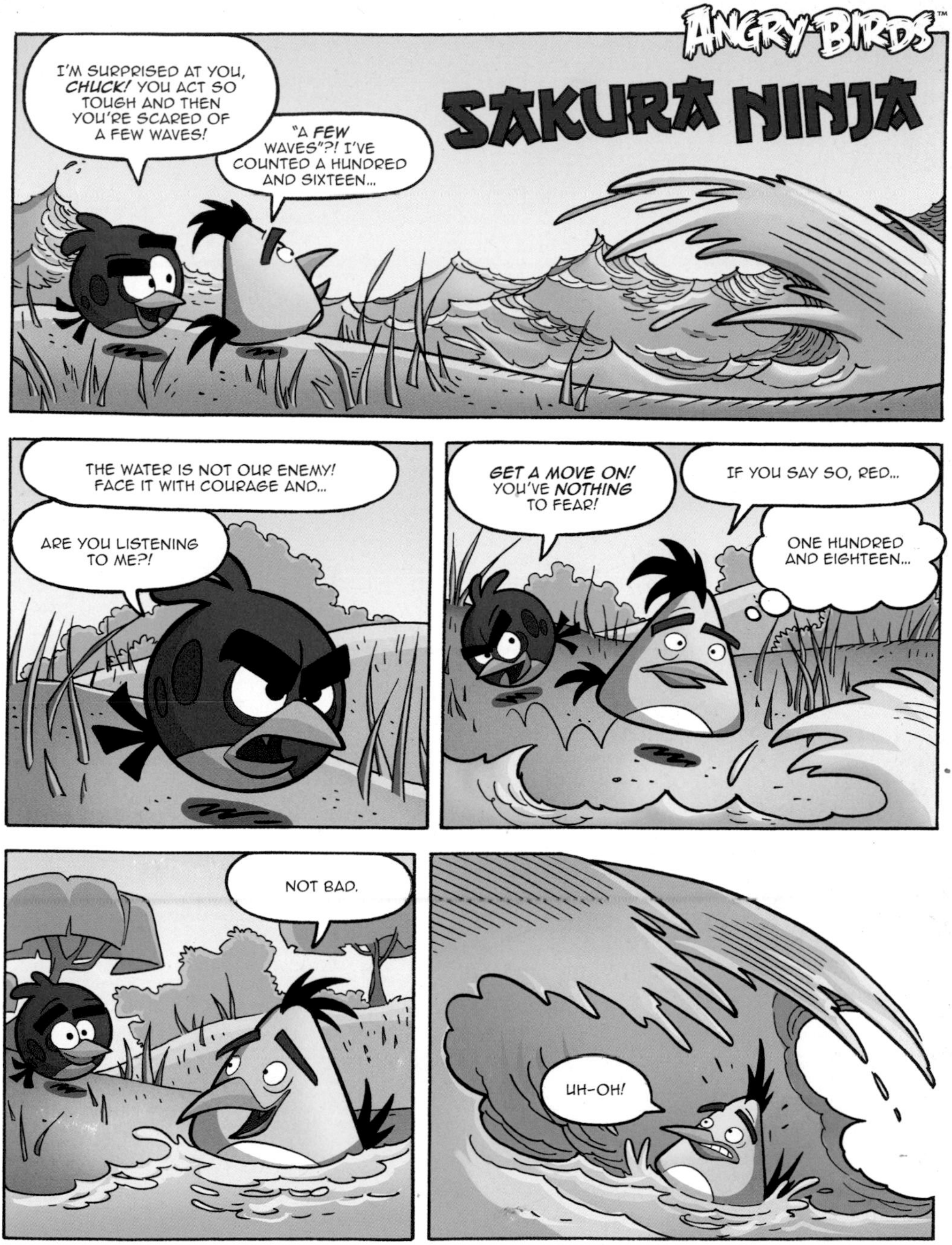
ANGRY BIRDS™
SAKURA NINJA
I'M SURPRISED AT YOU, *CHUCK!* YOU ACT SO TOUGH AND THEN YOU'RE SCARED OF A FEW WAVES!
"A *FEW* WAVES"?! I'VE COUNTED A HUNDRED AND SIXTEEN...
THE WATER IS NOT OUR ENEMY! FACE IT WITH COURAGE AND...
ARE YOU LISTENING TO ME?!
GET A MOVE ON! YOU'VE *NOTHING* TO FEAR!
IF YOU SAY SO, RED...
ONE HUNDRED AND EIGHTEEN...
NOT BAD.
UH-OH!

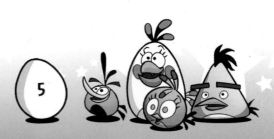

Written by: Tito Faraci
Art by: Giorgio Cavazzano
Colors by: Digikore
Letters by: Pisara Oy

DON'T WORRY! IT'S JUST WATER!
EHM...
THUMP!
URGH!
"JUST WATER"... "NOTHING TO FEAR"?!
I DON'T LIKE YOUR ATTITUDE!
QUICK! LET'S GET THIS TRUNK UP ON SHORE!
ONE HUNDRED AND EIGHTE... NO, NINETEEN!

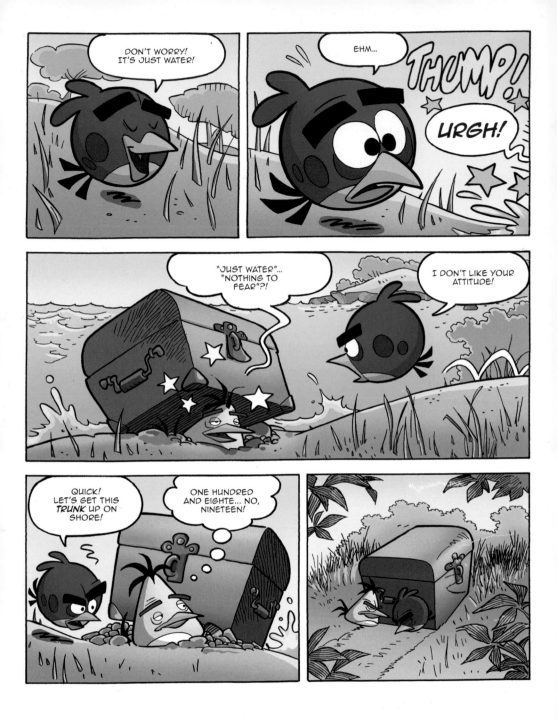

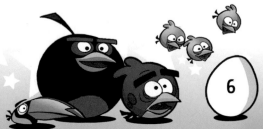

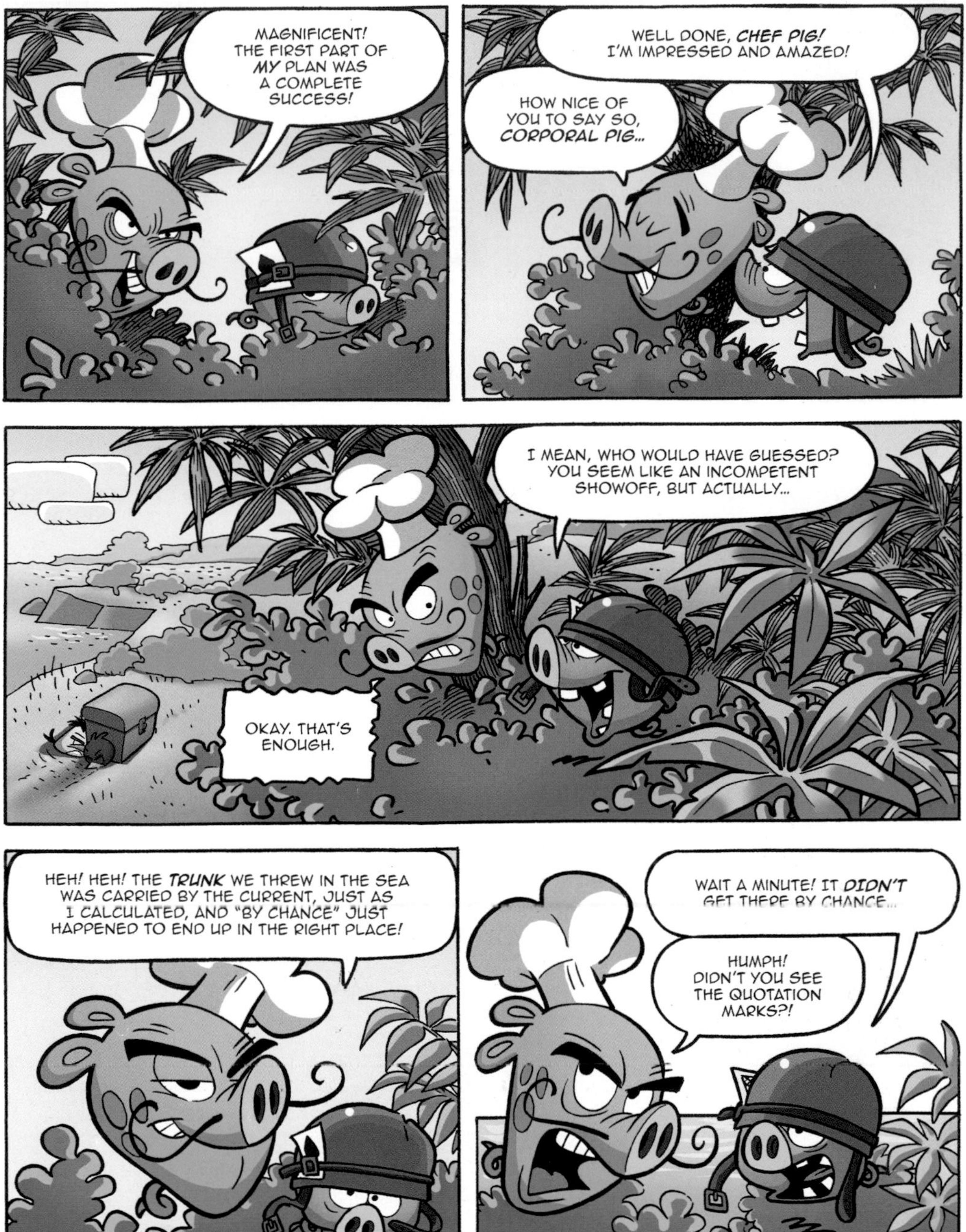
MAGNIFICENT! THE FIRST PART OF MY PLAN WAS A COMPLETE SUCCESS!
WELL DONE, CHEF PIG! I'M IMPRESSED AND AMAZED!
HOW NICE OF YOU TO SAY SO, CORPORAL PIG...
I MEAN, WHO WOULD HAVE GUESSED? YOU SEEM LIKE AN INCOMPETENT SHOWOFF, BUT ACTUALLY...
OKAY. THAT'S ENOUGH.
HEH! HEH! THE TRUNK WE THREW IN THE SEA WAS CARRIED BY THE CURRENT, JUST AS I CALCULATED, AND "BY CHANCE" JUST HAPPENED TO END UP IN THE RIGHT PLACE!
WAIT A MINUTE! IT DIDN'T GET THERE BY CHANCE...
HUMPH! DIDN'T YOU SEE THE QUOTATION MARKS?!

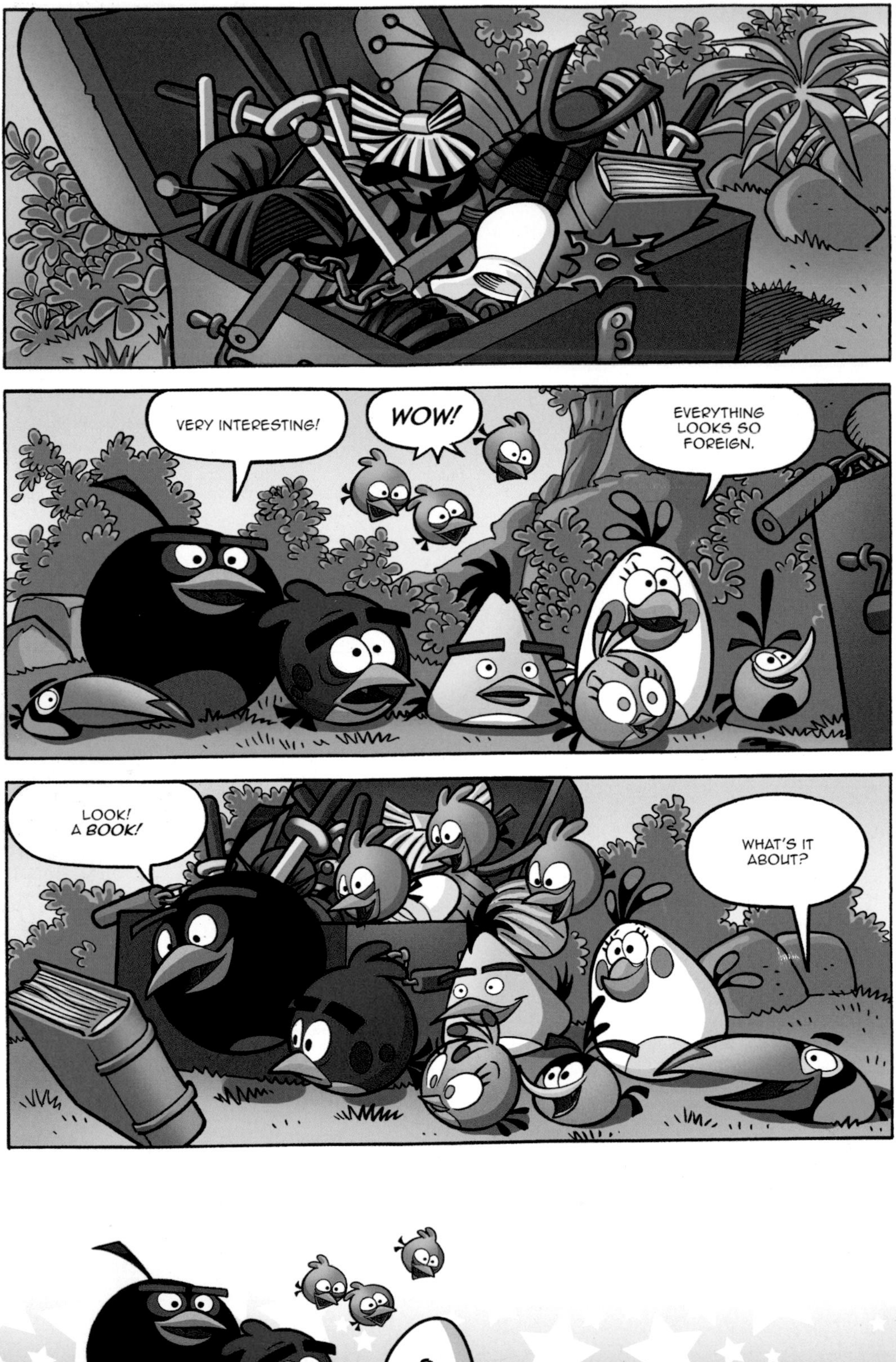
VERY INTERESTING!
WOW!
EVERYTHING LOOKS SO FOREIGN.
LOOK! A BOOK!
WHAT'S IT ABOUT?

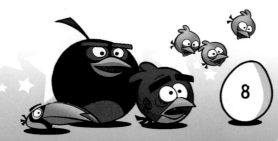

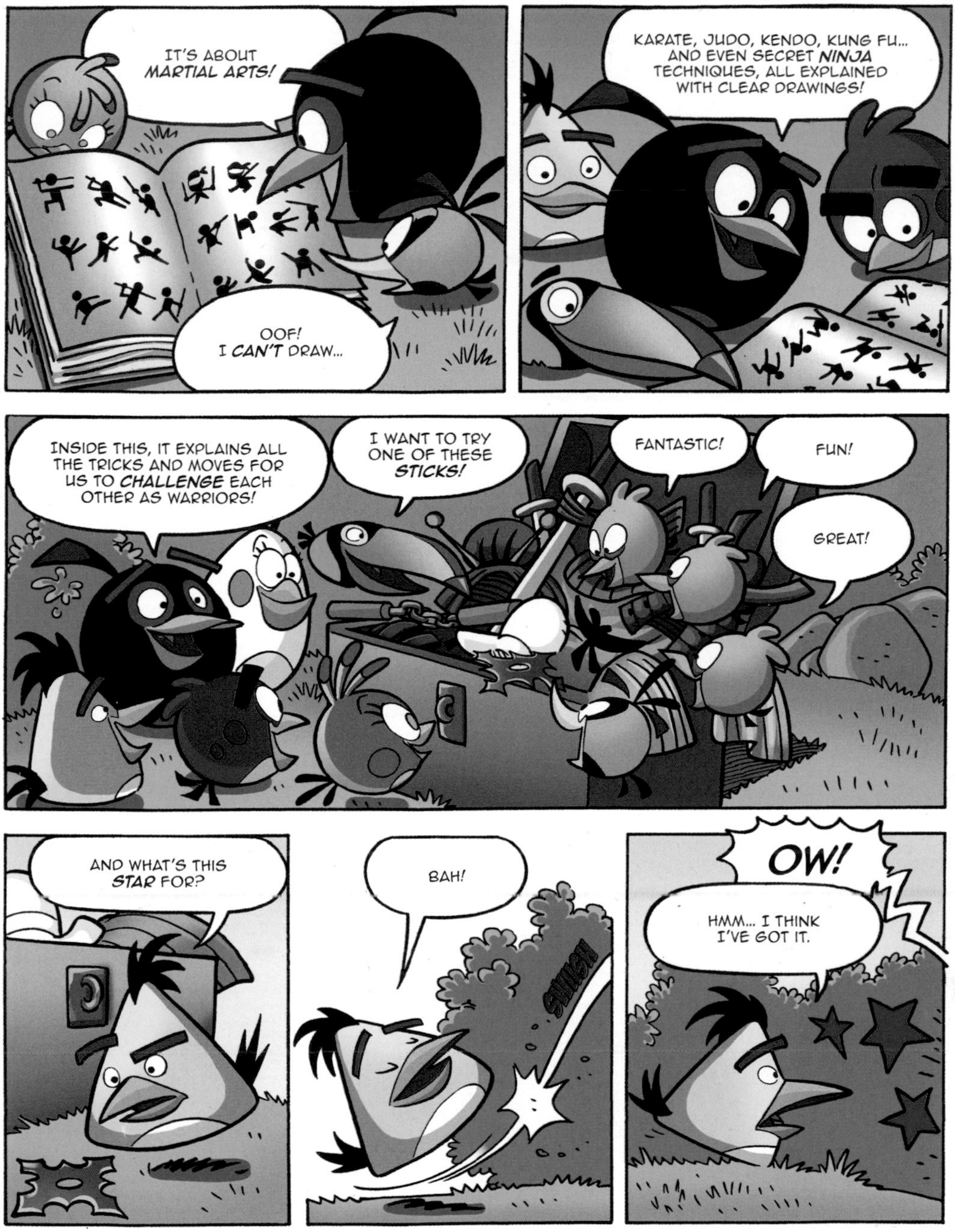
IT'S ABOUT MARTIAL ARTS!
OOF! I CAN'T DRAW...
KARATE, JUDO, KENDO, KUNG FU... AND EVEN SECRET NINJA TECHNIQUES, ALL EXPLAINED WITH CLEAR DRAWINGS!
INSIDE THIS, IT EXPLAINS ALL THE TRICKS AND MOVES FOR US TO CHALLENGE EACH OTHER AS WARRIORS!
I WANT TO TRY ONE OF THESE STICKS!
FANTASTIC!
FUN!
GREAT!
AND WHAT'S THIS STAR FOR?
BAH!
SHUSH
OW!
HMM... I THINK I'VE GOT IT.

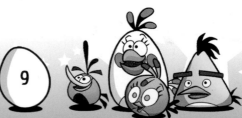

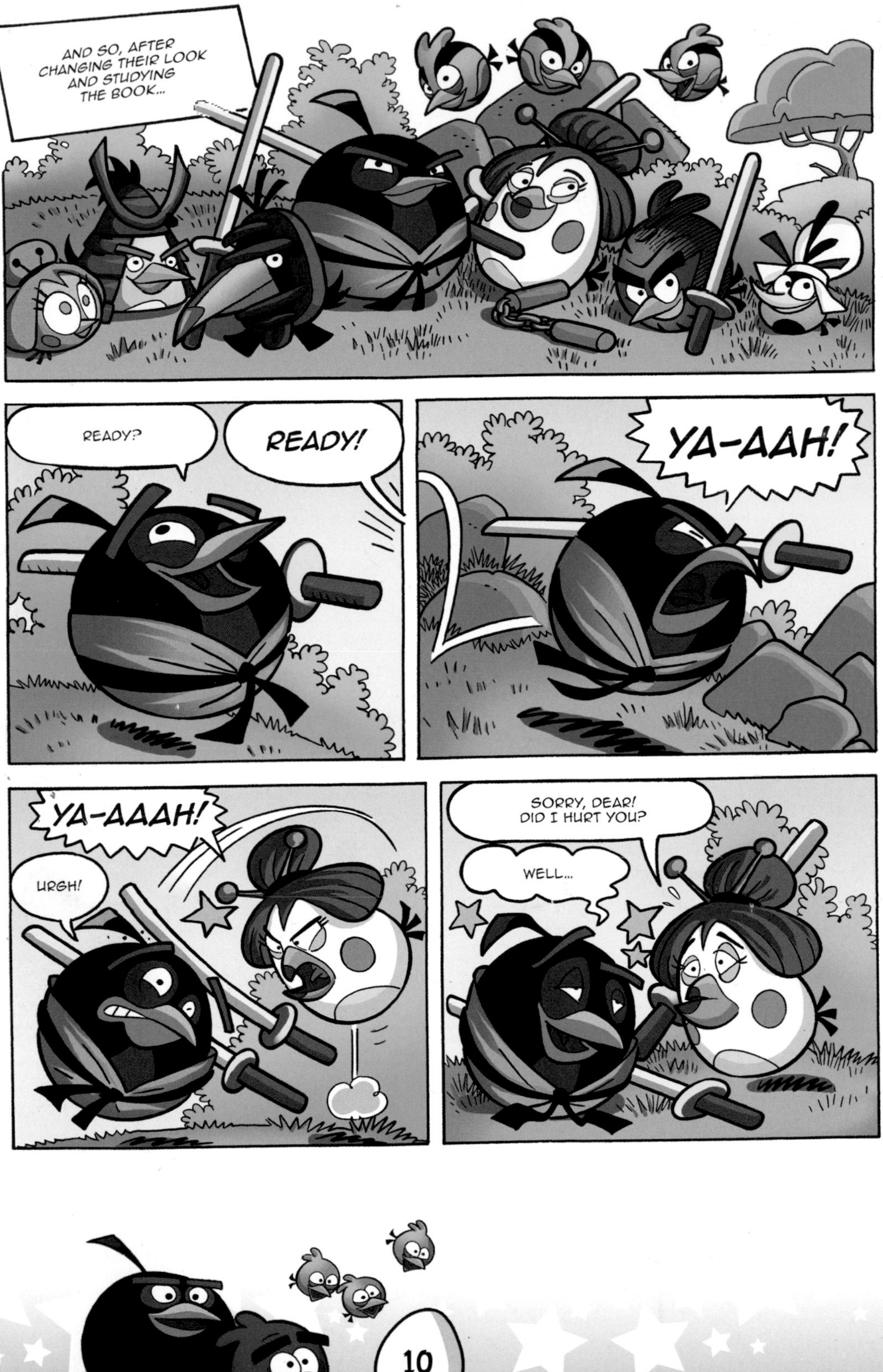
AND SO, AFTER CHANGING THEIR LOOK AND STUDYING THE BOOK...
READY?
READY!
YA-AAH!
YA-AAAH!
URGH!
SORRY, DEAR! DID I HURT YOU?
WELL...

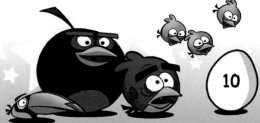

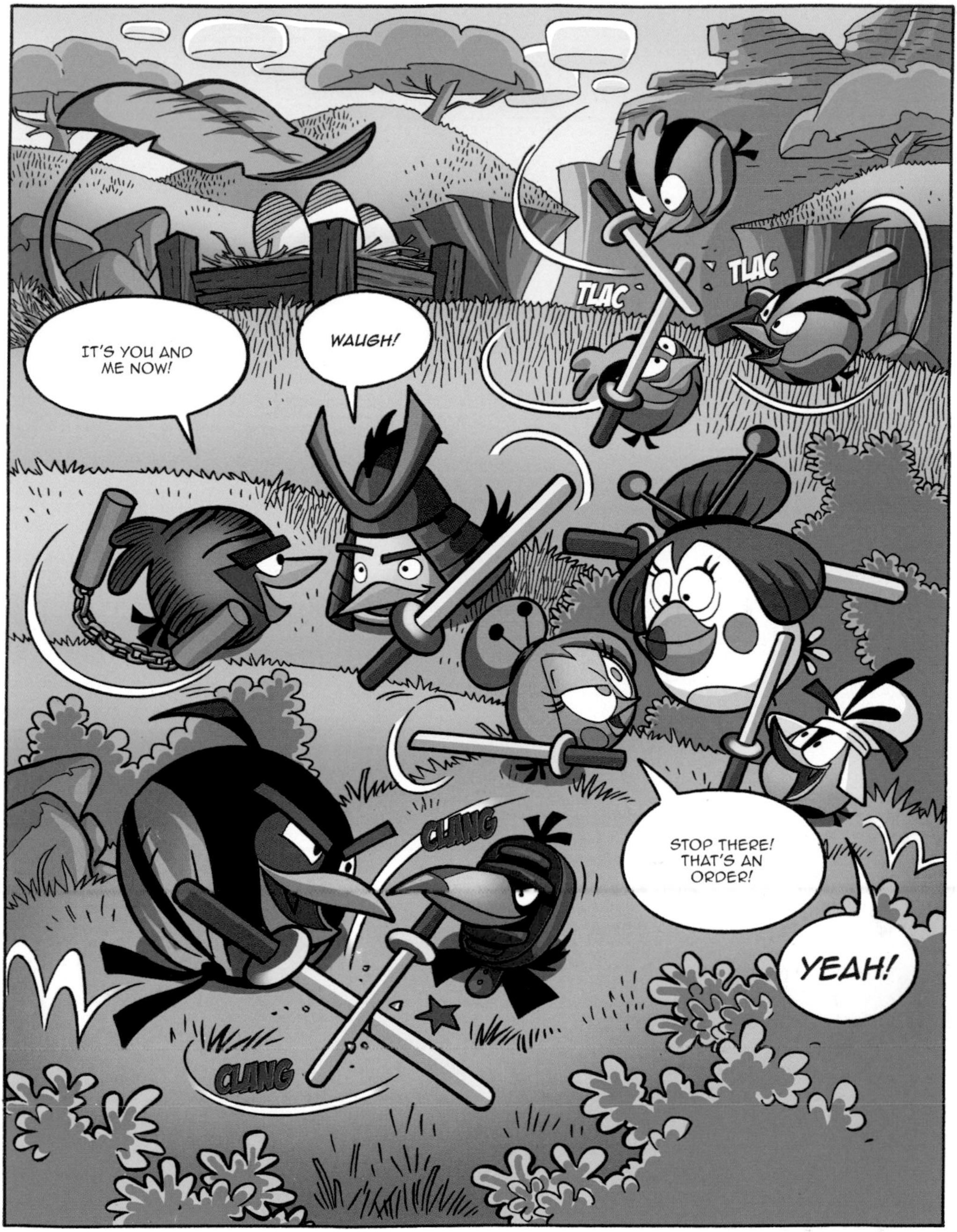
IT'S YOU AND ME NOW!
WAUGH!
TLAC
TLAC
CLANG
CLANG
STOP THERE! THAT'S AN ORDER!
YEAH!

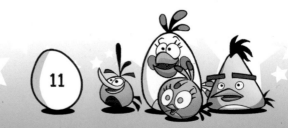

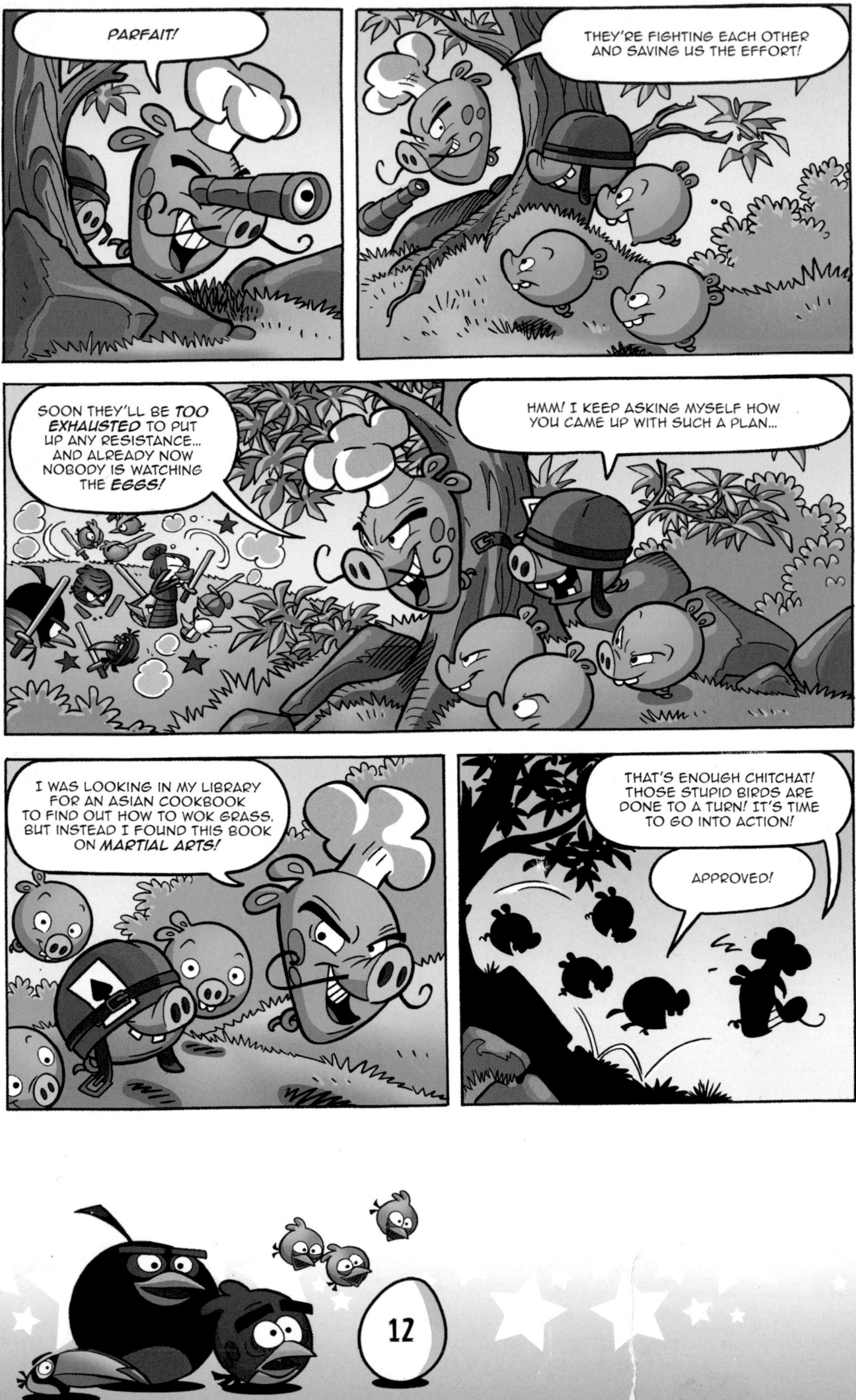
PARFAIT!
THEY'RE FIGHTING EACH OTHER AND SAVING US THE EFFORT!
SOON THEY'LL BE TOO EXHAUSTED TO PUT UP ANY RESISTANCE... AND ALREADY NOW NOBODY IS WATCHING THE EGGS!
HMM! I KEEP ASKING MYSELF HOW YOU CAME UP WITH SUCH A PLAN...
I WAS LOOKING IN MY LIBRARY FOR AN ASIAN COOKBOOK TO FIND OUT HOW TO WOK GRASS, BUT INSTEAD I FOUND THIS BOOK ON MARTIAL ARTS!
THAT'S ENOUGH CHITCHAT! THOSE STUPID BIRDS ARE DONE TO A TURN! IT'S TIME TO GO INTO ACTION!
APPROVED!

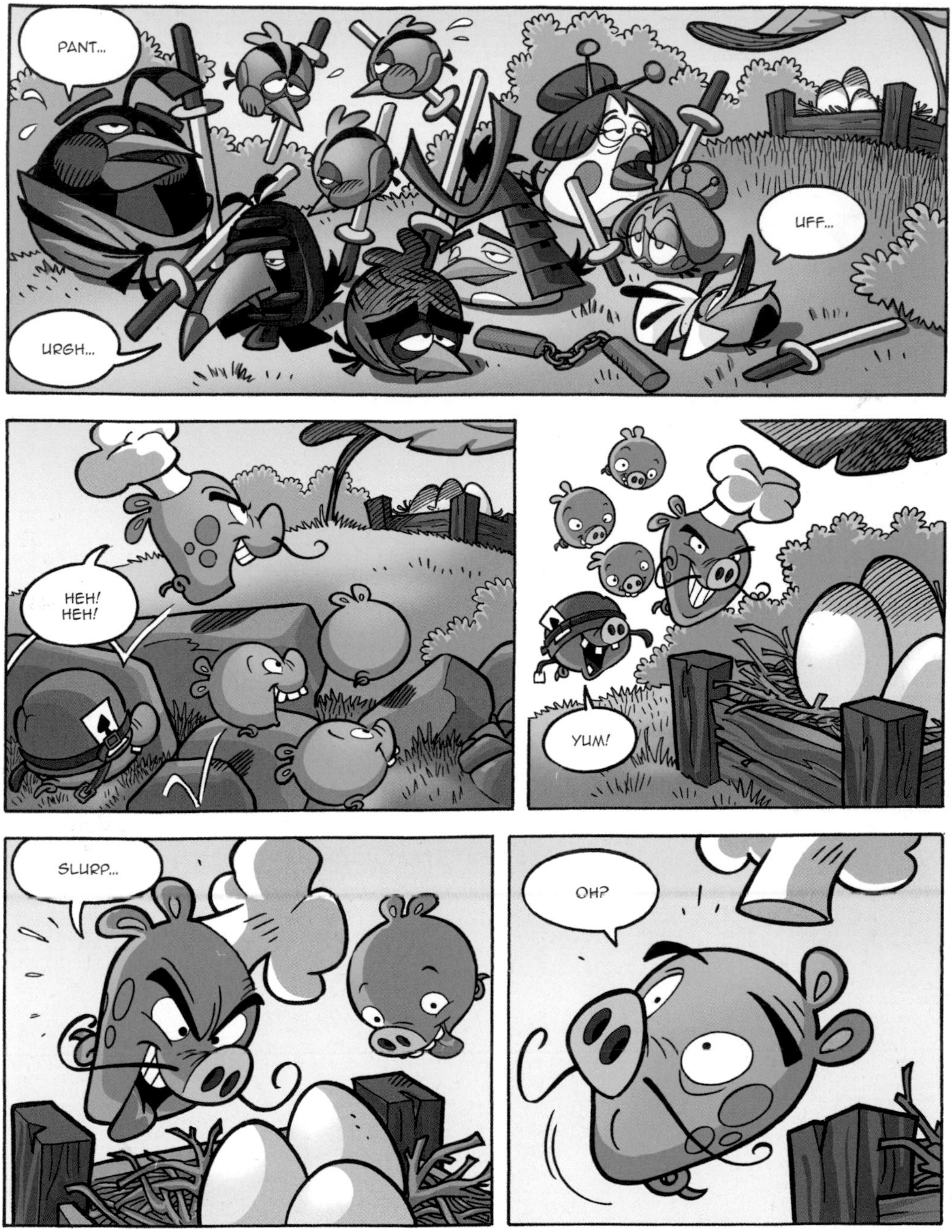
PANT...
URGH...
UFF...
HEH! HEH!
YUM!
SLURP...
OH?

OH NO! HEAVY-
WEIGHT ALERT!
AHEM!
I REALLY NEED
TO GO! I LEFT A
GRASS SOUFFLÉ
IN THE OVEN...
URGH!
WHAT'S GOING
ON THERE?
FIIIIIII!

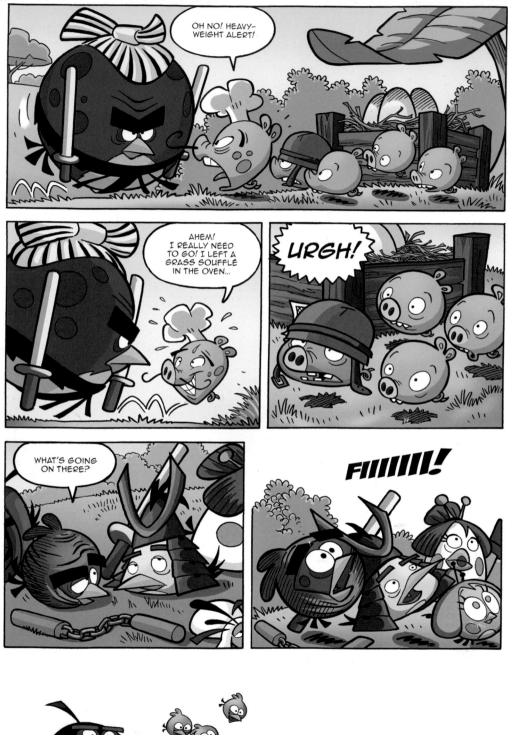

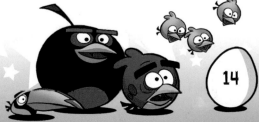

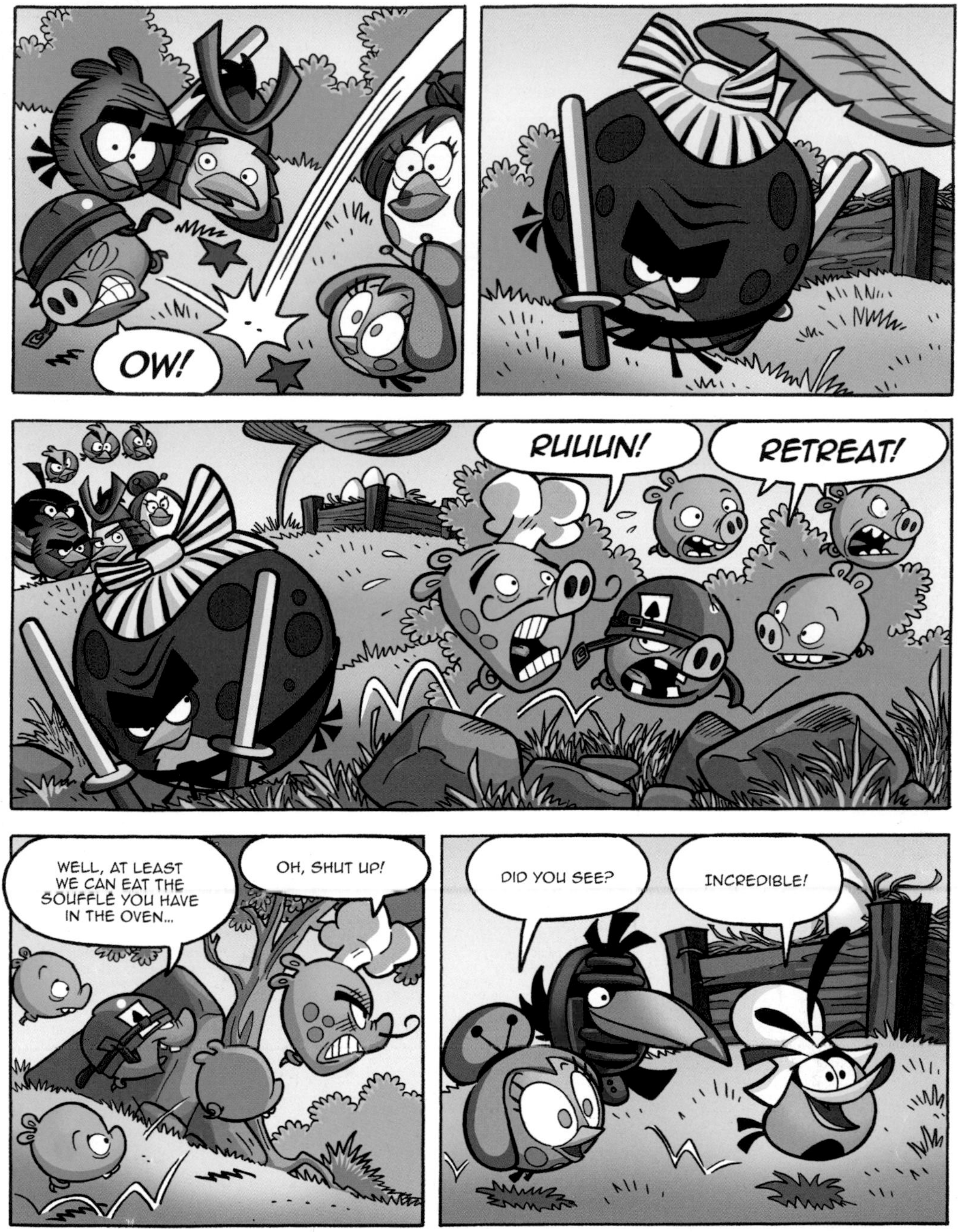
OW!
RUUUN!
RETREAT!
WELL, AT LEAST WE CAN EAT THE SOUFFLÉ YOU HAVE IN THE OVEN...
OH, SHUT UP!
DID YOU SEE?
INCREDIBLE!

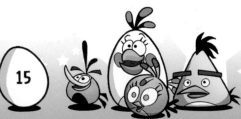

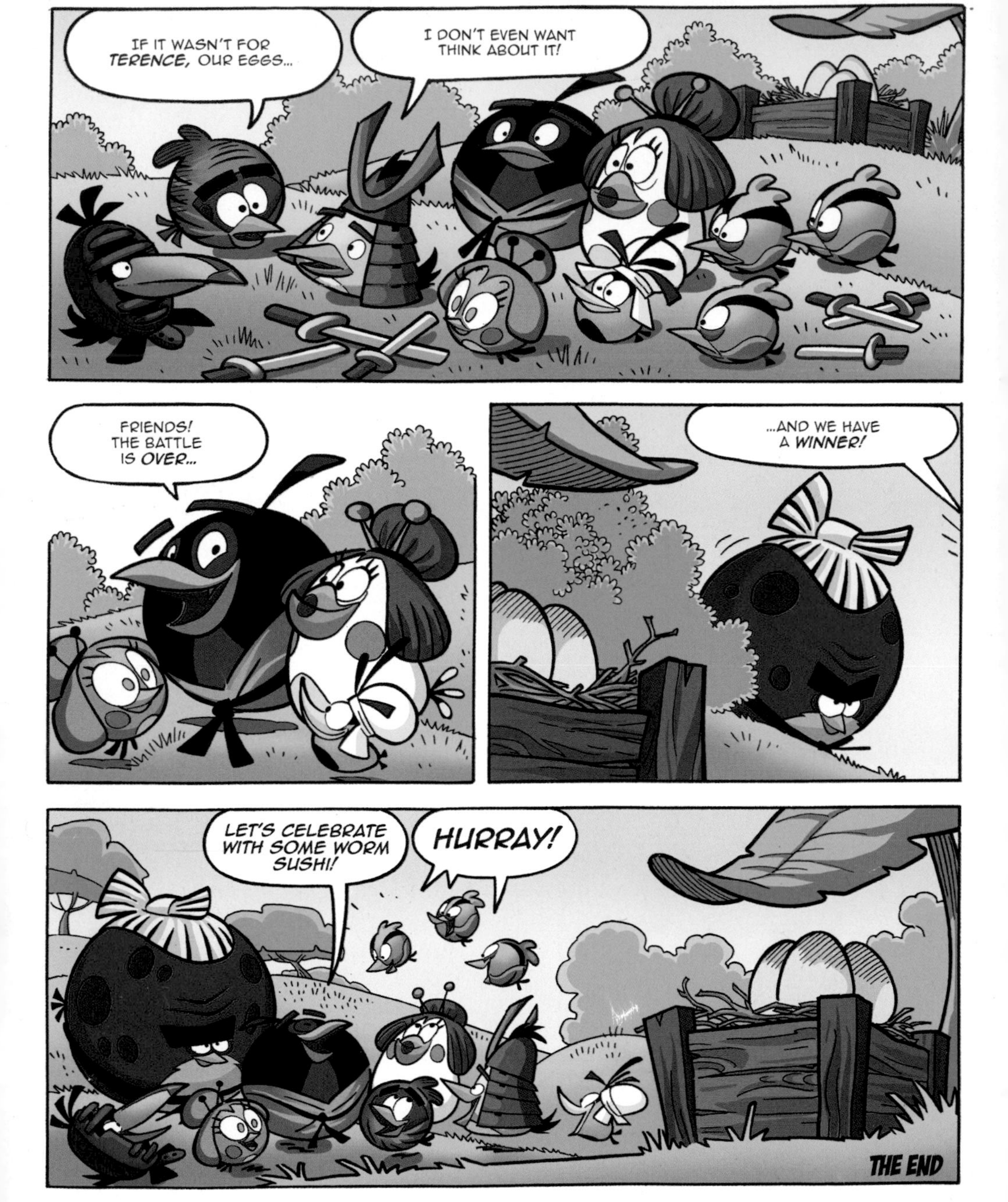
IF IT WASN'T FOR TERENCE, OUR EGGS...
I DON'T EVEN WANT THINK ABOUT IT!
FRIENDS! THE BATTLE IS OVER...
...AND WE HAVE A WINNER!
LET'S CELEBRATE WITH SOME WORM SUSHI!
HURRAY!
THE END

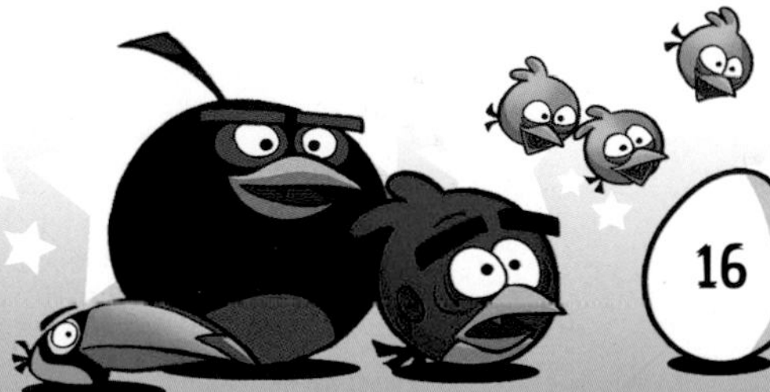

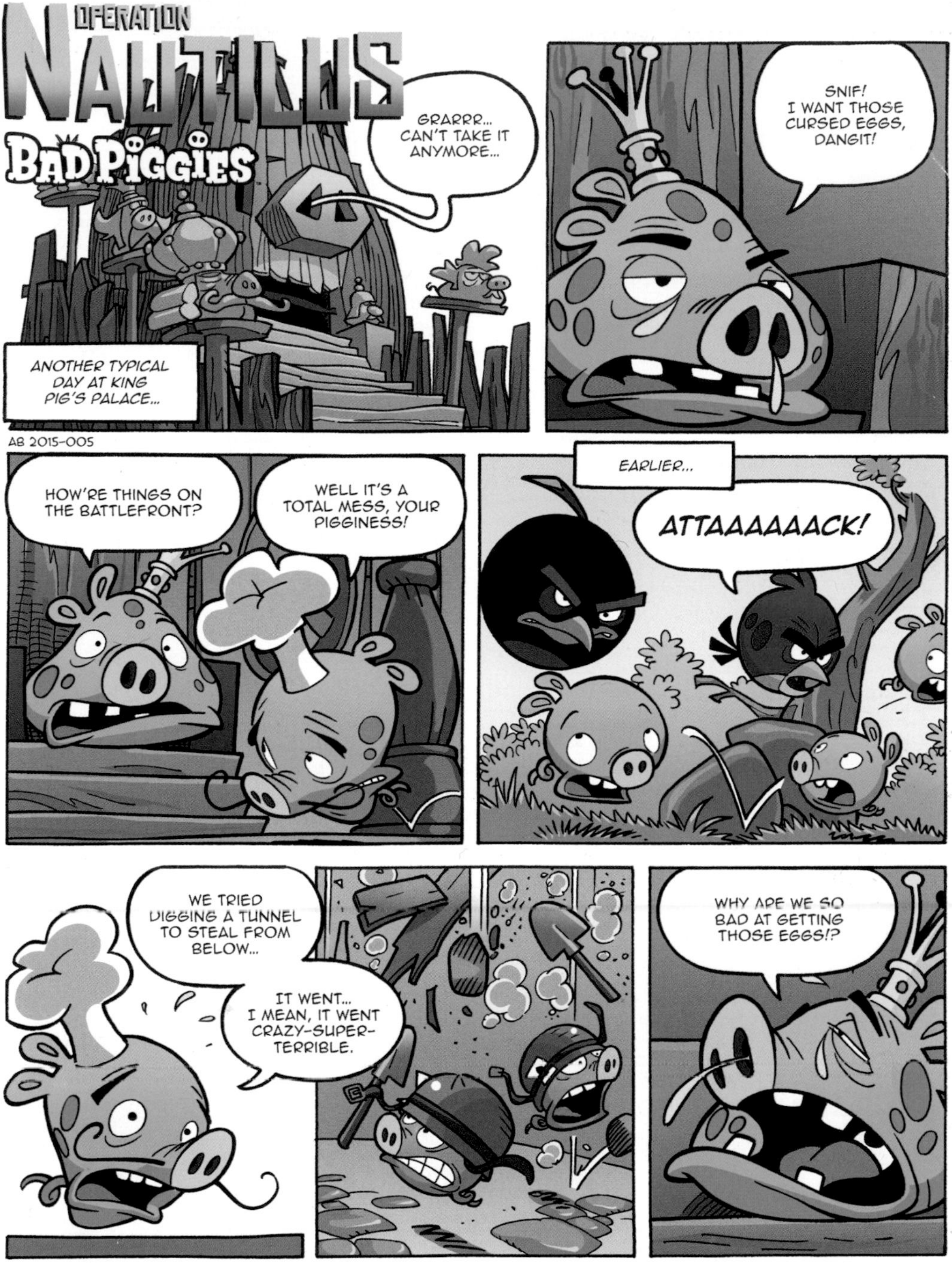
OPERATION
NAUTILUS
BAD PIGGIES
ANOTHER TYPICAL DAY AT KING PIG'S PALACE...
GRARRR... CAN'T TAKE IT ANYMORE...
SNIF! I WANT THOSE CURSED EGGS, DANGIT!
AB 2015-005
HOW'RE THINGS ON THE BATTLEFRONT?
WELL IT'S A TOTAL MESS, YOUR PIGGINESS!
EARLIER...
ATTAAAAAAACK!
WE TRIED DIGGING A TUNNEL TO STEAL FROM BELOW...
IT WENT... I MEAN, IT WENT CRAZY-SUPER-TERRIBLE.
WHY ARE WE SO BAD AT GETTING THOSE EGGS!?

Written by: Francois Corteggiani
Art by: Giorgio Cavazzano
Colors by: Digikore
Letters by: Pisara Oy

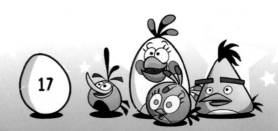

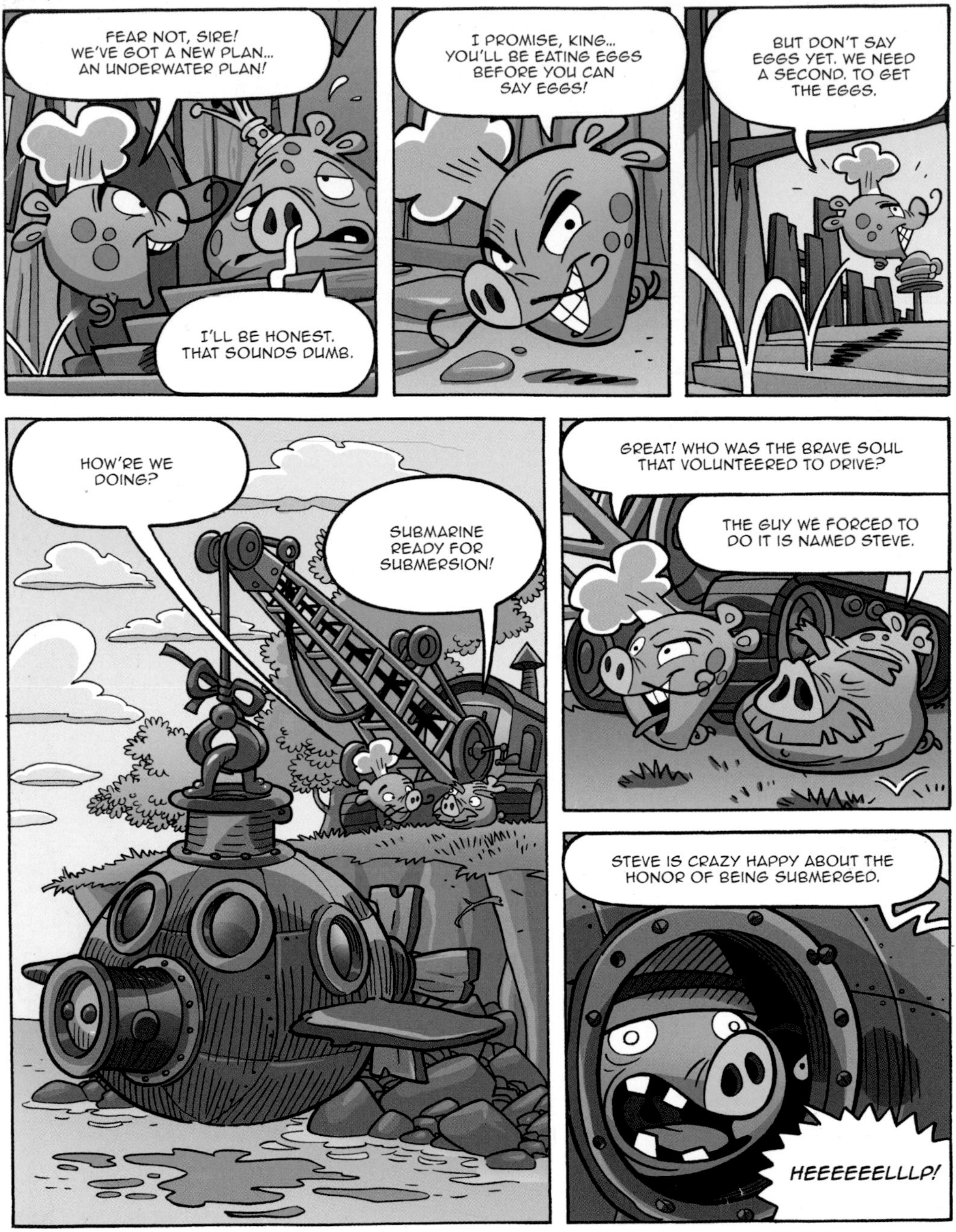
FEAR NOT, SIRE! WE'VE GOT A NEW PLAN... AN UNDERWATER PLAN!
I'LL BE HONEST. THAT SOUNDS DUMB.
I PROMISE, KING... YOU'LL BE EATING EGGS BEFORE YOU CAN SAY EGGS!
BUT DON'T SAY EGGS YET. WE NEED A SECOND. TO GET THE EGGS.
HOW'RE WE DOING?
SUBMARINE READY FOR SUBMERSION!
GREAT! WHO WAS THE BRAVE SOUL THAT VOLUNTEERED TO DRIVE?
THE GUY WE FORCED TO DO IT IS NAMED STEVE.
STEVE IS CRAZY HAPPY ABOUT THE HONOR OF BEING SUBMERGED.
HEEEEEELLLLP!

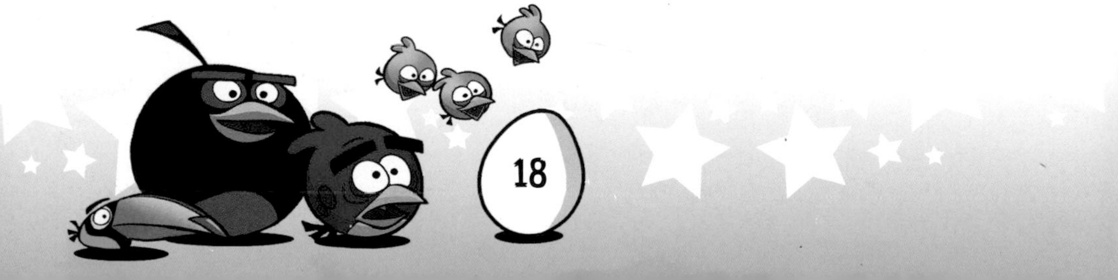

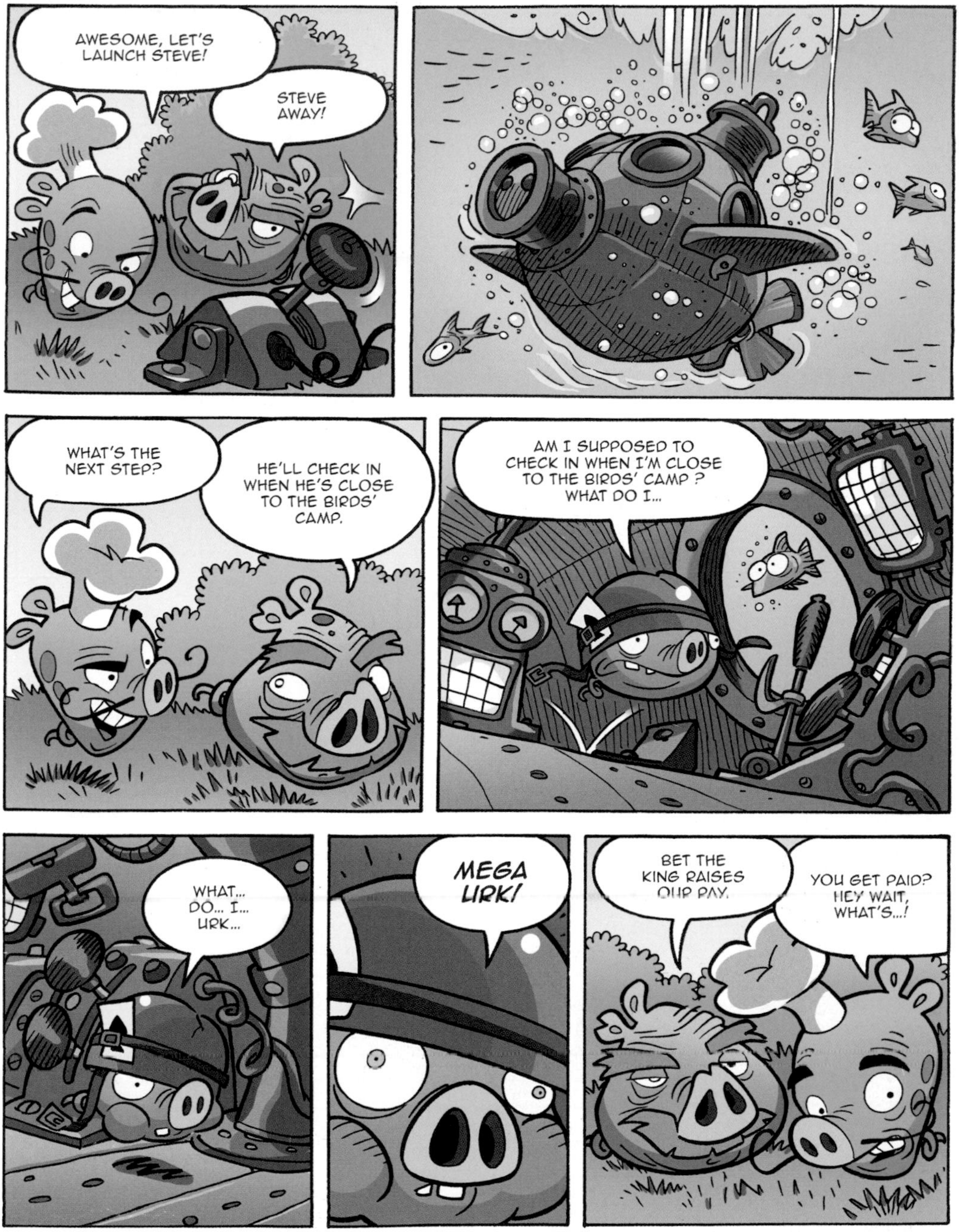
AWESOME, LET'S LAUNCH STEVE!
STEVE AWAY!
WHAT'S THE NEXT STEP?
HE'LL CHECK IN WHEN HE'S CLOSE TO THE BIRDS' CAMP.
AM I SUPPOSED TO CHECK IN WHEN I'M CLOSE TO THE BIRDS' CAMP ? WHAT DO I...
WHAT... DO... I... URK...
MEGA URK!
BET THE KING RAISES OUR PAY.
YOU GET PAID? HEY WAIT, WHAT'S...!

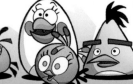

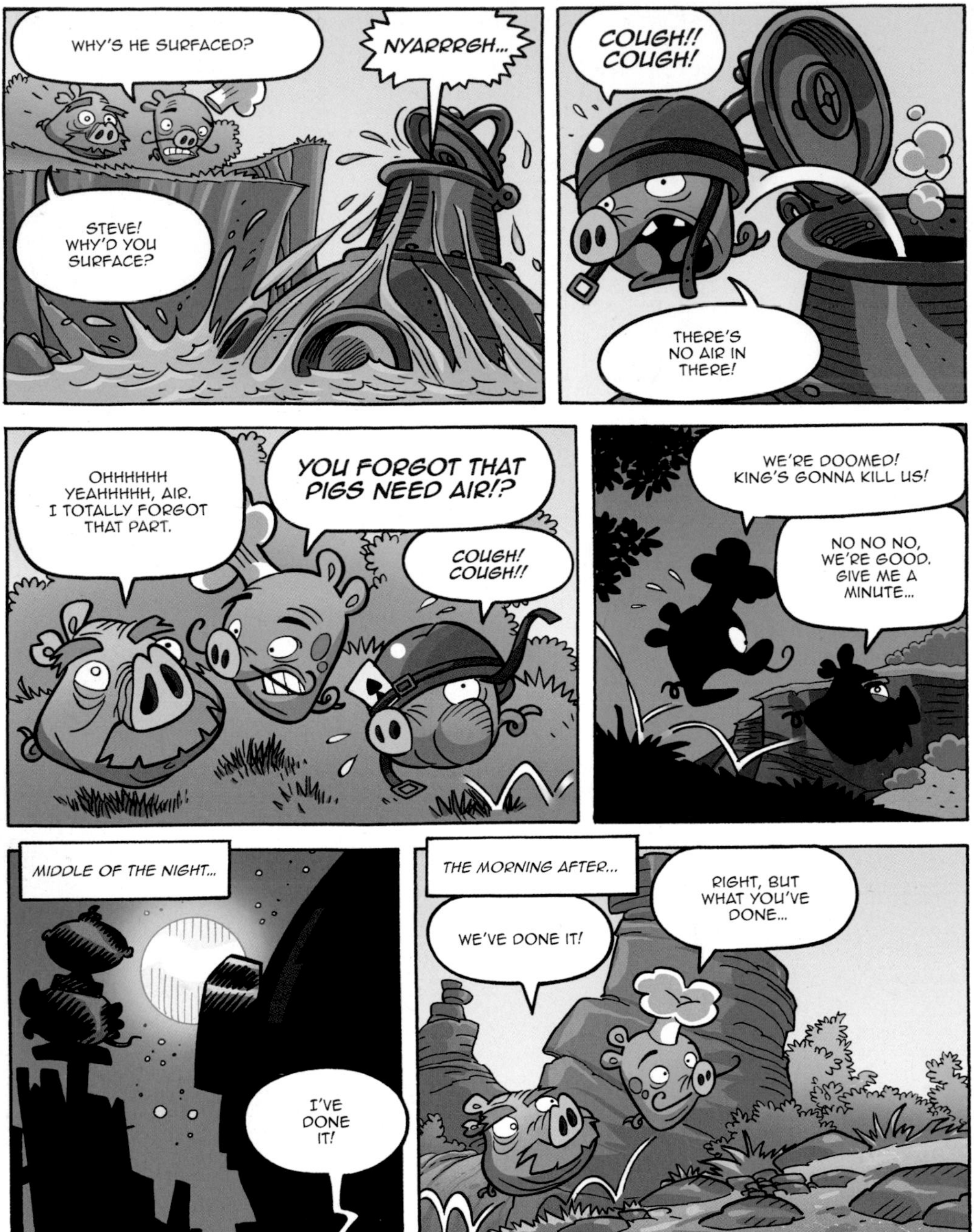
WHY'S HE SURFACED?
NYARRRGH...
STEVE! WHY'D YOU SURFACE?
COUGH!! COUGH!
THERE'S NO AIR IN THERE!
OHHHHHH YEAHHHHHH, AIR. I TOTALLY FORGOT THAT PART.
YOU FORGOT THAT PIGS NEED AIR!?
COUGH! COUGH!!
WE'RE DOOMED! KING'S GONNA KILL US!
NO NO NO, WE'RE GOOD. GIVE ME A MINUTE...
MIDDLE OF THE NIGHT...
I'VE DONE IT!
THE MORNING AFTER...
WE'VE DONE IT!
RIGHT, BUT WHAT YOU'VE DONE...

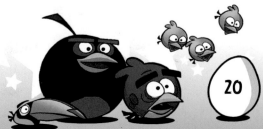

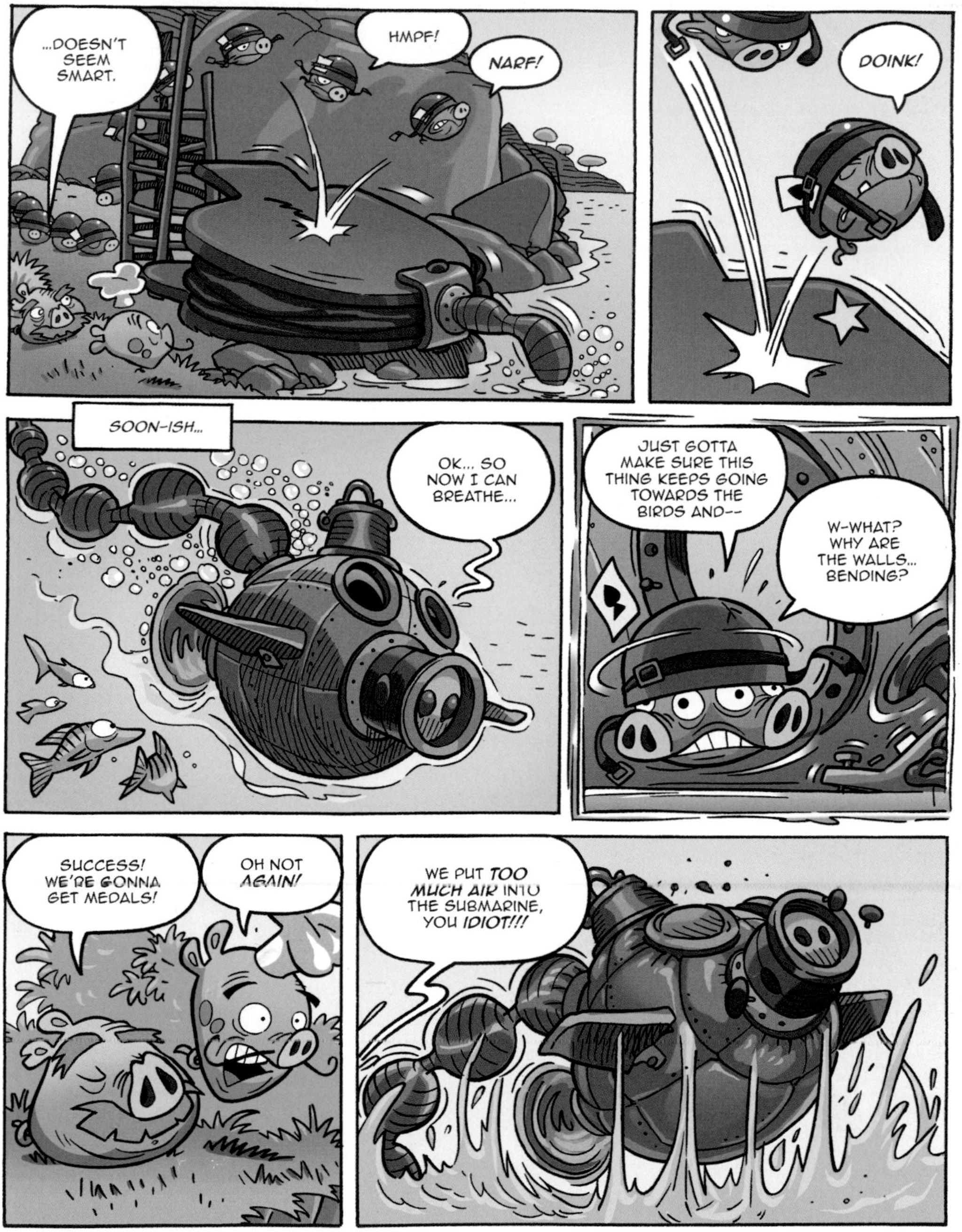
...DOESN'T SEEM SMART.
HMPF!
NARF!
DOINK!
SOON-ISH...
OK... SO NOW I CAN BREATHE...
JUST GOTTA MAKE SURE THIS THING KEEPS GOING TOWARDS THE BIRDS AND--
W-WHAT? WHY ARE THE WALLS... BENDING?
SUCCESS! WE'RE GONNA GET MEDALS!
OH NOT AGAIN!
WE PUT TOO MUCH AIR INTO THE SUBMARINE, YOU IDIOT!!!

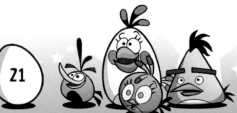

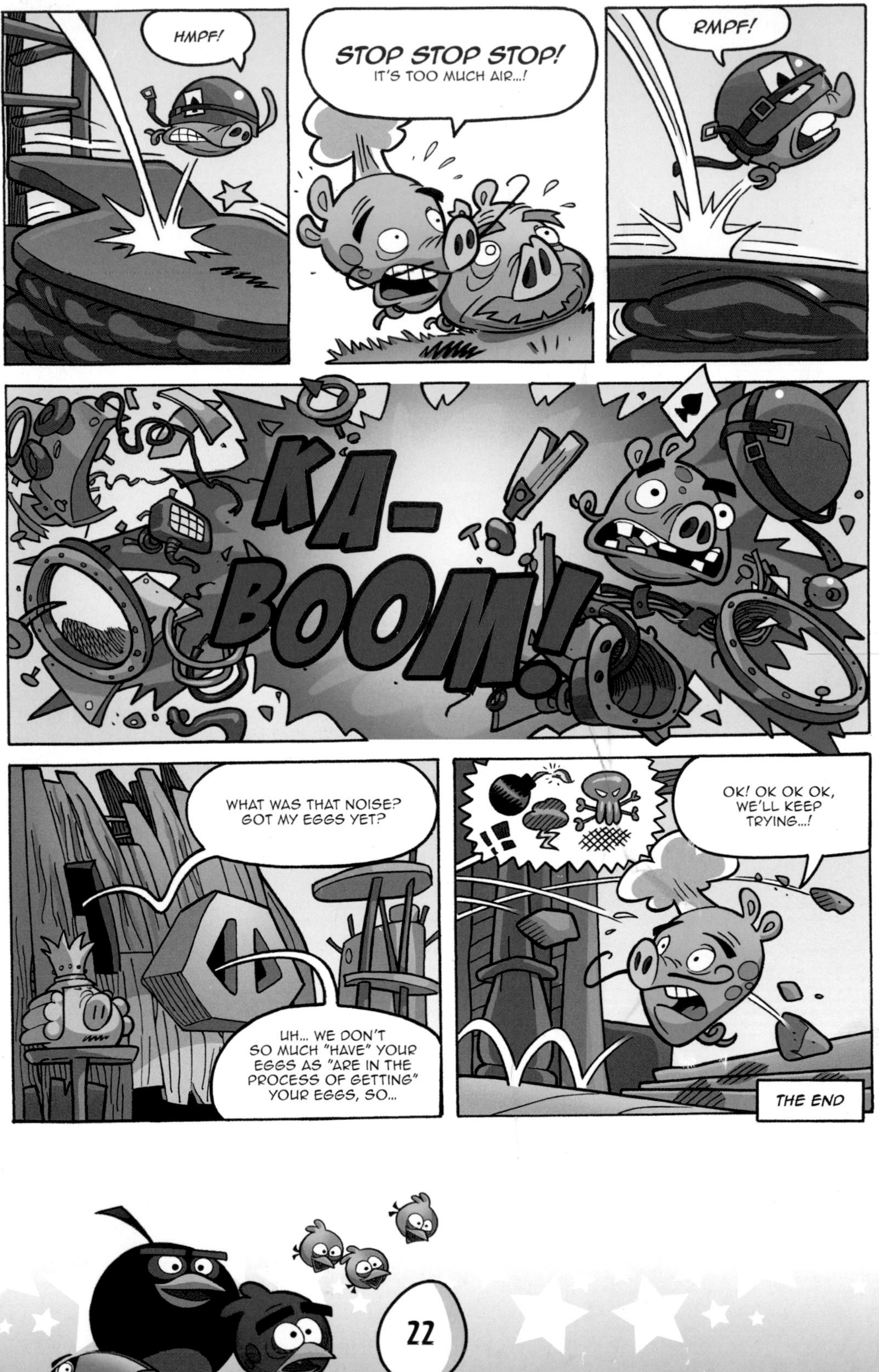
HMPF!
STOP STOP STOP! IT'S TOO MUCH AIR...!
RMPF!
KA-BOOM!
WHAT WAS THAT NOISE? GOT MY EGGS YET?
UH... WE DON'T SO MUCH "HAVE" YOUR EGGS AS "ARE IN THE PROCESS OF GETTING" YOUR EGGS, SO...
OK! OK OK OK, WE'LL KEEP TRYING...!
THE END

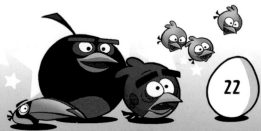

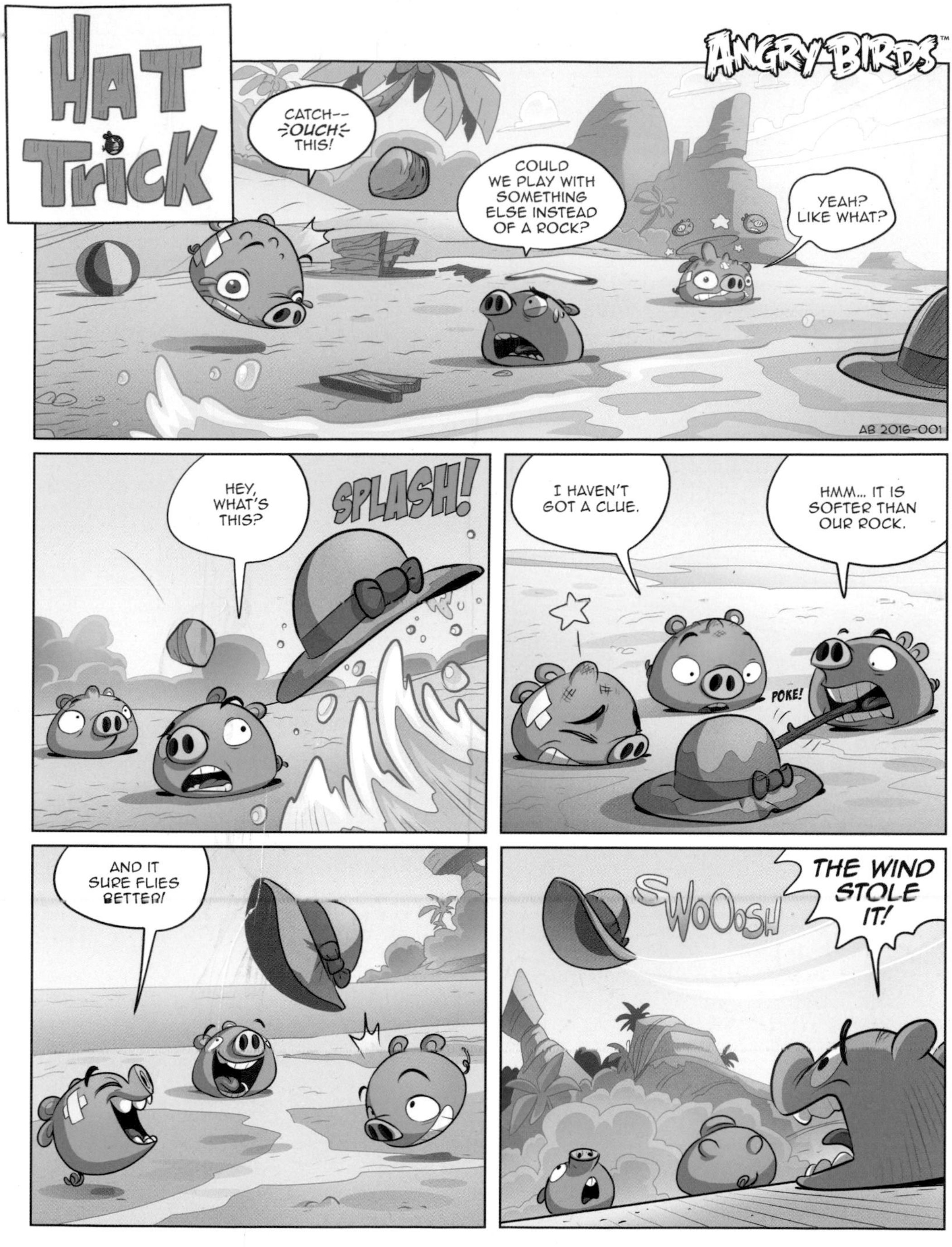
HAT TRICK
ANGRY BIRDS
CATCH-- OUCH THIS!
COULD WE PLAY WITH SOMETHING ELSE INSTEAD OF A ROCK?
YEAH? LIKE WHAT?
AB 2016-001
HEY, WHAT'S THIS?
SPLASH!
I HAVEN'T GOT A CLUE.
HMM... IT IS SOFTER THAN OUR ROCK.
POKE!
AND IT SURE FLIES BETTER!
SWOOOSH
THE WIND STOLE IT!

WRITTEN BY: JANNE TORISEVA
ART BY: ANTONELLO DALENA
COLORS BY: PAOLO MADDALENI
LETTERS BY: PISARA OY

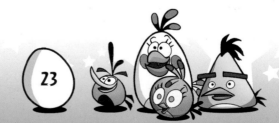

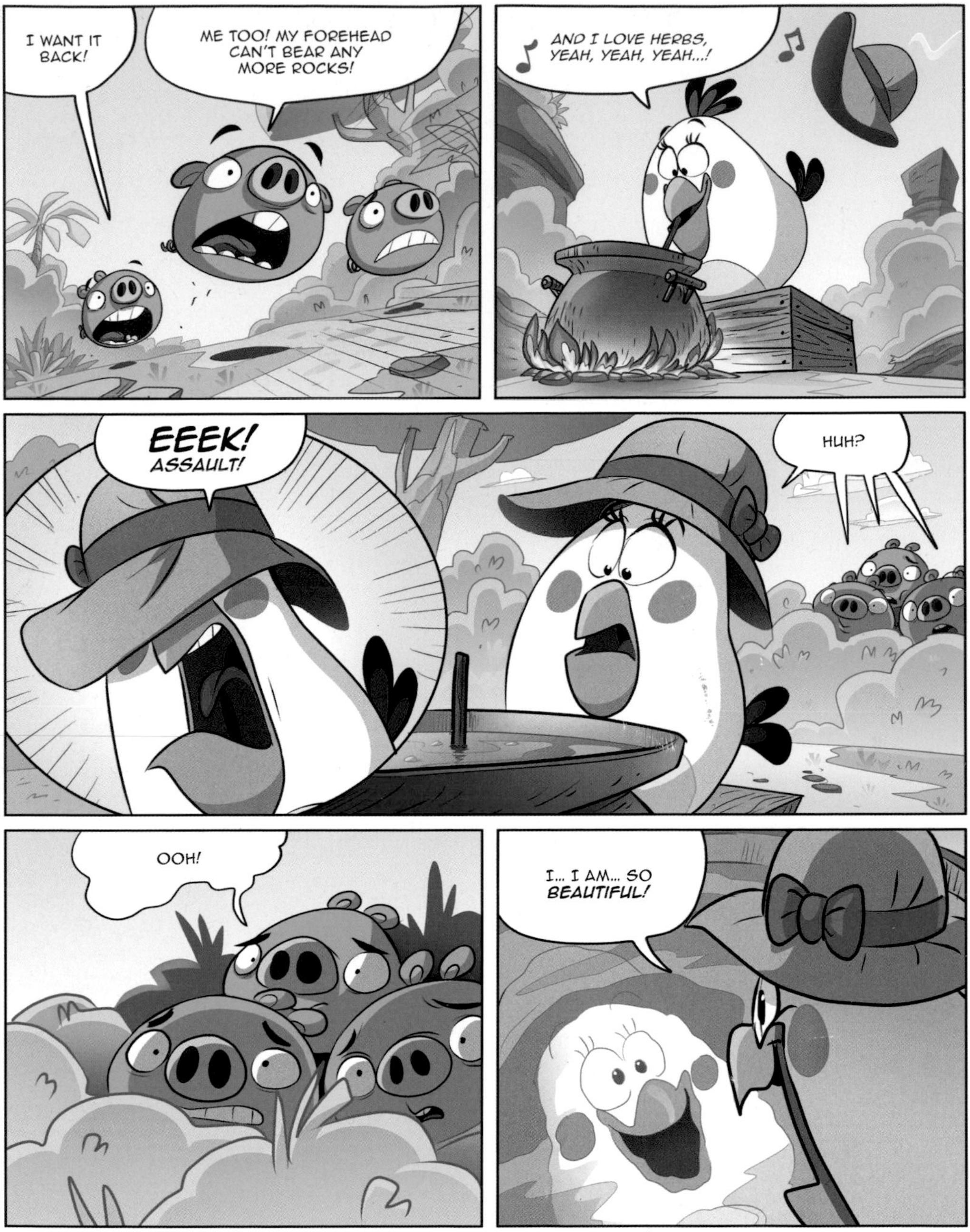
I WANT IT BACK!
ME TOO! MY FOREHEAD CAN'T BEAR ANY MORE ROCKS!
AND I LOVE HERBS, YEAH, YEAH, YEAH...!
EEEK! ASSAULT!
HUH?
OOH!
I... I AM... SO BEAUTIFUL!

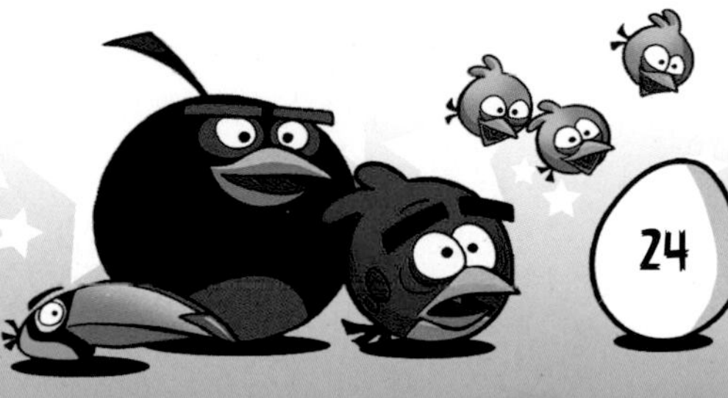

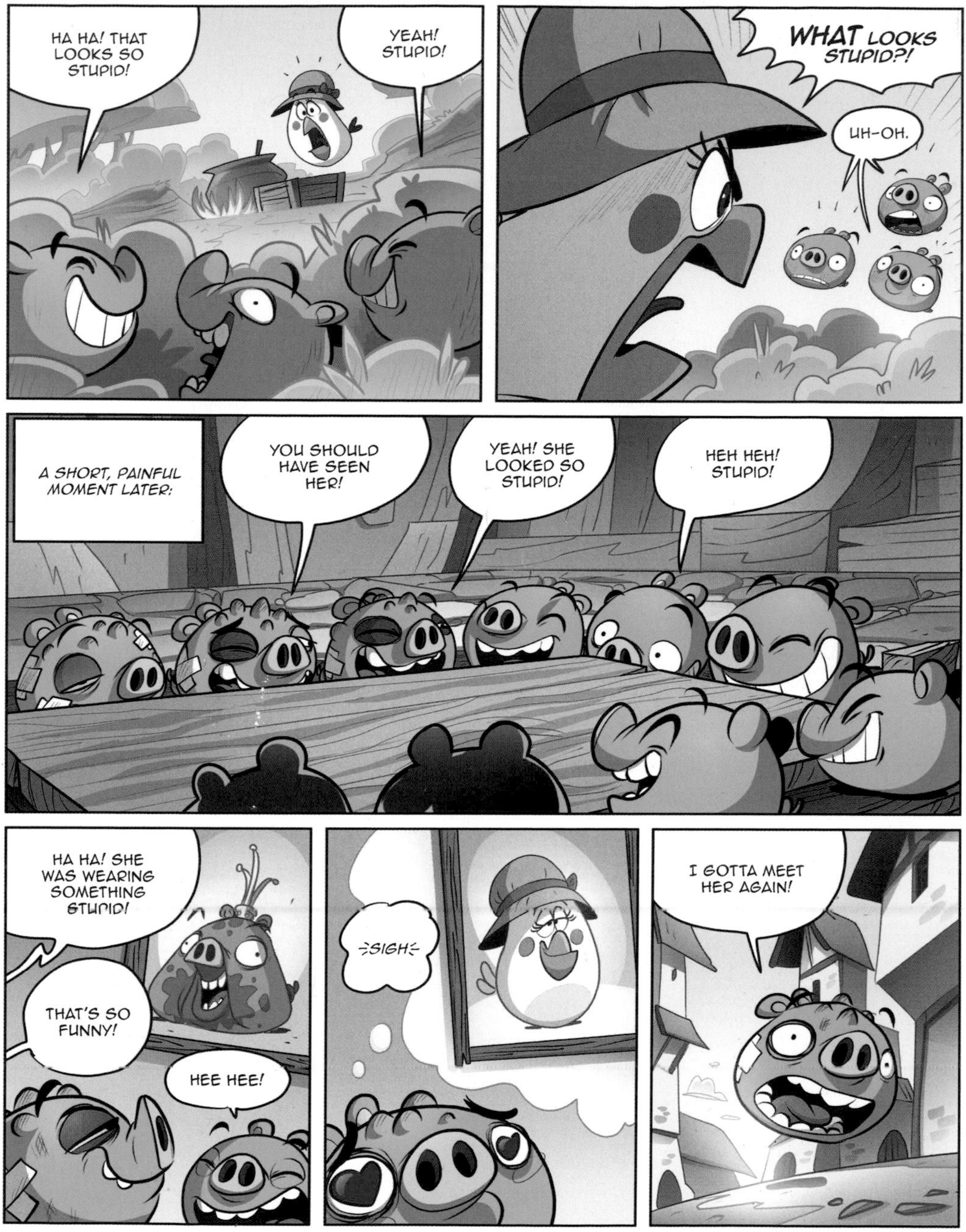
HA HA! THAT LOOKS SO STUPID!
YEAH! STUPID!
WHAT LOOKS STUPID?!
UH-OH.
A SHORT, PAINFUL MOMENT LATER:
YOU SHOULD HAVE SEEN HER!
YEAH! SHE LOOKED SO STUPID!
HEH HEH! STUPID!
HA HA! SHE WAS WEARING SOMETHING STUPID!
THAT'S SO FUNNY!
HEE HEE!
-SIGH-
I GOTTA MEET HER AGAIN!

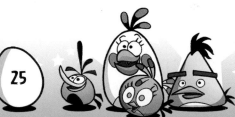

WHAT DO YOU WANT?!
UH... I BOUGHT YOU THESE FLOWERS.
FLOWERS? FOR ME?
YOUR SOUP SMELLS DELICIOUS. MAY I TASTE IT?
REALLY?
SLURP YOU KNOW, YOU LOOK BEAUTIFUL WITH THAT THING ON YOUR HEAD.
WELL... YES, I DO!
LATER:
CATCH ME IF YOU CAN!
BURP IT'S HARD WITH A BELLY FULL OF SOUP!
IT'S GETTING LATE. I THINK I MUST HEAD BACK TO THE CASTLE.
WELL, I COULD FIX A SMALL SUPPER BEFORE YOU GO...

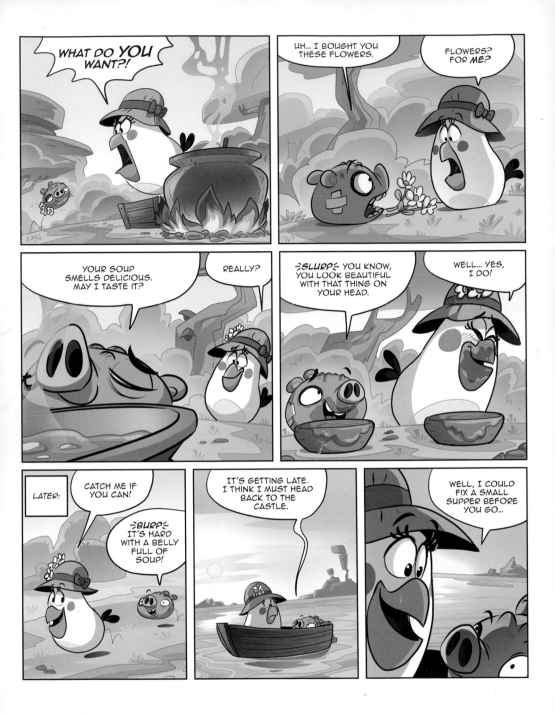

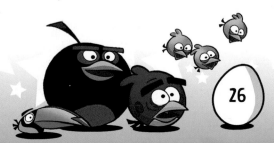

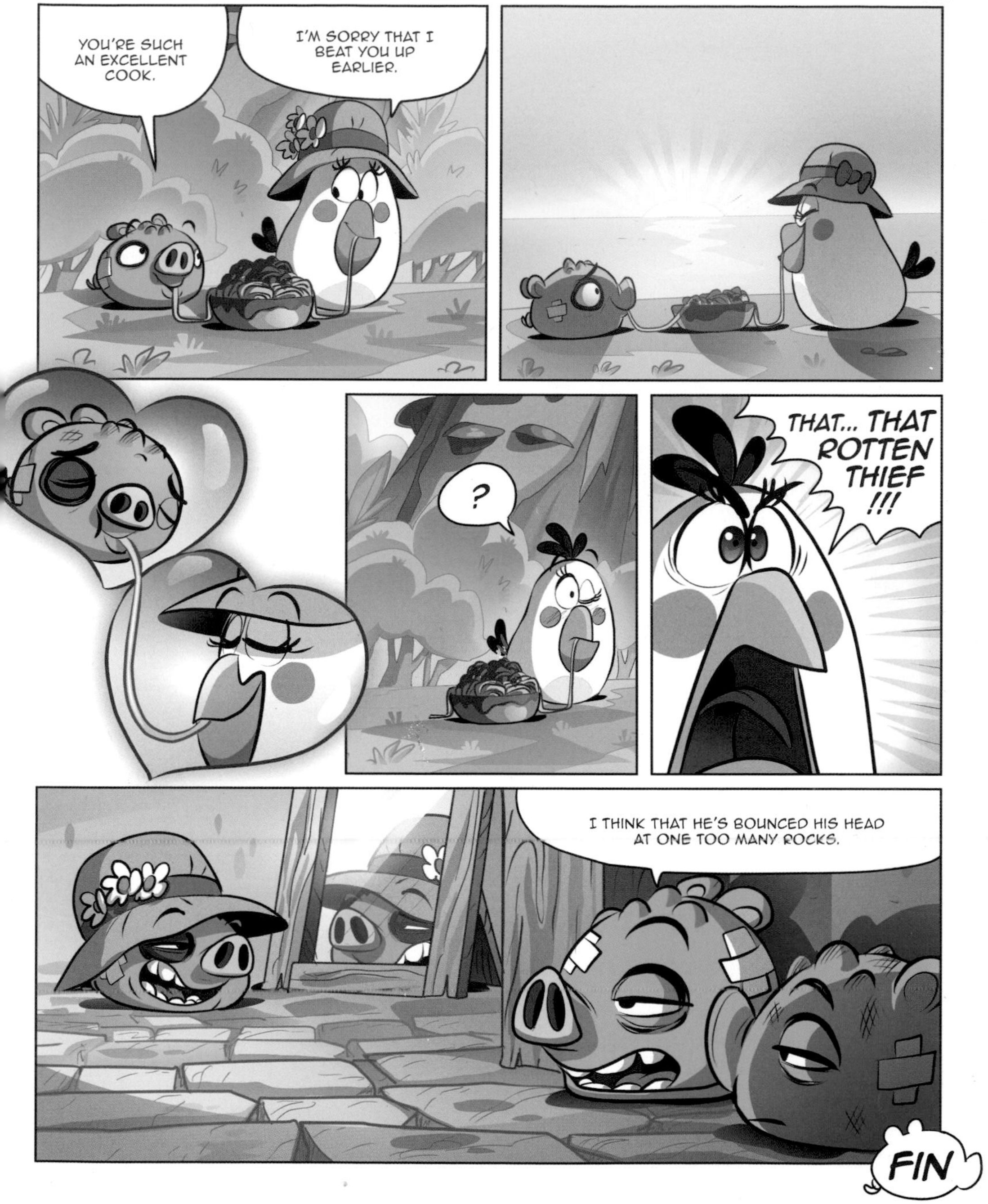
YOU'RE SUCH AN EXCELLENT COOK.
I'M SORRY THAT I BEAT YOU UP EARLIER.
?
THAT... THAT ROTTEN THIEF !!!
I THINK THAT HE'S BOUNCED HIS HEAD AT ONE TOO MANY ROCKS.
FIN

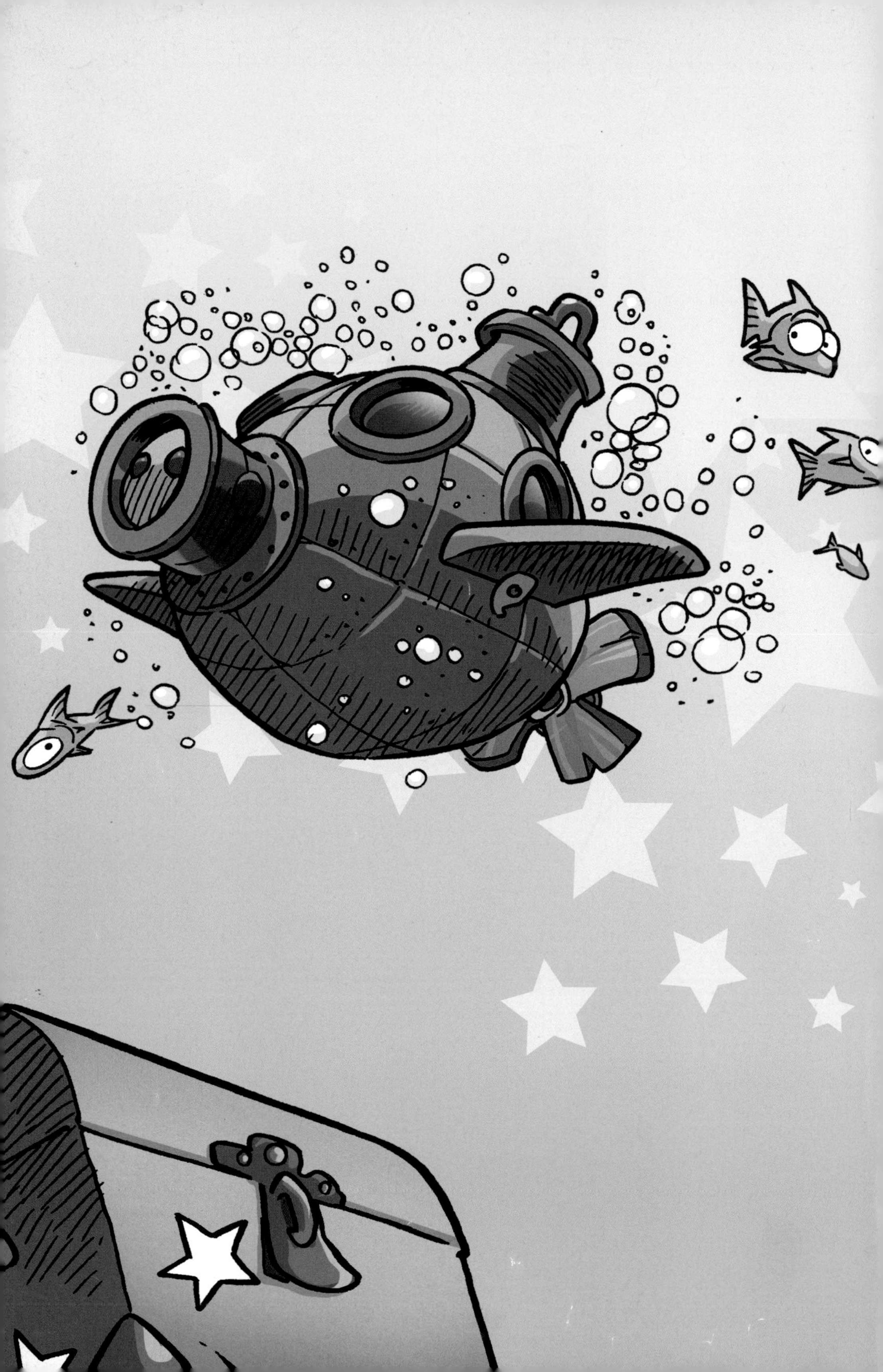

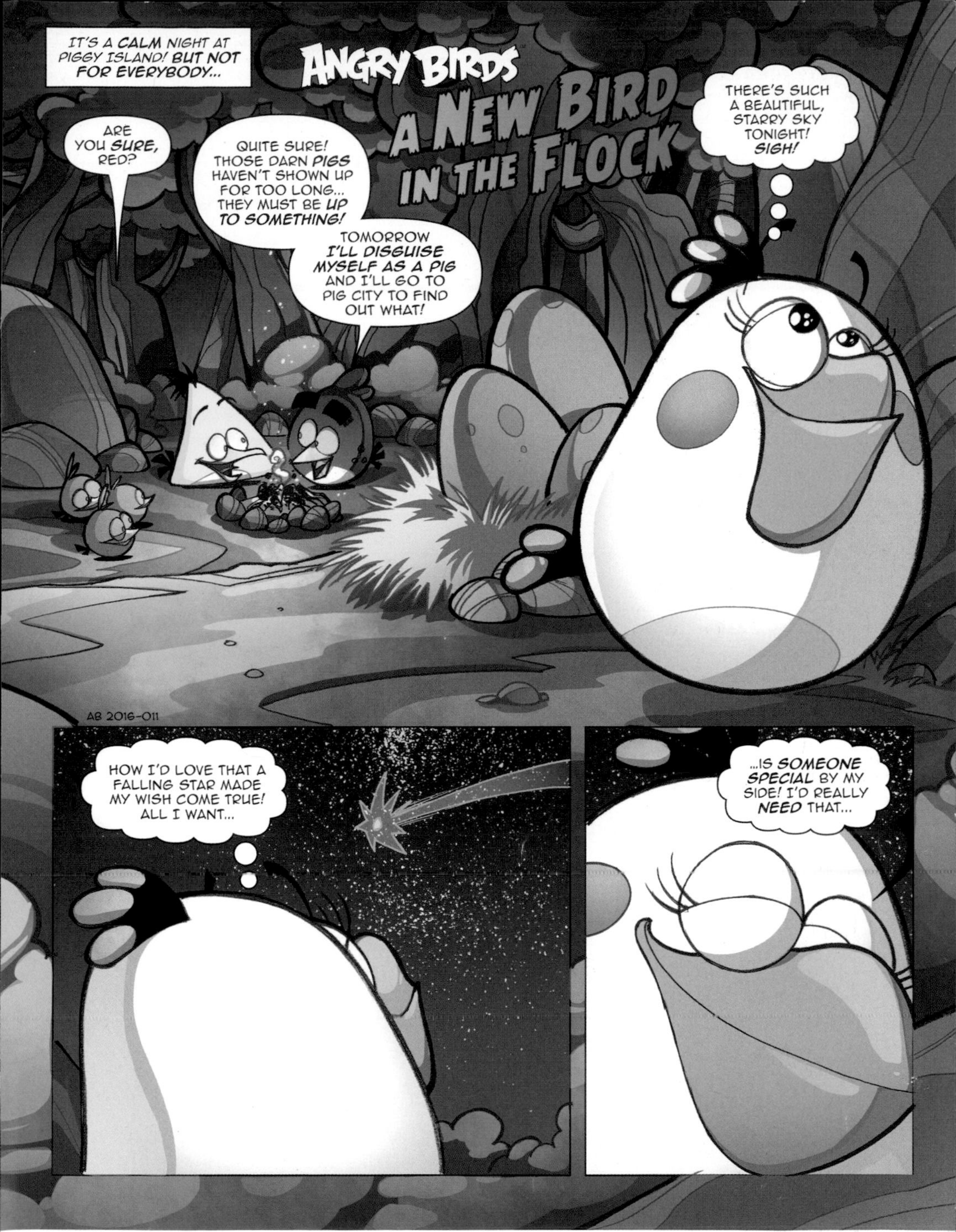
IT'S A CALM NIGHT AT PIGGY ISLAND! BUT NOT FOR EVERYBODY...
ANGRY BIRDS
A NEW BIRD IN THE FLOCK
ARE YOU SURE, RED?
QUITE SURE! THOSE DARN PIGS HAVEN'T SHOWN UP FOR TOO LONG... THEY MUST BE UP TO SOMETHING!
TOMORROW I'LL DISGUISE MYSELF AS A PIG AND I'LL GO TO PIG CITY TO FIND OUT WHAT!
THERE'S SUCH A BEAUTIFUL, STARRY SKY TONIGHT! SIGH!
AB 2016-011
HOW I'D LOVE THAT A FALLING STAR MADE MY WISH COME TRUE! ALL I WANT...
...IS SOMEONE SPECIAL BY MY SIDE! I'D REALLY NEED THAT...

Written by: Monica Manzoni
Art by: David Baldeon
Colors by: David Garcia
Letters by: Pisara Oy

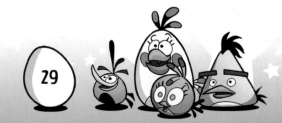

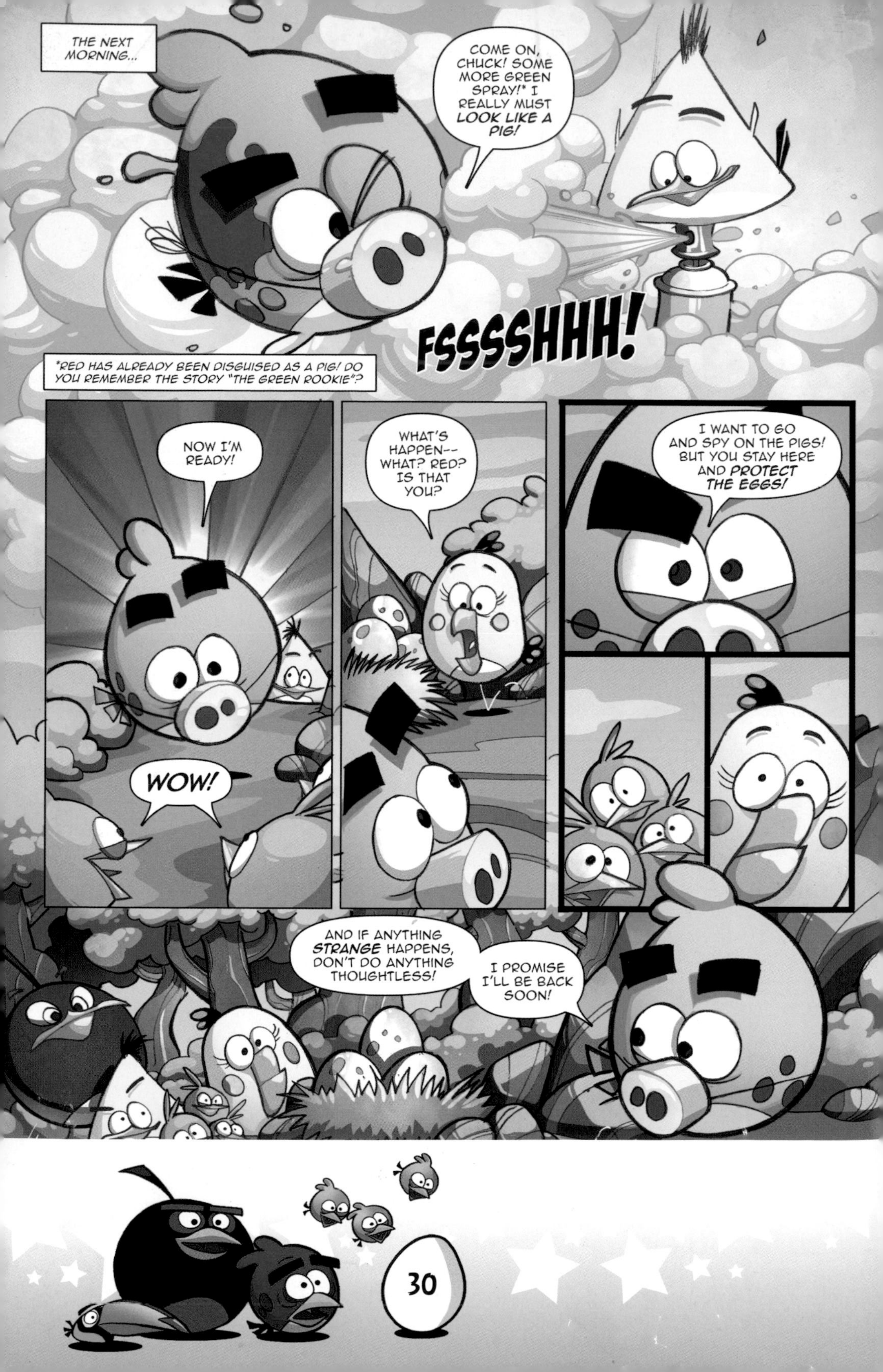
THE NEXT MORNING...
COME ON, CHUCK! SOME MORE GREEN SPRAY!* I REALLY MUST LOOK LIKE A PIG!
FSSSSHHH!
*RED HAS ALREADY BEEN DISGUISED AS A PIG! DO YOU REMEMBER THE STORY "THE GREEN ROOKIE"?
NOW I'M READY!
WOW!
WHAT'S HAPPEN-- WHAT? RED? IS THAT YOU?
I WANT TO GO AND SPY ON THE PIGS! BUT YOU STAY HERE AND PROTECT THE EGGS!
AND IF ANYTHING STRANGE HAPPENS, DON'T DO ANYTHING THOUGHTLESS!
I PROMISE I'LL BE BACK SOON!

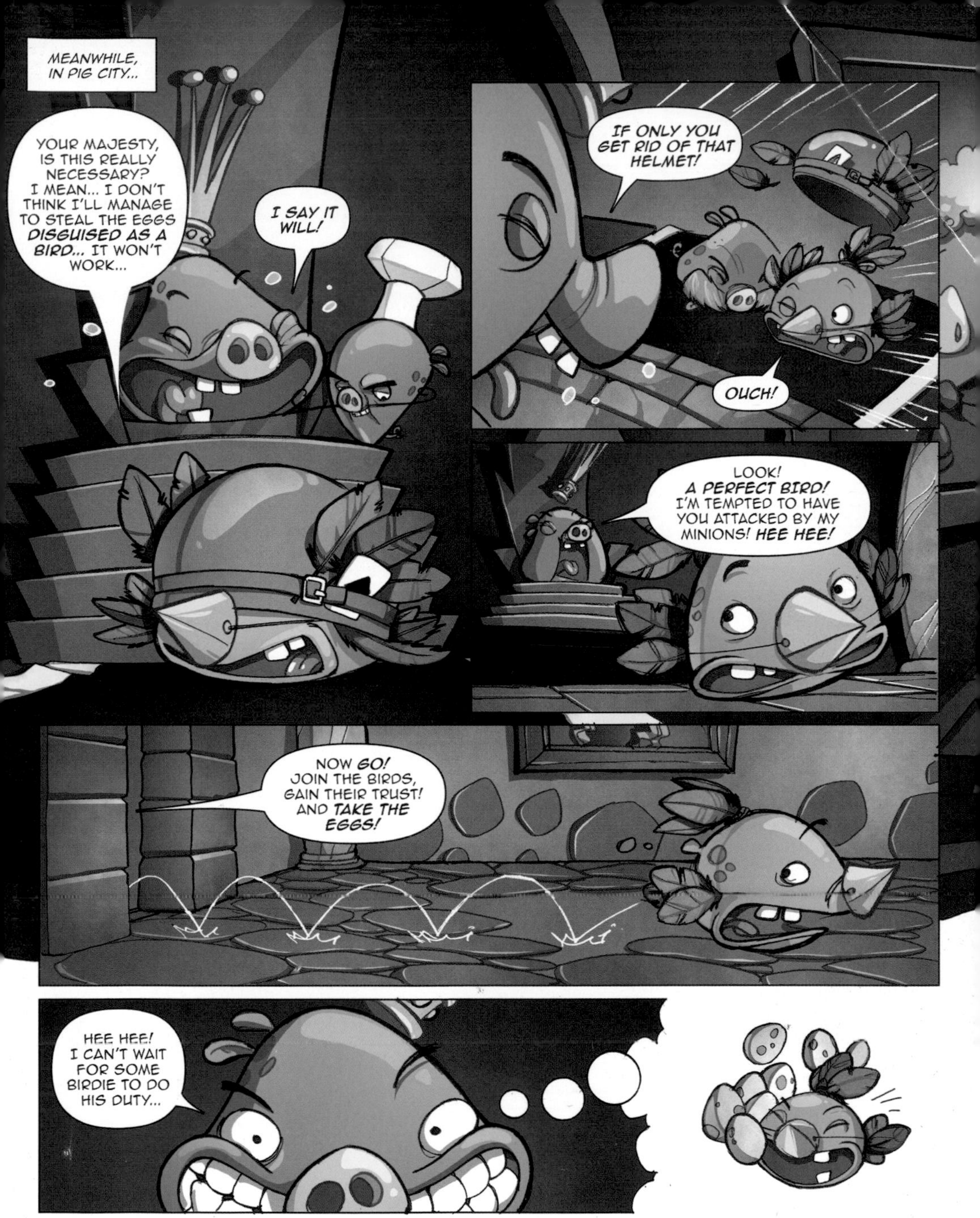
MEANWHILE, IN PIG CITY...
YOUR MAJESTY, IS THIS REALLY NECESSARY? I MEAN... I DON'T THINK I'LL MANAGE TO STEAL THE EGGS DISGUISED AS A BIRD... IT WON'T WORK...
I SAY IT WILL!
IF ONLY YOU GET RID OF THAT HELMET!
OUCH!
LOOK! A PERFECT BIRD! I'M TEMPTED TO HAVE YOU ATTACKED BY MY MINIONS! HEE HEE!
NOW GO! JOIN THE BIRDS, GAIN THEIR TRUST! AND TAKE THE EGGS!
HEE HEE! I CAN'T WAIT FOR SOME BIRDIE TO DO HIS DUTY...

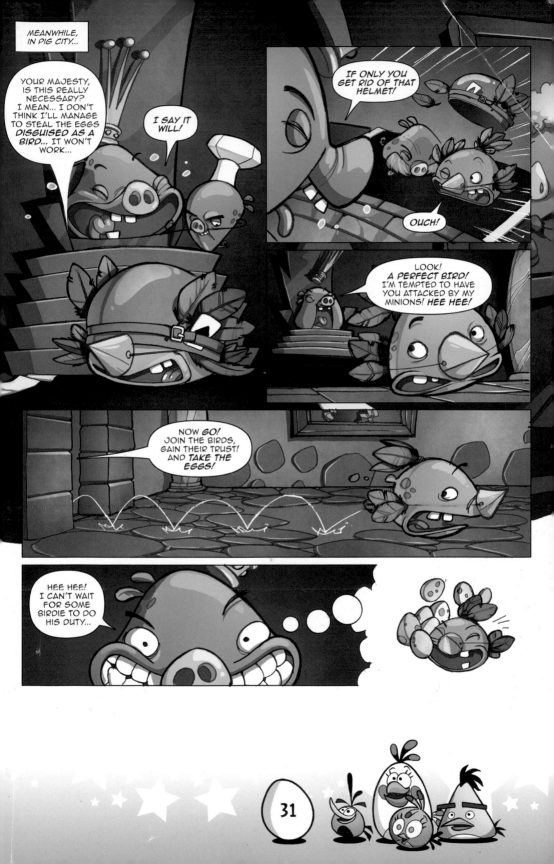

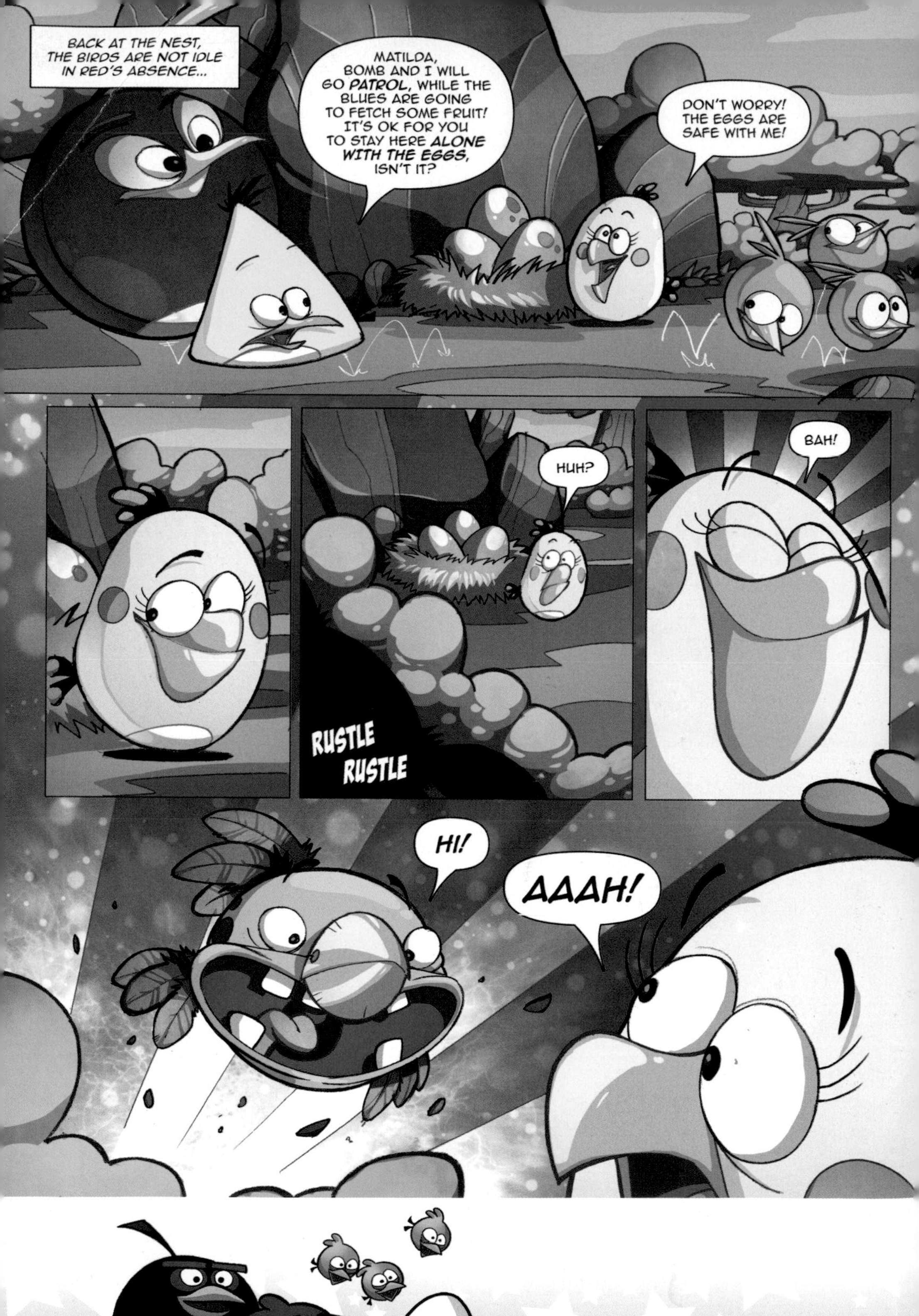

BACK AT THE NEST, THE BIRDS ARE NOT IDLE IN RED'S ABSENCE...
MATILDA, BOMB AND I WILL GO PATROL, WHILE THE BLUES ARE GOING TO FETCH SOME FRUIT! IT'S OK FOR YOU TO STAY HERE ALONE WITH THE EGGS, ISN'T IT?
DON'T WORRY! THE EGGS ARE SAFE WITH ME!
HUH?
RUSTLE
RUSTLE
BAH!
HI!
AAAH!

WHO ARE YOU?

I'VE *NEVER* SEEN YOU ON THIS ISLAND!

I AM *ALONE!* AND I'M LOOKING FOR *SOMEONE TO BE WITH...*

MY NAME'S... ERR... *PLUMPY!* I THINK I'VE GOT *LOST!*

RR... I MEAN... A *FLOCK!*

OH, REALLY?!

LATER...

EVERYBODY MEET PLUMPY! WE'RE *REALLY HAPPY* THAT OUR FLOCK HAS A *NEW MEMBER* NOW!

ERR... THOSE ARE... *EGGS!* AREN'T THEY?

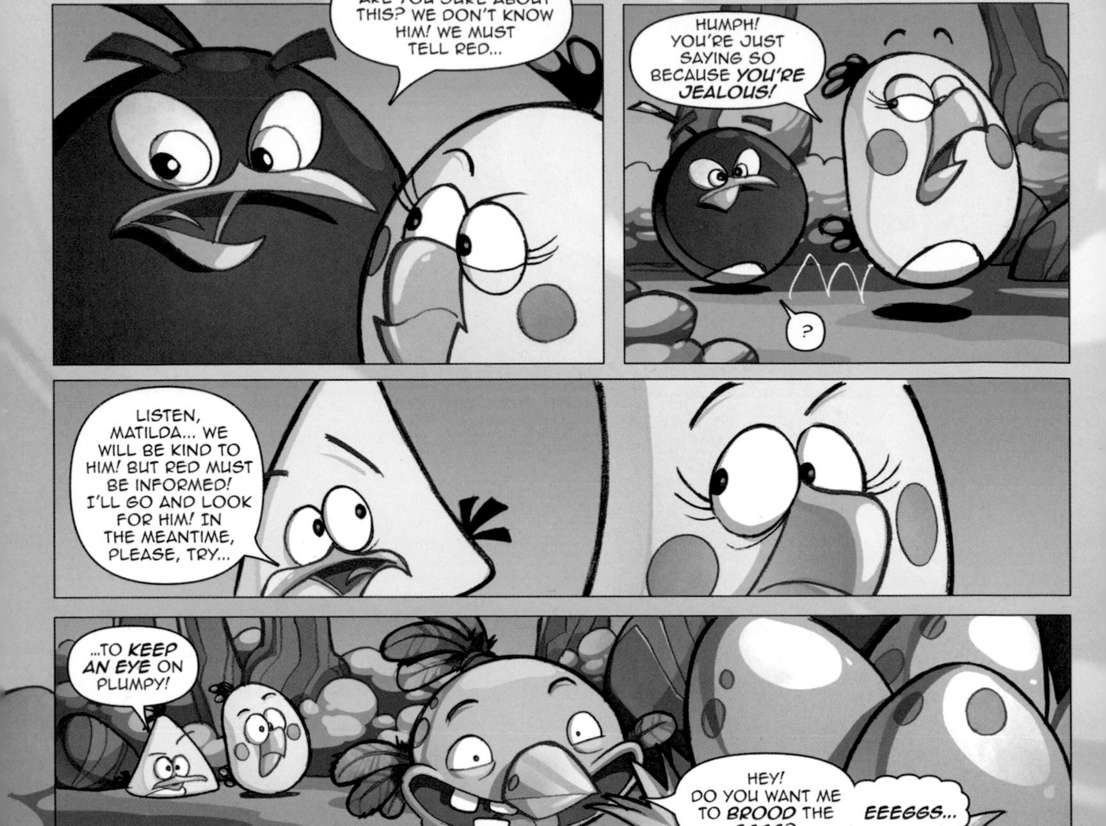
ERR... MATILDA... ARE YOU SURE ABOUT THIS? WE DON'T KNOW HIM! WE MUST TELL RED...
HUMPH! YOU'RE JUST SAYING SO BECAUSE YOU'RE JEALOUS!
?
LISTEN, MATILDA... WE WILL BE KIND TO HIM! BUT RED MUST BE INFORMED! I'LL GO AND LOOK FOR HIM! IN THE MEANTIME, PLEASE, TRY...
...TO KEEP AN EYE ON PLUMPY!
HEY! DO YOU WANT ME TO BROOD THE EGGS?
EEEGGS...
SO, BOMB AND I WILL FIND RED! THE BLUES AND YOU WILL STAY HERE WITH PLUMPY... AND THE EGGS! ALL RIGHT?
ALL RIGHT, ALL RIGHT... BUT I'M SURE THERE'S NOTHING TO WORRY ABOUT!

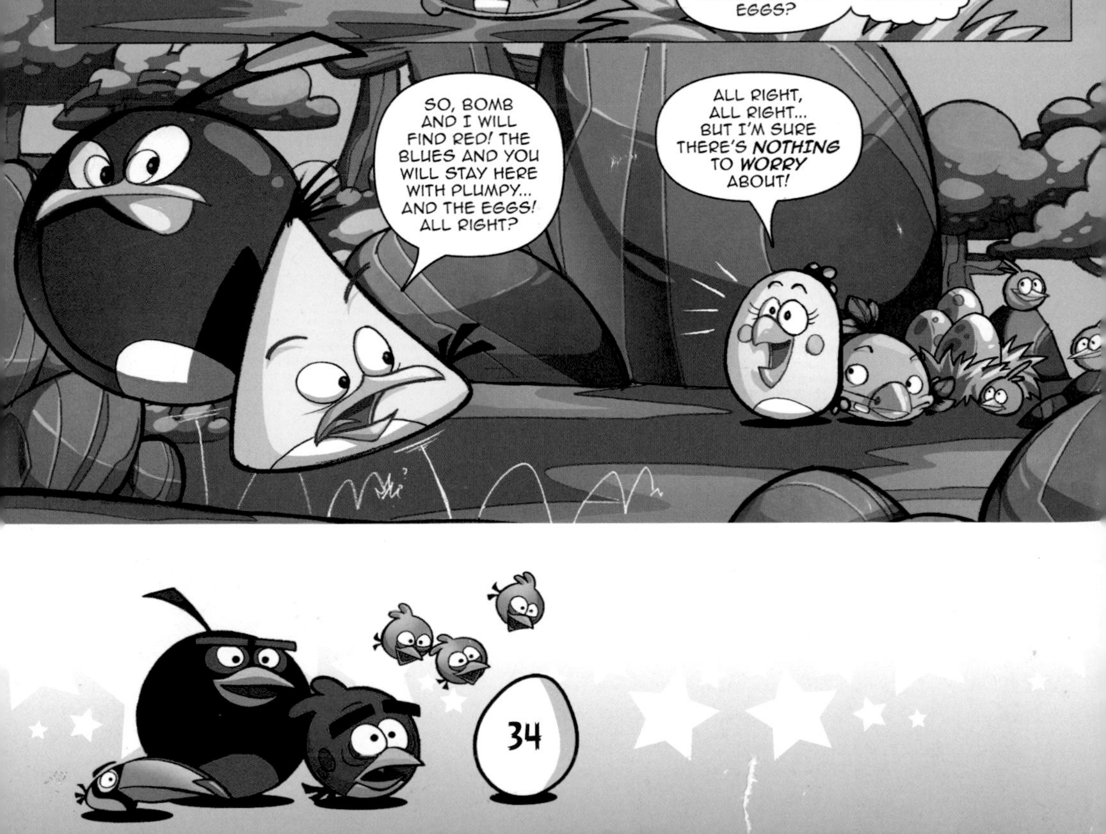

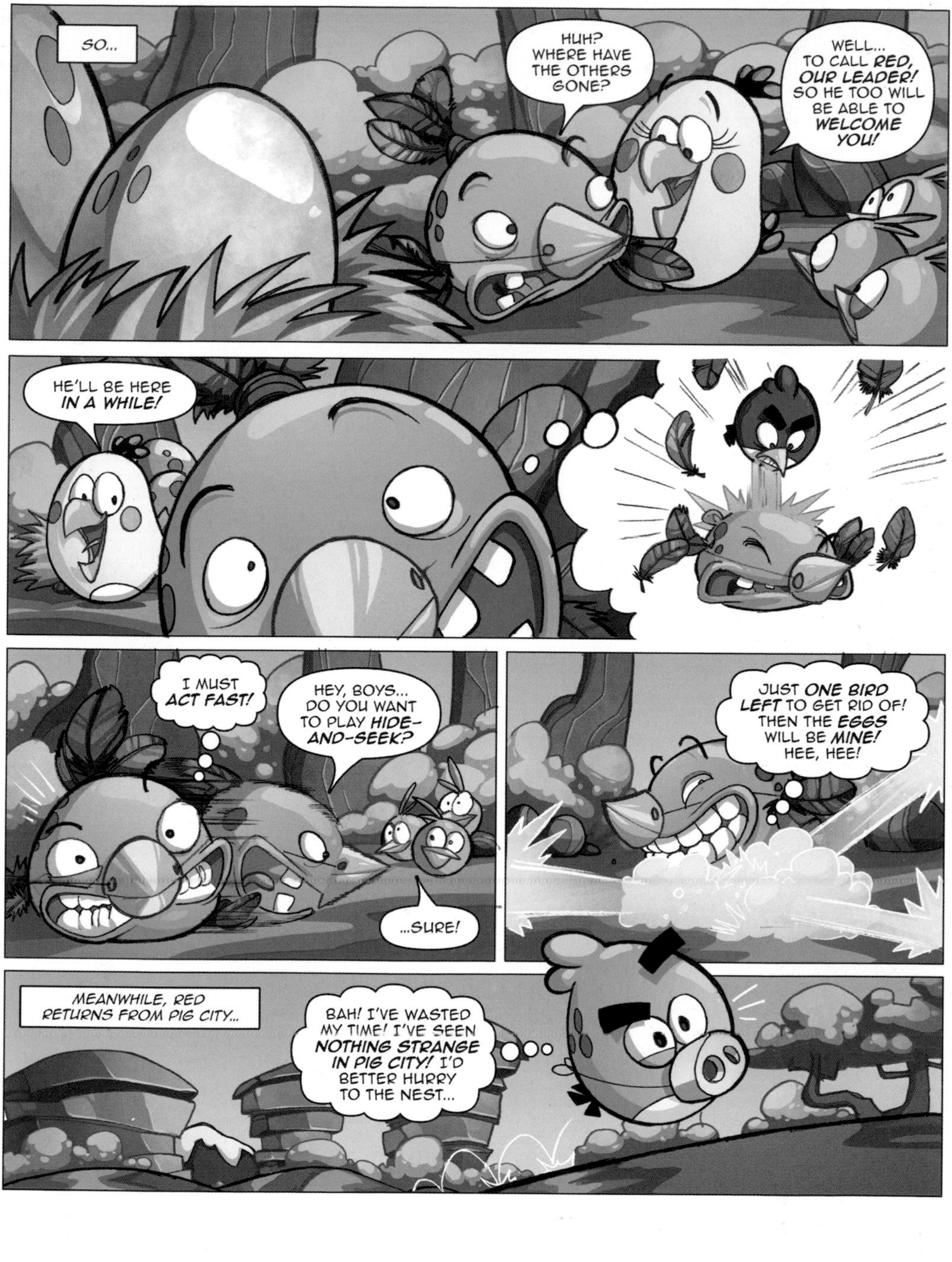
SO...
HUH? WHERE HAVE THE OTHERS GONE?
WELL... TO CALL RED, OUR LEADER! SO HE TOO WILL BE ABLE TO WELCOME YOU!
HE'LL BE HERE IN A WHILE!
I MUST ACT FAST!
HEY, BOYS... DO YOU WANT TO PLAY HIDE-AND-SEEK?
...SURE!
JUST ONE BIRD LEFT TO GET RID OF! THEN THE EGGS WILL BE MINE! HEE, HEE!
MEANWHILE, RED RETURNS FROM PIG CITY...
BAH! I'VE WASTED MY TIME! I'VE SEEN NOTHING STRANGE IN PIG CITY! I'D BETTER HURRY TO THE NEST...

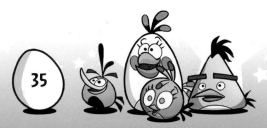

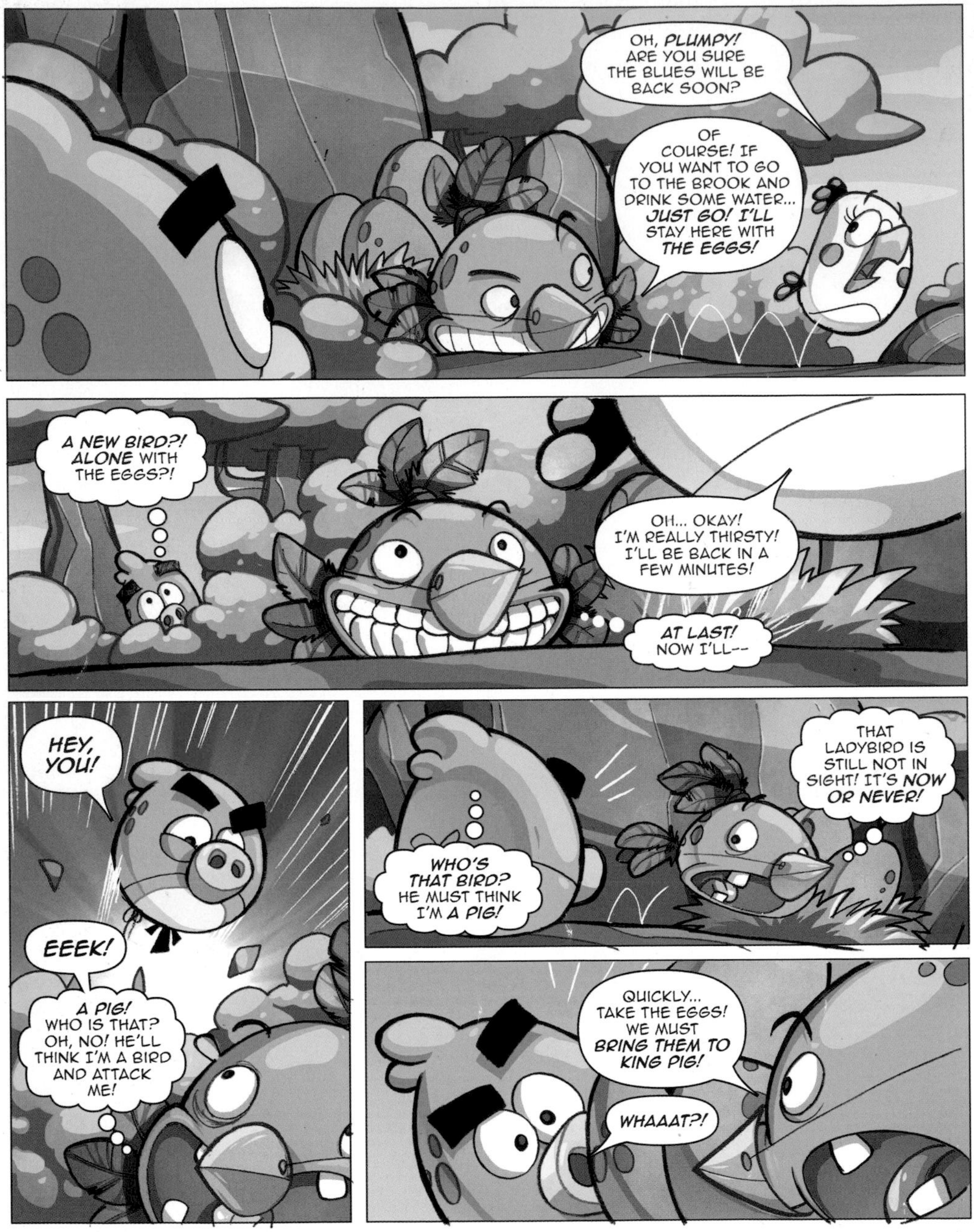
OH, PLUMPY! ARE YOU SURE THE BLUES WILL BE BACK SOON?
OF COURSE! IF YOU WANT TO GO TO THE BROOK AND DRINK SOME WATER... JUST GO! I'LL STAY HERE WITH THE EGGS!
A NEW BIRD?! ALONE WITH THE EGGS?!
OH... OKAY! I'M REALLY THIRSTY! I'LL BE BACK IN A FEW MINUTES!
AT LAST! NOW I'LL--
HEY, YOU!
EEEK!
A PIG! WHO IS THAT? OH, NO! HE'LL THINK I'M A BIRD AND ATTACK ME!
WHO'S THAT BIRD? HE MUST THINK I'M A PIG!
THAT LADYBIRD IS STILL NOT IN SIGHT! IT'S NOW OR NEVER!
QUICKLY... TAKE THE EGGS! WE MUST BRING THEM TO KING PIG!
WHAAAT?!

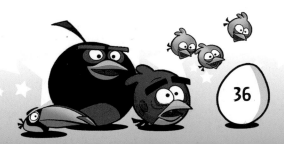

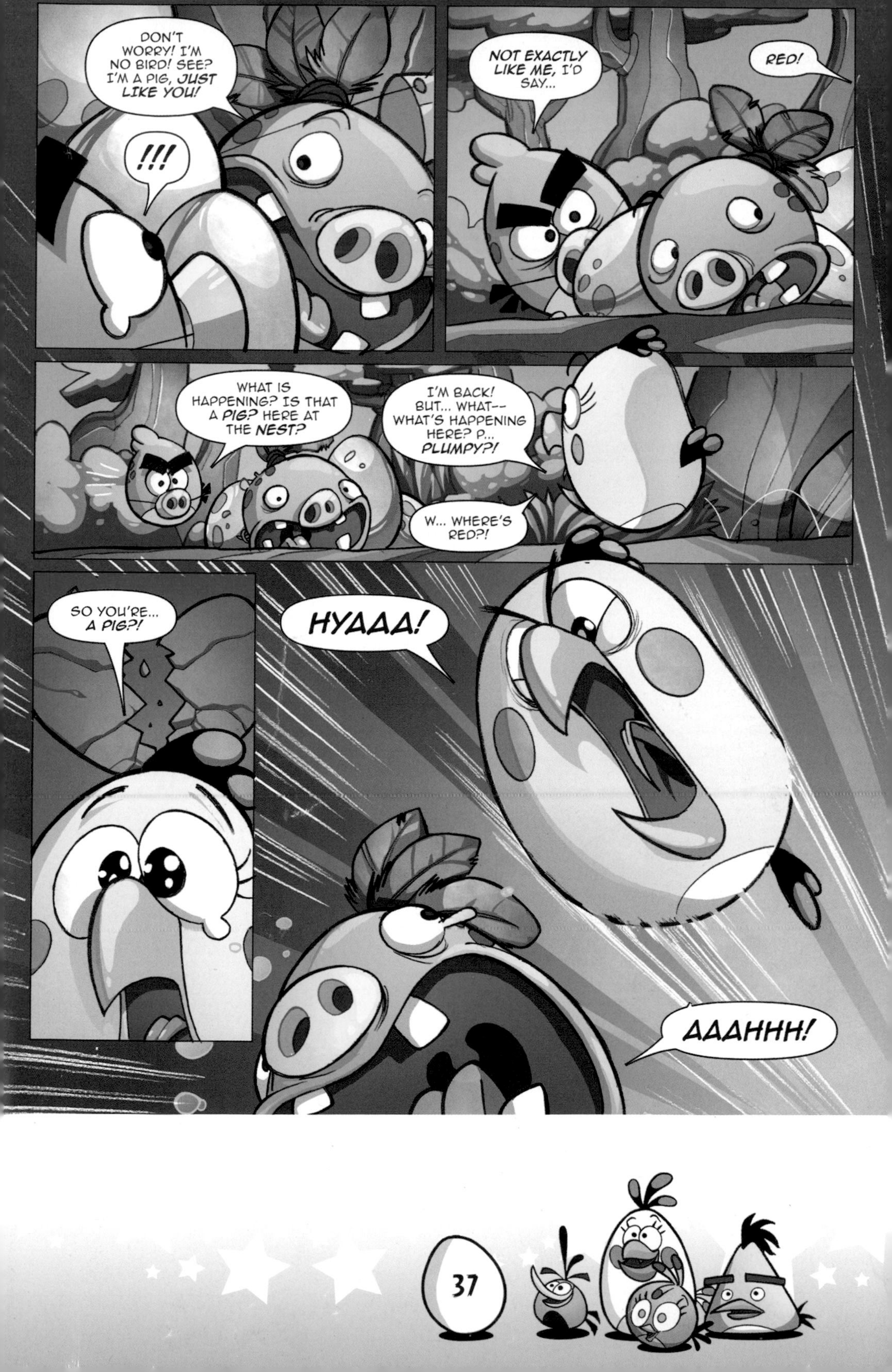
DON'T WORRY! I'M NO BIRD! SEE? I'M A PIG, JUST LIKE YOU!
!!!
NOT EXACTLY LIKE ME, I'D SAY...
RED!
WHAT IS HAPPENING? IS THAT A PIG? HERE AT THE NEST?
I'M BACK! BUT... WHAT-- WHAT'S HAPPENING HERE? P... PLUMPY?!
W... WHERE'S RED?!
SO YOU'RE... A PIG?!
HYAAA!
AAAHHH!

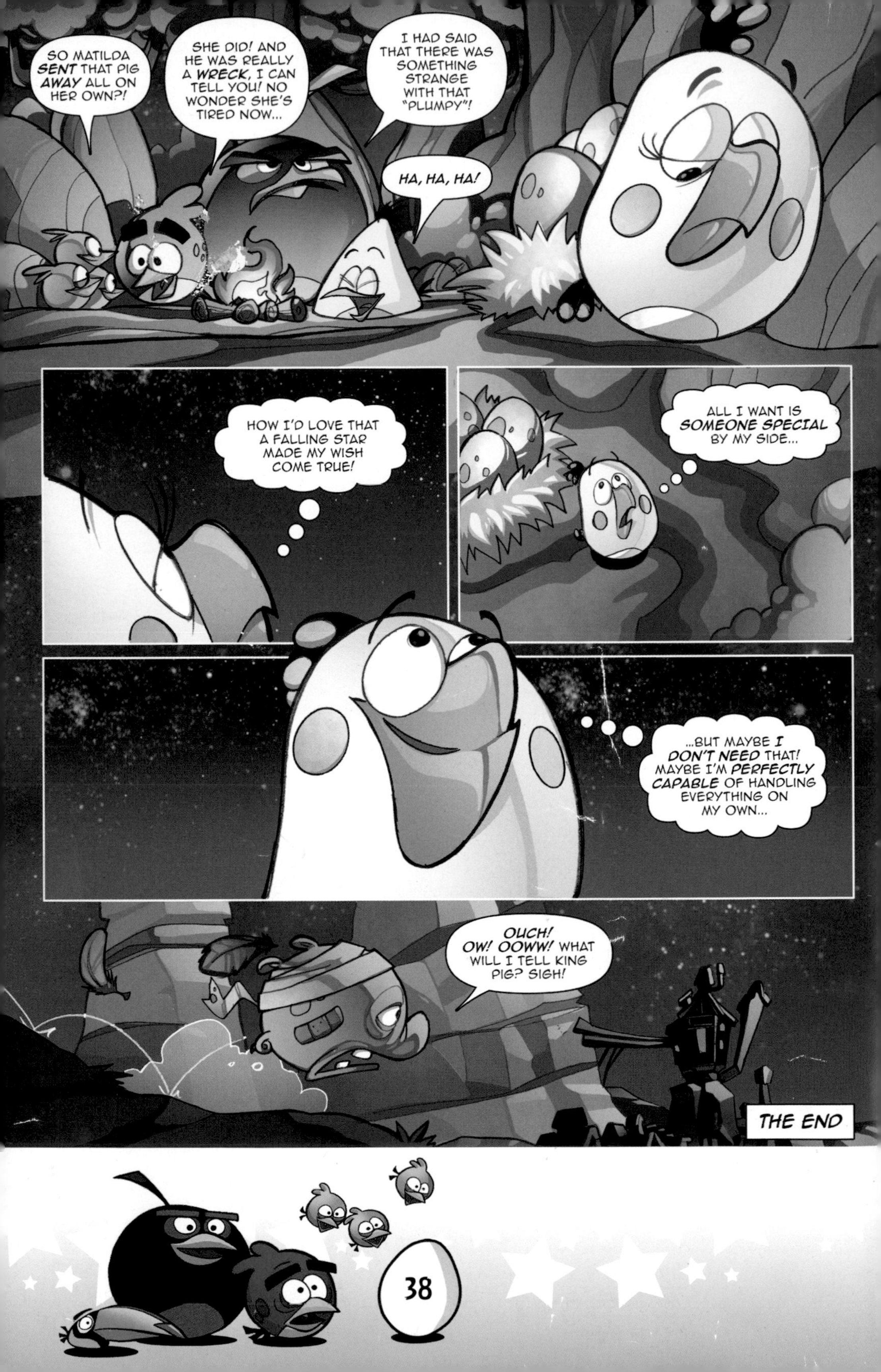
SO MATILDA SENT THAT PIG AWAY ALL ON HER OWN?!
SHE DID! AND HE WAS REALLY A WRECK, I CAN TELL YOU! NO WONDER SHE'S TIRED NOW...
I HAD SAID THAT THERE WAS SOMETHING STRANGE WITH THAT "PLUMPY"!
HA, HA, HA!
HOW I'D LOVE THAT A FALLING STAR MADE MY WISH COME TRUE!
ALL I WANT IS SOMEONE SPECIAL BY MY SIDE...
...BUT MAYBE I DON'T NEED THAT! MAYBE I'M PERFECTLY CAPABLE OF HANDLING EVERYTHING ON MY OWN...
OUCH! OW! OOWW! WHAT WILL I TELL KING PIG? SIGH!
THE END

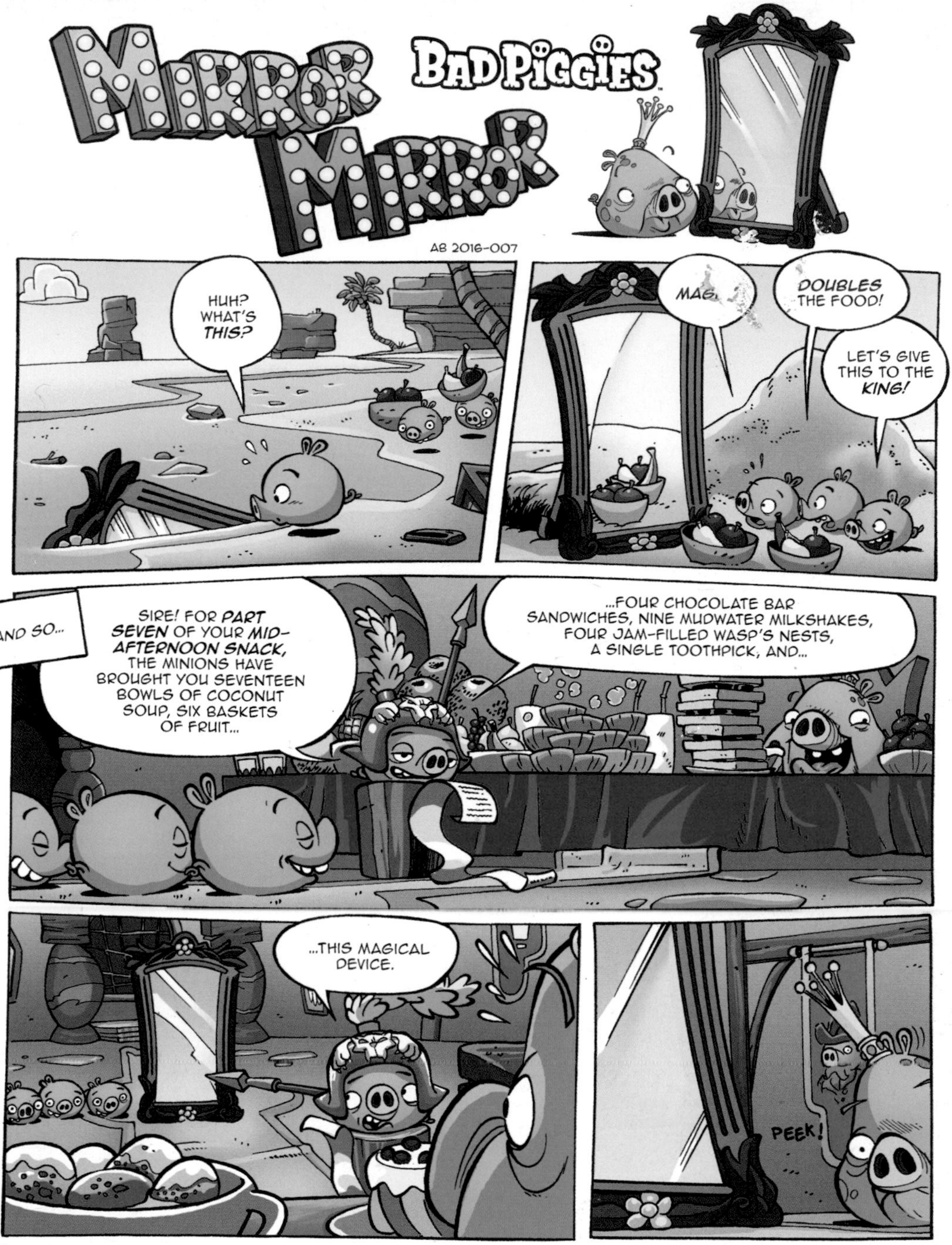
MIRROR MIRROR
BAD PIGGIES
AB 2016-007
HUH? WHAT'S THIS?
MAG
DOUBLES THE FOOD!
LET'S GIVE THIS TO THE KING!
AND SO...
SIRE! FOR PART SEVEN OF YOUR MID-AFTERNOON SNACK, THE MINIONS HAVE BROUGHT YOU SEVENTEEN BOWLS OF COCONUT SOUP, SIX BASKETS OF FRUIT...
...FOUR CHOCOLATE BAR SANDWICHES, NINE MUDWATER MILKSHAKES, FOUR JAM-FILLED WASP'S NESTS, A SINGLE TOOTHPICK, AND...
...THIS MAGICAL DEVICE.
PEEK!

Written by: Paul Tobin
Art by: Paco Rodriques
Colors by: Digikore
Letters by: Pisara Oy

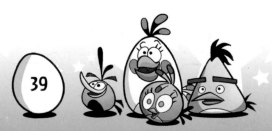

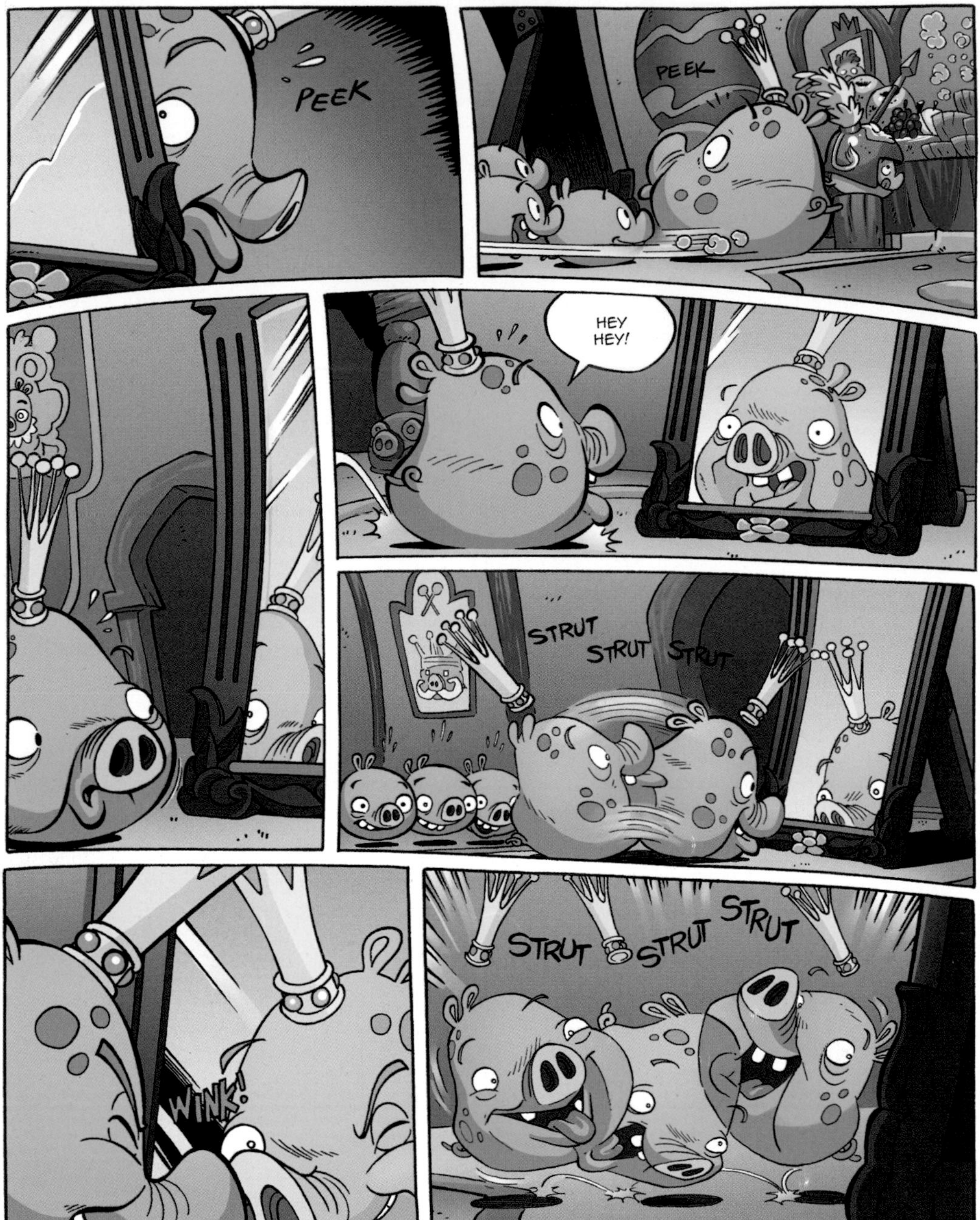
PEEK
PEEK
HEY HEY!
STRUT
STRUT
STRUT
WINK!
STRUT
STRUT
STRUT

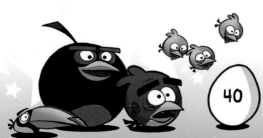

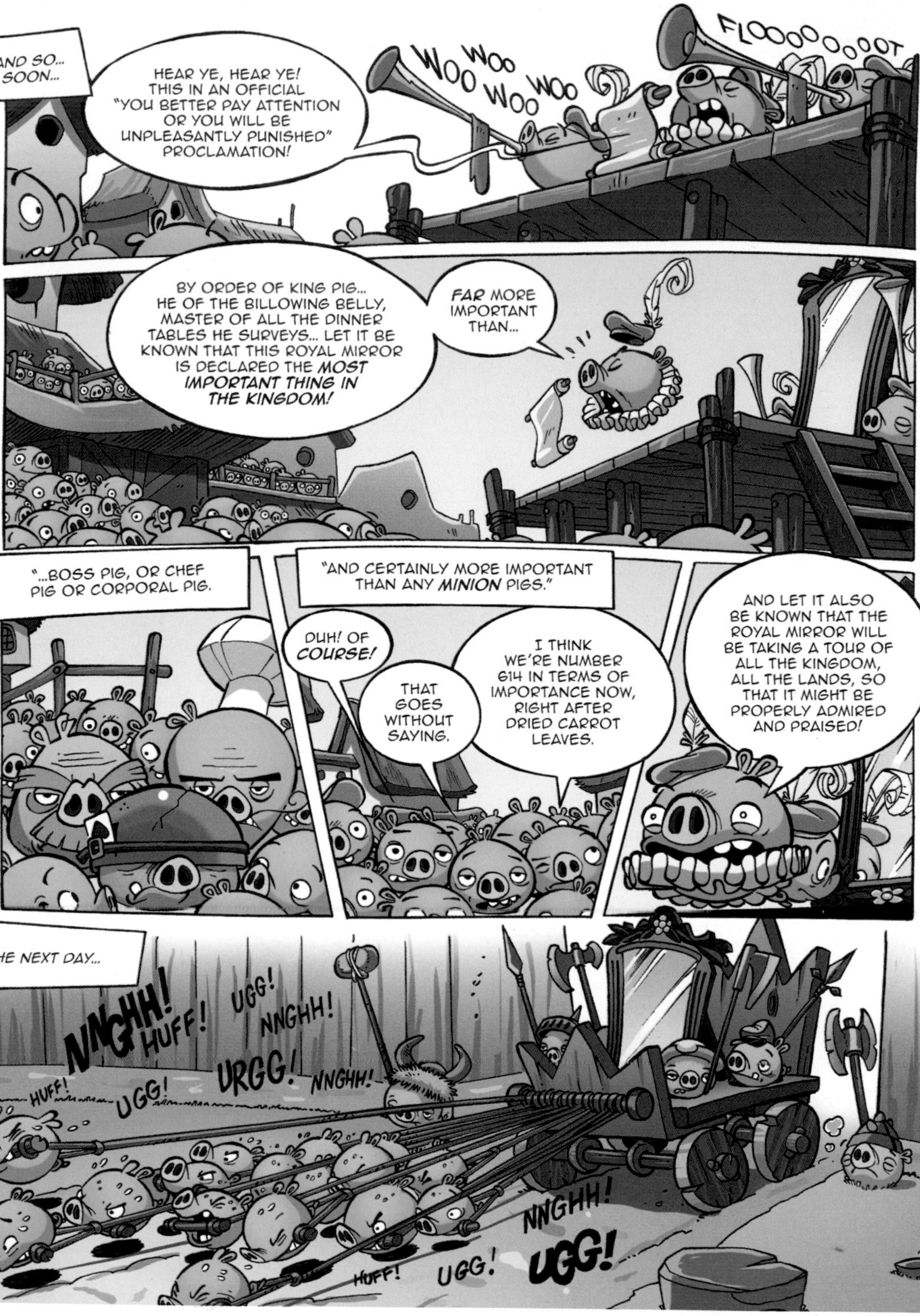

AND SO... SOON...
HEAR YE, HEAR YE! THIS IN AN OFFICIAL "YOU BETTER PAY ATTENTION OR YOU WILL BE UNPLEASANTLY PUNISHED" PROCLAMATION!
WOO WOO WOO WOO WOO
FLOOOOOOOOOT
BY ORDER OF KING PIG... HE OF THE BILLOWING BELLY, MASTER OF ALL THE DINNER TABLES HE SURVEYS... LET IT BE KNOWN THAT THIS ROYAL MIRROR IS DECLARED THE MOST IMPORTANT THING IN THE KINGDOM!
FAR MORE IMPORTANT THAN...
"...BOSS PIG, OR CHEF PIG OR CORPORAL PIG.
"AND CERTAINLY MORE IMPORTANT THAN ANY MINION PIGS."
DUH! OF COURSE!
THAT GOES WITHOUT SAYING.
I THINK WE'RE NUMBER 614 IN TERMS OF IMPORTANCE NOW, RIGHT AFTER DRIED CARROT LEAVES.
AND LET IT ALSO BE KNOWN THAT THE ROYAL MIRROR WILL BE TAKING A TOUR OF ALL THE KINGDOM, ALL THE LANDS, SO THAT IT MIGHT BE PROPERLY ADMIRED AND PRAISED!
THE NEXT DAY...
NNGHH! HUFF! UGG! NNGHH!
URGG! NNGHH!
HUFF! UGG!
NNGHH!
HUFF! UGG! UGG!

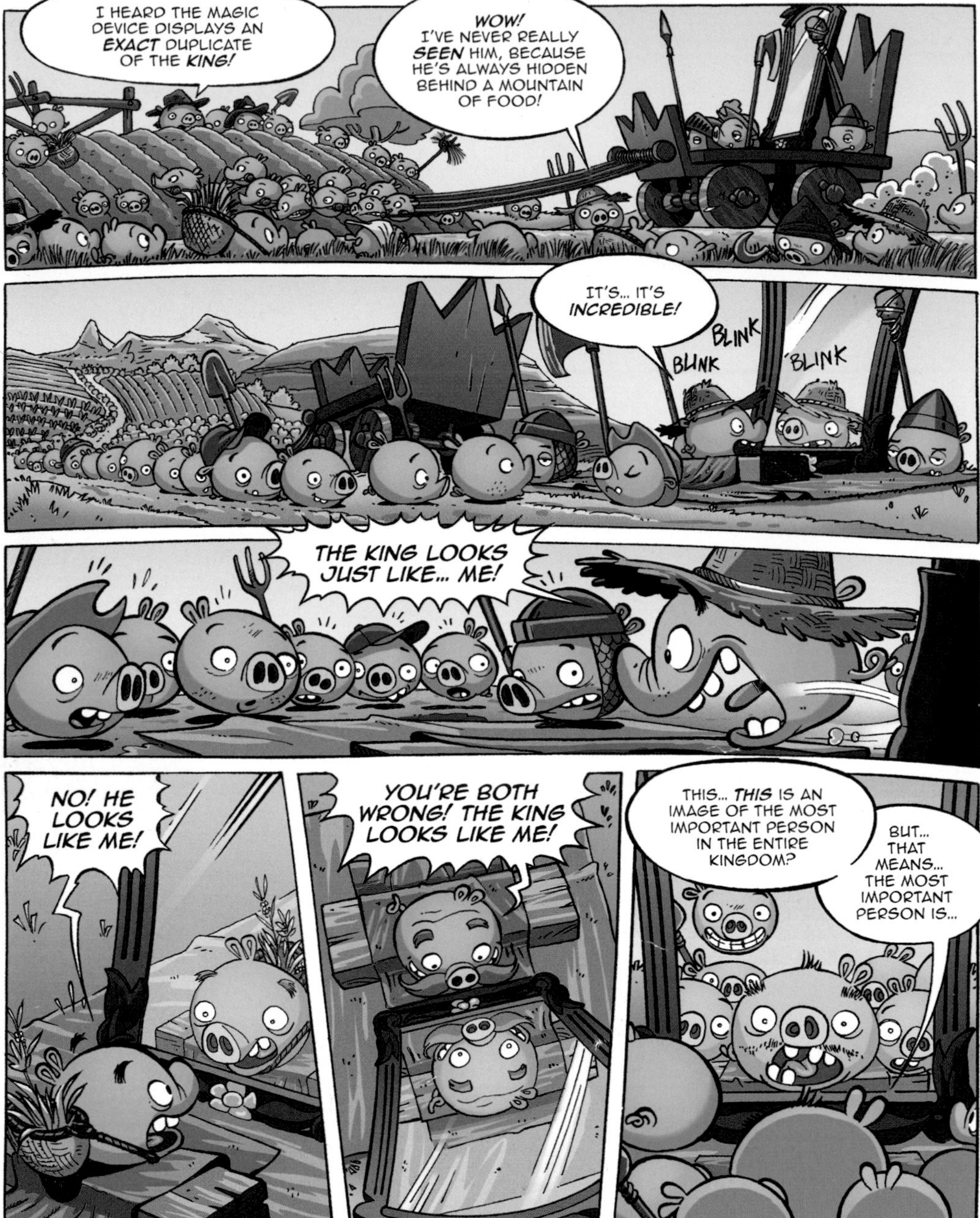
I HEARD THE MAGIC DEVICE DISPLAYS AN EXACT DUPLICATE OF THE KING!
WOW! I'VE NEVER REALLY SEEN HIM, BECAUSE HE'S ALWAYS HIDDEN BEHIND A MOUNTAIN OF FOOD!
IT'S... IT'S INCREDIBLE!
BLINK
BLINK
BLINK
THE KING LOOKS JUST LIKE... ME!
NO! HE LOOKS LIKE ME!
YOU'RE BOTH WRONG! THE KING LOOKS LIKE ME!
THIS... THIS IS AN IMAGE OF THE MOST IMPORTANT PERSON IN THE ENTIRE KINGDOM?
BUT... THAT MEANS... THE MOST IMPORTANT PERSON IS...

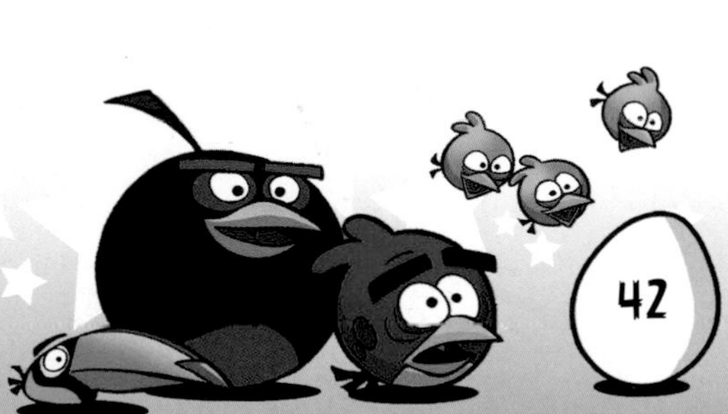

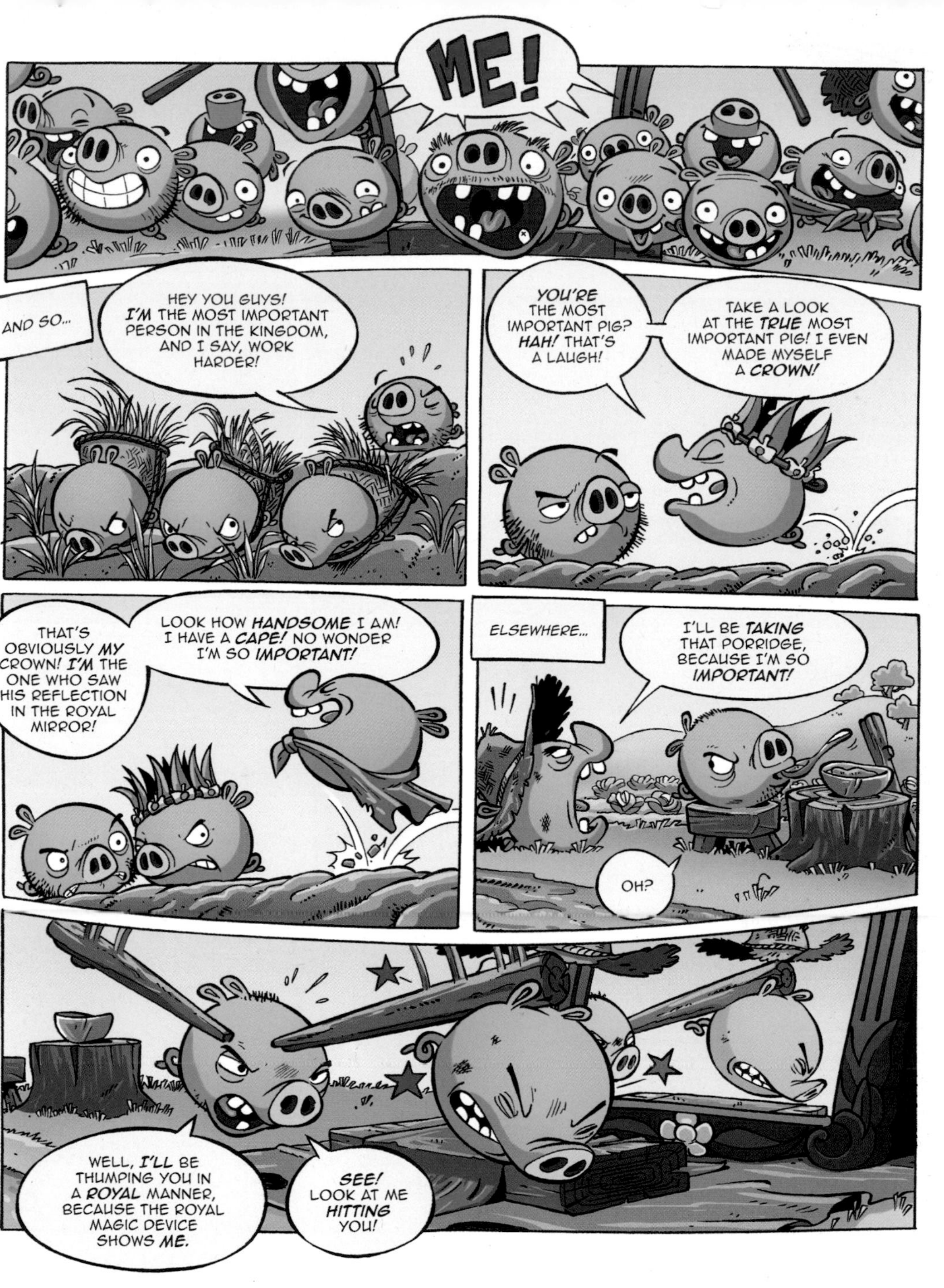
ME!
AND SO...
HEY YOU GUYS! I'M THE MOST IMPORTANT PERSON IN THE KINGDOM, AND I SAY, WORK HARDER!
YOU'RE THE MOST IMPORTANT PIG? HAH! THAT'S A LAUGH!
TAKE A LOOK AT THE TRUE MOST IMPORTANT PIG! I EVEN MADE MYSELF A CROWN!
THAT'S OBVIOUSLY MY CROWN! I'M THE ONE WHO SAW HIS REFLECTION IN THE ROYAL MIRROR!
LOOK HOW HANDSOME I AM! I HAVE A CAPE! NO WONDER I'M SO IMPORTANT!
ELSEWHERE...
I'LL BE TAKING THAT PORRIDGE, BECAUSE I'M SO IMPORTANT!
OH?
WELL, I'LL BE THUMPING YOU IN A ROYAL MANNER, BECAUSE THE ROYAL MAGIC DEVICE SHOWS ME.
SEE! LOOK AT ME HITTING YOU!

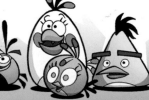

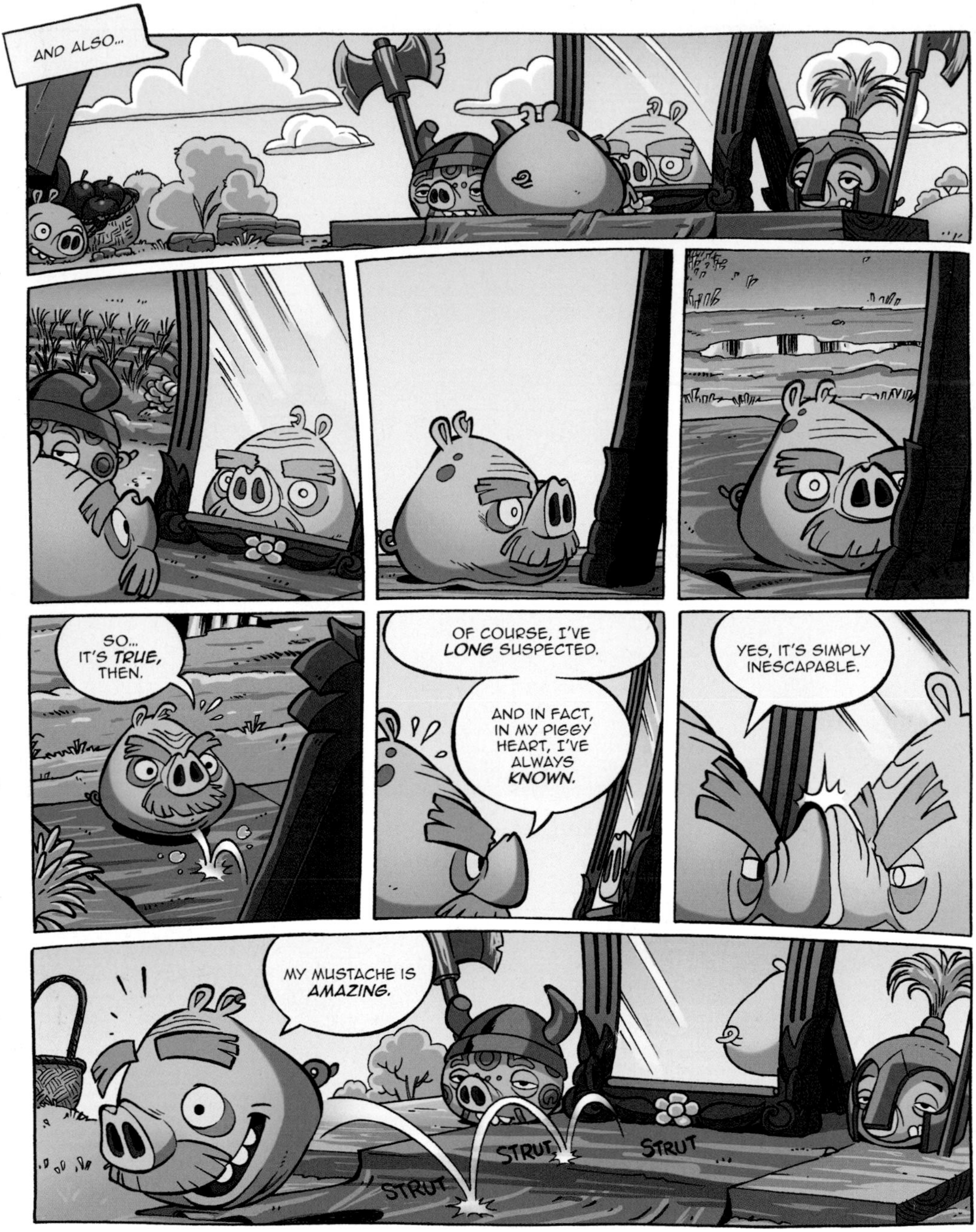
AND ALSO...
SO... IT'S *TRUE,* THEN.
OF COURSE, I'VE *LONG* SUSPECTED.
AND IN FACT, IN MY PIGGY HEART, I'VE ALWAYS *KNOWN.*
YES, IT'S SIMPLY INESCAPABLE.
MY MUSTACHE IS *AMAZING.*
STRUT
STRUT
STRUT

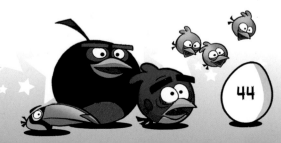

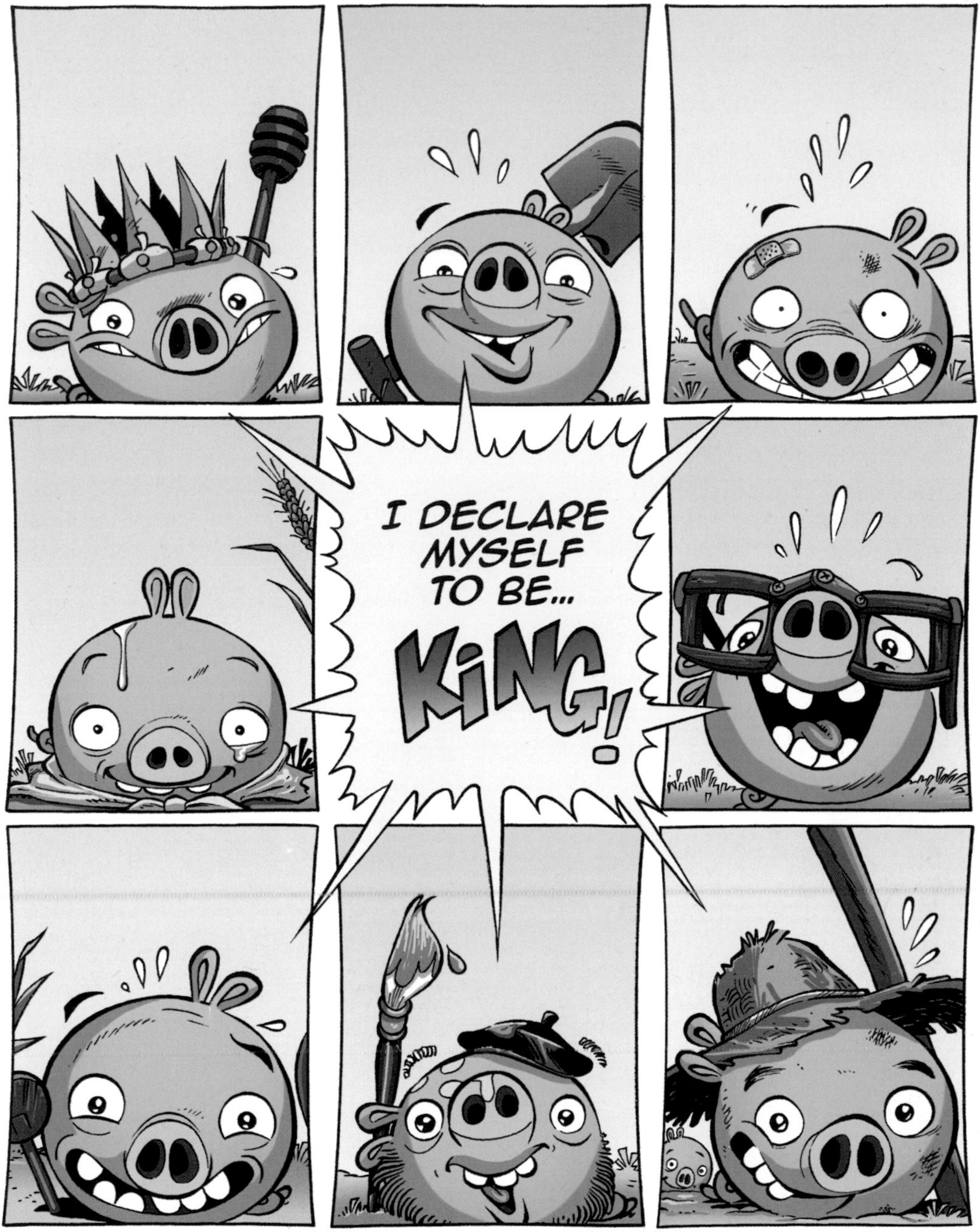
I DECLARE MYSELF TO BE...
KING!

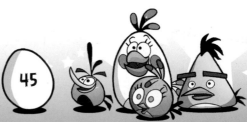

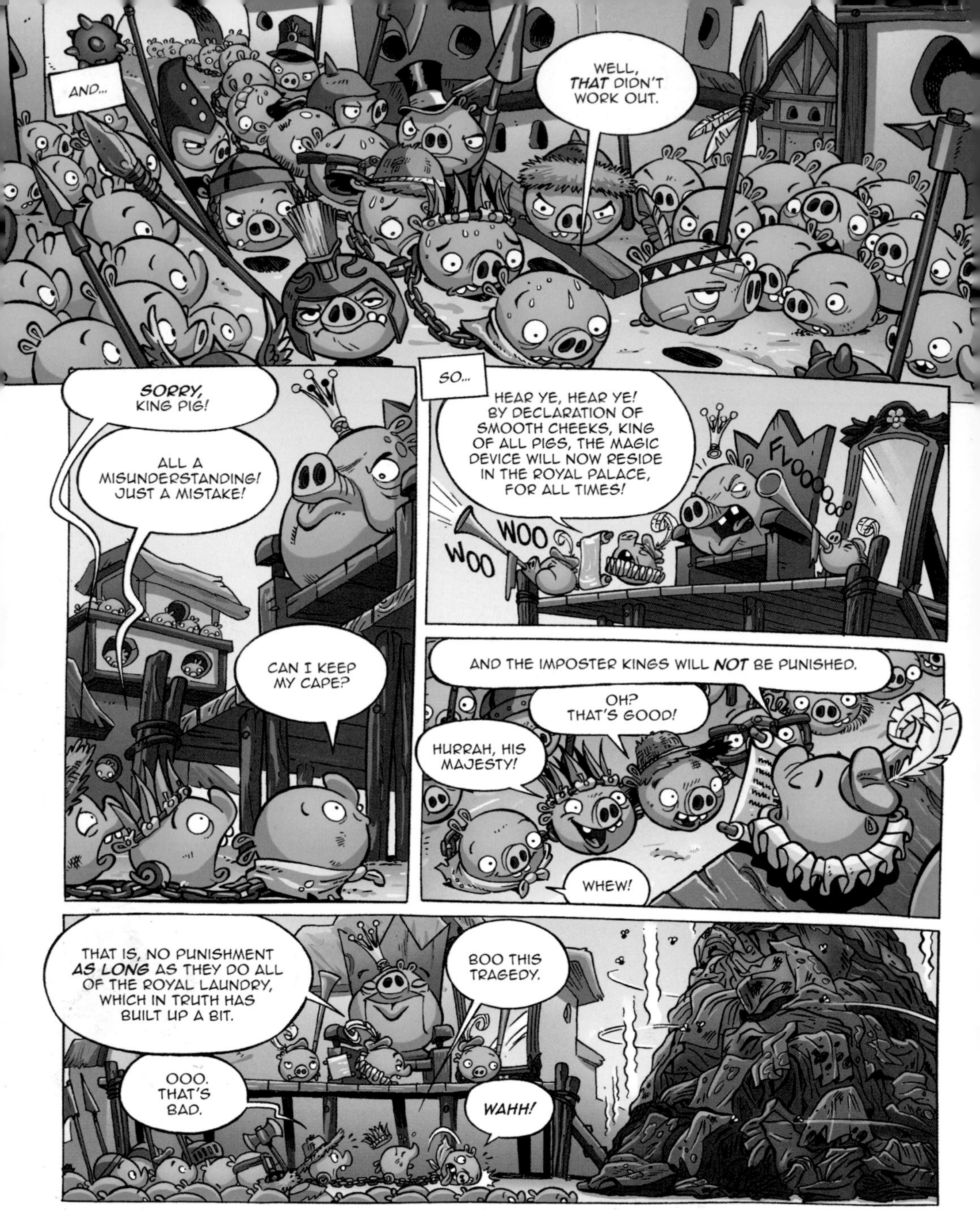

AND...
WELL, THAT DIDN'T WORK OUT.
SORRY, KING PIG!
ALL A MISUNDERSTANDING! JUST A MISTAKE!
CAN I KEEP MY CAPE?
SO...
HEAR YE, HEAR YE! BY DECLARATION OF SMOOTH CHEEKS, KING OF ALL PIGS, THE MAGIC DEVICE WILL NOW RESIDE IN THE ROYAL PALACE, FOR ALL TIMES!
WOO
WOO
AND THE IMPOSTER KINGS WILL NOT BE PUNISHED.
OH? THAT'S GOOD!
HURRAH, HIS MAJESTY!
WHEW!
THAT IS, NO PUNISHMENT AS LONG AS THEY DO ALL OF THE ROYAL LAUNDRY, WHICH IN TRUTH HAS BUILT UP A BIT.
BOO THIS TRAGEDY.
OOO. THAT'S BAD.
WAHH!

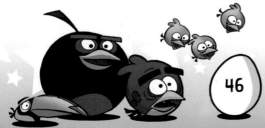

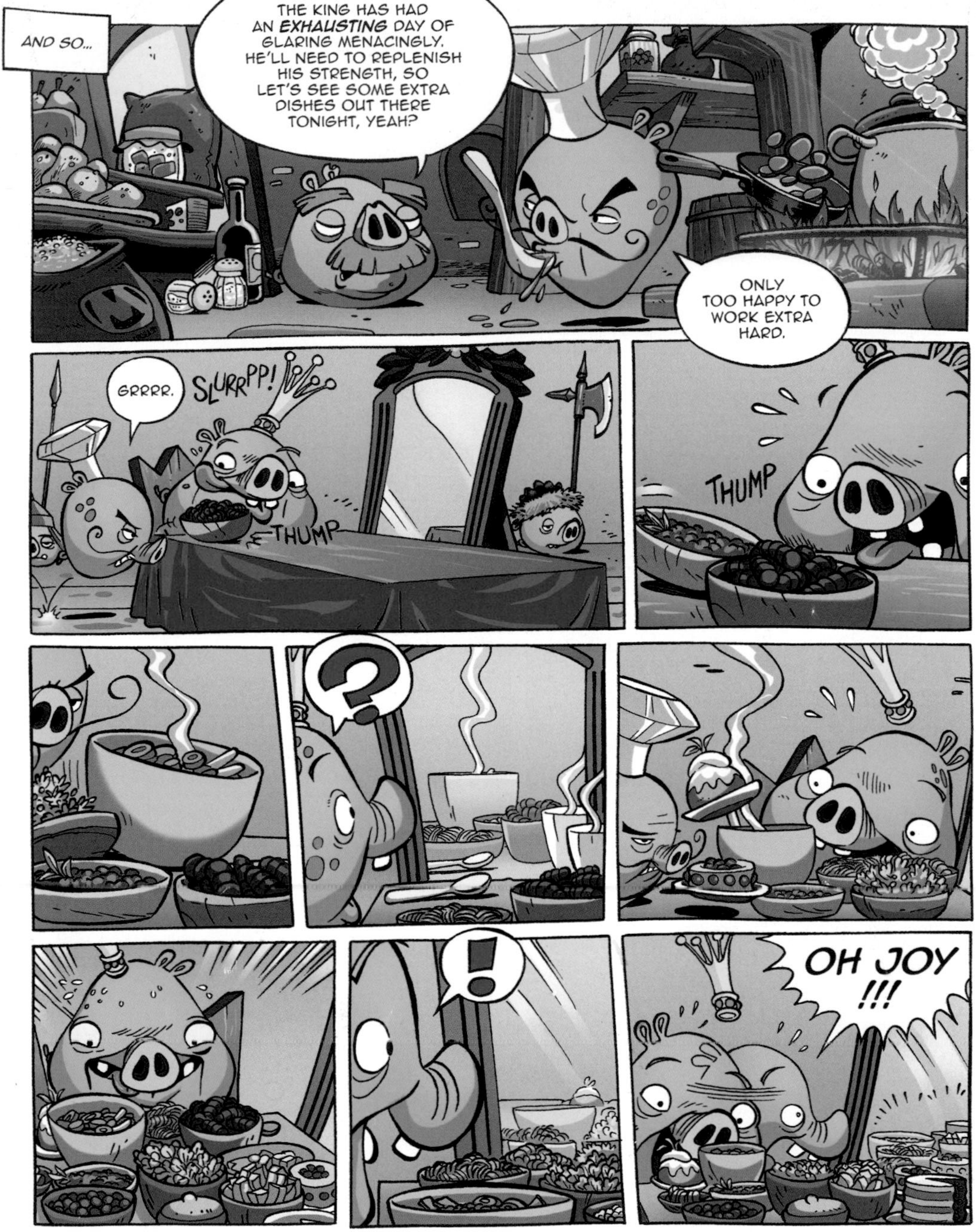
AND SO...
THE KING HAS HAD AN EXHAUSTING DAY OF GLARING MENACINGLY. HE'LL NEED TO REPLENISH HIS STRENGTH, SO LET'S SEE SOME EXTRA DISHES OUT THERE TONIGHT, YEAH?
ONLY TOO HAPPY TO WORK EXTRA HARD.
GRRRR.
SLURRPP!
THUMP
THUMP
?
!
OH JOY !!!

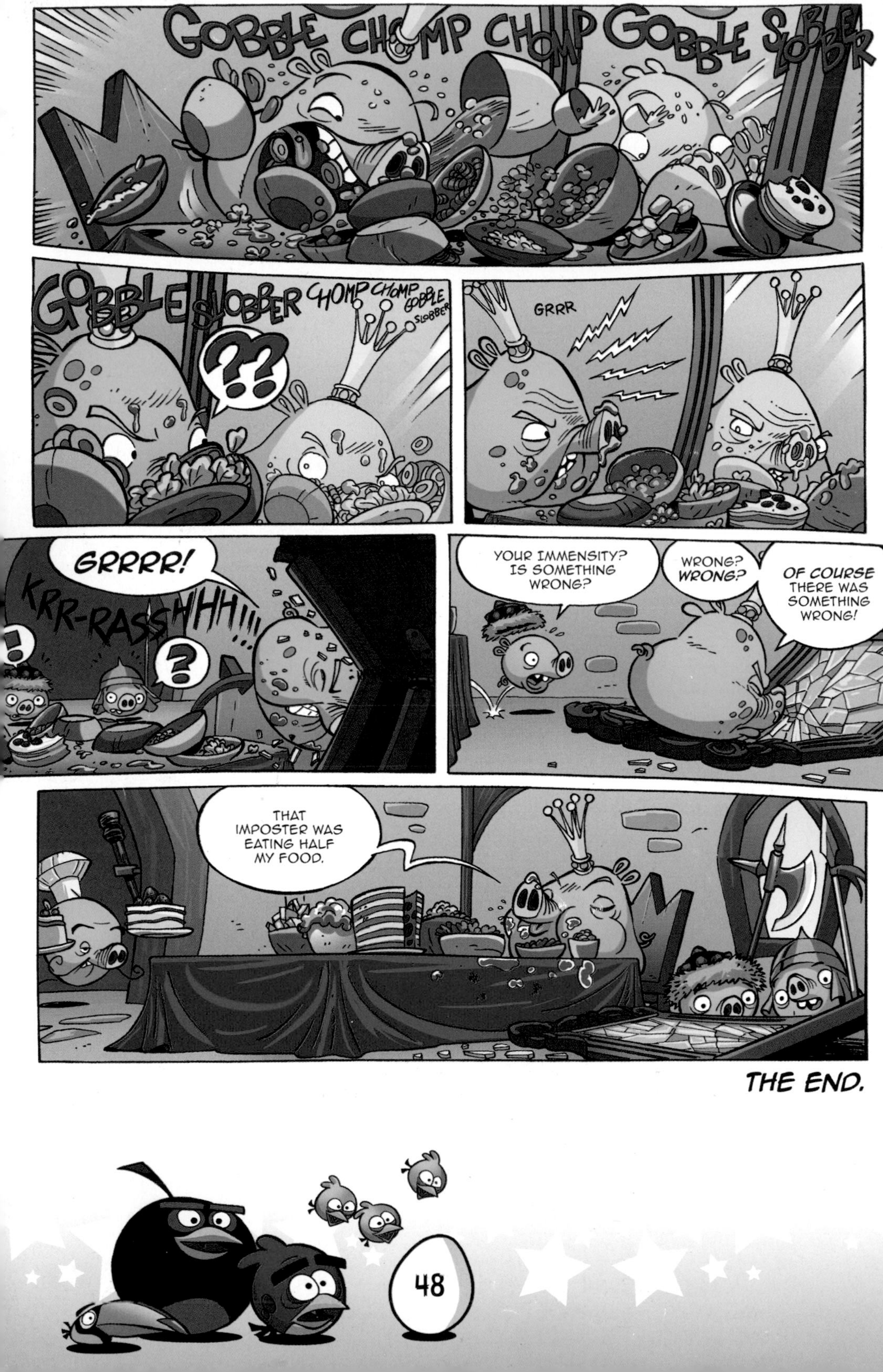
GOBBLE CHOMP CHOMP GOBBLE SLOBBER
GOBBLE SLOBBER CHOMP CHOMP GOBBLE SLOBBER
??
GRRR
GRRRR!
KRR-RASSHHH!!!
!
?
YOUR IMMENSITY? IS SOMETHING WRONG?
WRONG? WRONG?
OF COURSE THERE WAS SOMETHING WRONG!
THAT IMPOSTER WAS EATING HALF MY FOOD.
THE END.

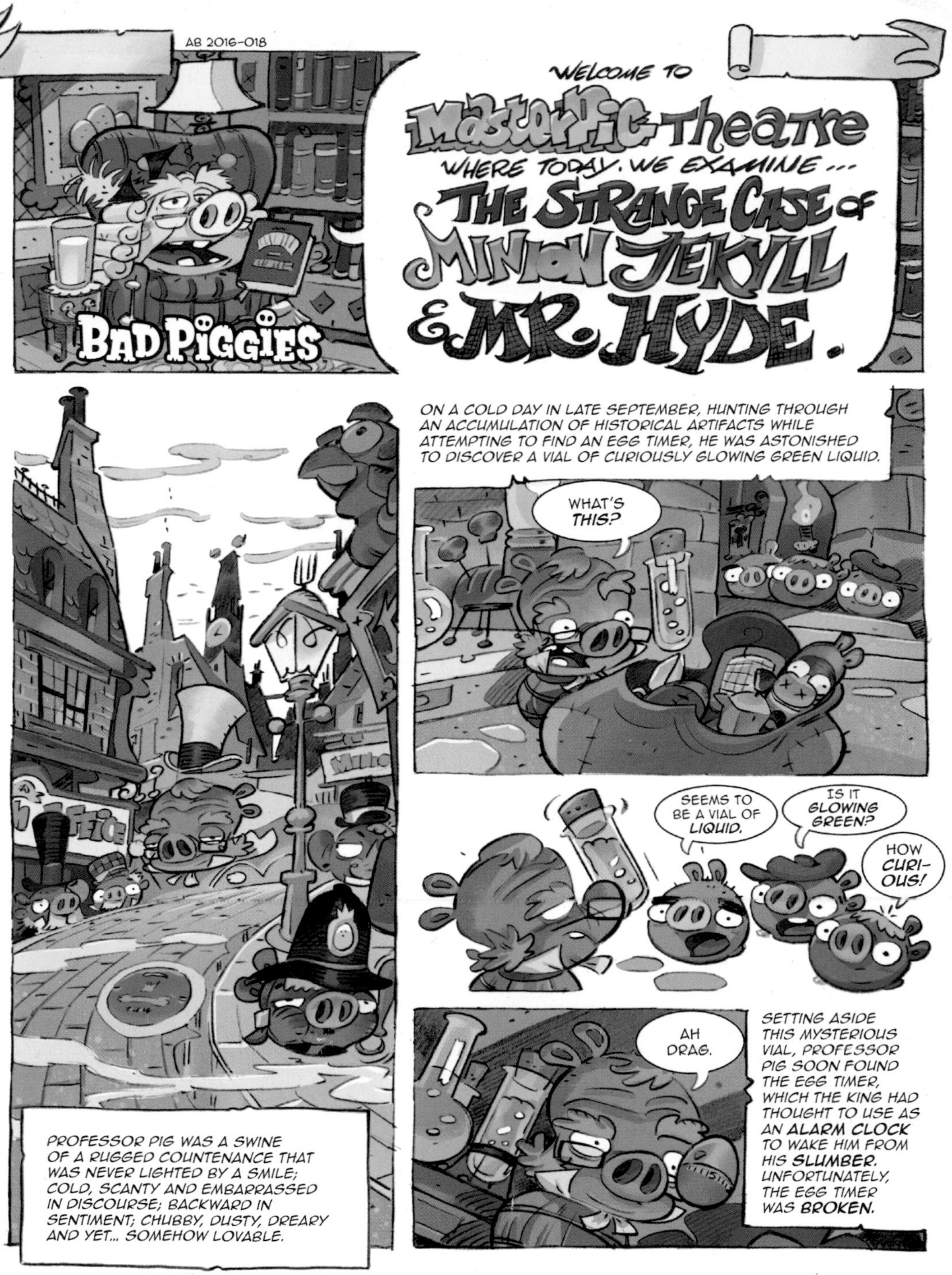
AB 2016-018
WELCOME TO
MASTERPIG THEATRE
WHERE TODAY, WE EXAMINE...
THE STRANGE CASE OF
MINION JEKYLL
& MR. HYDE.
BAD PIGGIES
PROFESSOR PIG WAS A SWINE OF A RUGGED COUNTENANCE THAT WAS NEVER LIGHTED BY A SMILE; COLD, SCANTY AND EMBARRASSED IN DISCOURSE; BACKWARD IN SENTIMENT; CHUBBY, DUSTY, DREARY AND YET... SOMEHOW LOVABLE.
ON A COLD DAY IN LATE SEPTEMBER, HUNTING THROUGH AN ACCUMULATION OF HISTORICAL ARTIFACTS WHILE ATTEMPTING TO FIND AN EGG TIMER, HE WAS ASTONISHED TO DISCOVER A VIAL OF CURIOUSLY GLOWING GREEN LIQUID.
WHAT'S THIS?
SEEMS TO BE A VIAL OF LIQUID.
IS IT GLOWING GREEN?
HOW CURI-OUS!
AH DRAG.
SETTING ASIDE THIS MYSTERIOUS VIAL, PROFESSOR PIG SOON FOUND THE EGG TIMER, WHICH THE KING HAD THOUGHT TO USE AS AN ALARM CLOCK TO WAKE HIM FROM HIS SLUMBER. UNFORTUNATELY, THE EGG TIMER WAS BROKEN.

WRITTEN BY: PAUL TOBIN
ART BY: STEFANO INTINI
COLORS BY: NICOLA PASQUETTO
LETTERS BY: PISARA OY

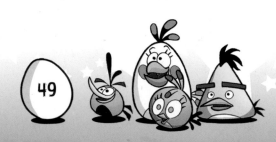

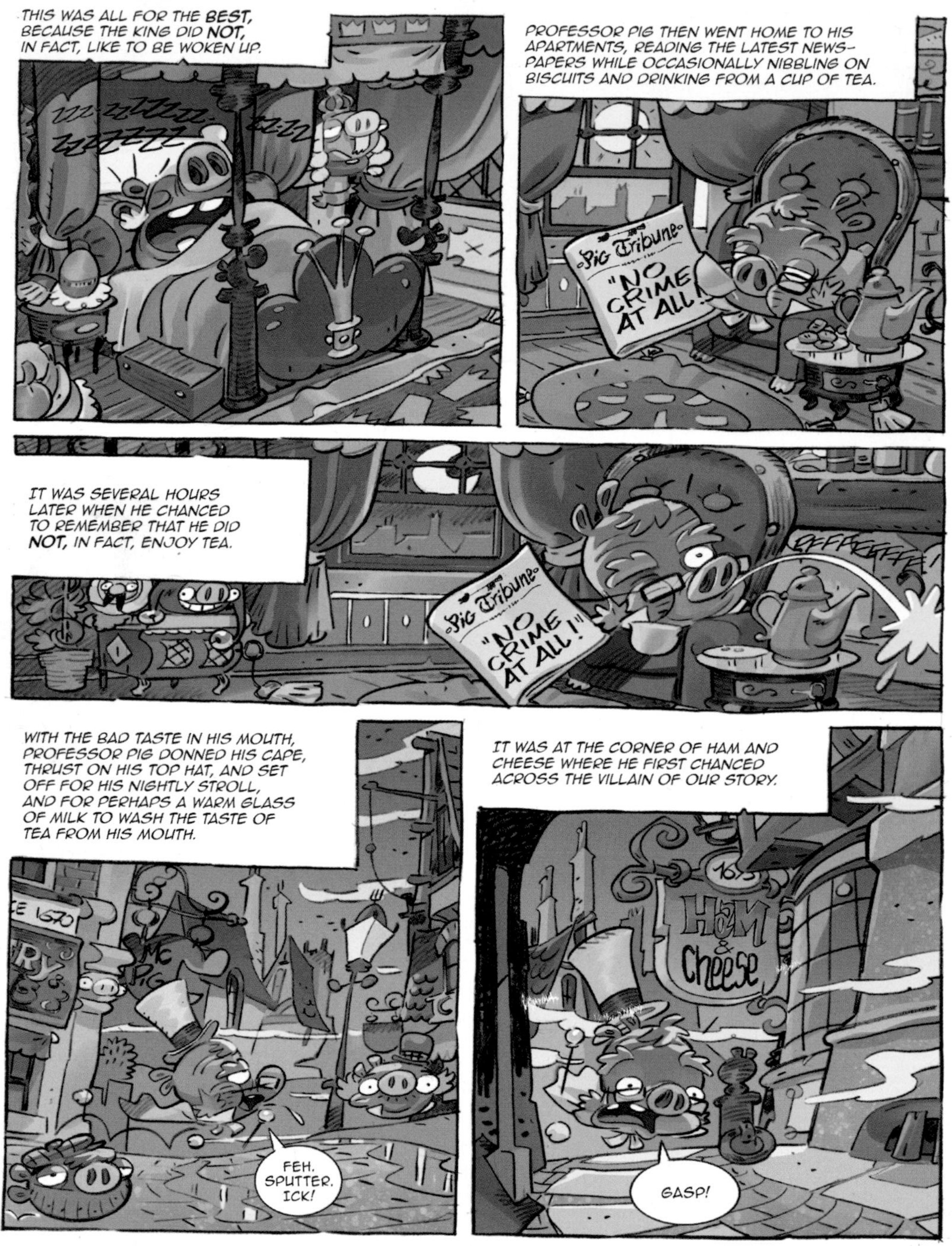
THIS WAS ALL FOR THE **BEST,** BECAUSE THE KING DID **NOT,** IN FACT, LIKE TO BE WOKEN UP.
PROFESSOR PIG THEN WENT HOME TO HIS APARTMENTS, READING THE LATEST NEWS-PAPERS WHILE OCCASIONALLY NIBBLING ON BISCUITS AND DRINKING FROM A CUP OF TEA.
Pig Tribune
"NO CRIME AT ALL!"
IT WAS SEVERAL HOURS LATER WHEN HE CHANCED TO REMEMBER THAT HE DID **NOT,** IN FACT, ENJOY TEA.
Pig Tribune
"NO CRIME AT ALL!"
WITH THE BAD TASTE IN HIS MOUTH, PROFESSOR PIG DONNED HIS CAPE, THRUST ON HIS TOP HAT, AND SET OFF FOR HIS NIGHTLY STROLL, AND FOR PERHAPS A WARM GLASS OF MILK TO WASH THE TASTE OF TEA FROM HIS MOUTH.
FEH. SPUTTER. ICK!
IT WAS AT THE CORNER OF HAM AND CHEESE WHERE HE FIRST CHANCED ACROSS THE VILLAIN OF OUR STORY.
HAM & CHEESE
GASP!

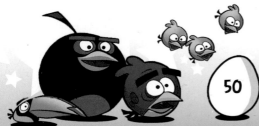

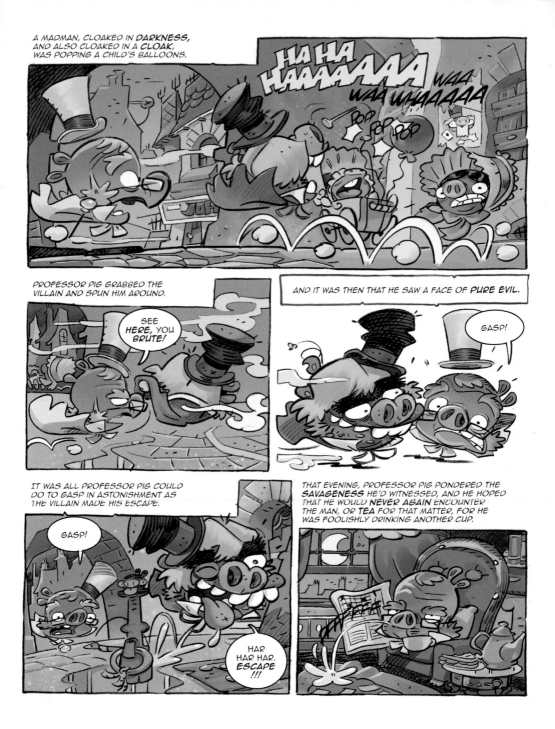

A MADMAN, CLOAKED IN **DARKNESS**, AND ALSO CLOAKED IN A **CLOAK**, WAS POPPING A CHILD'S BALLOONS.

HA HA HAAAAAAAA WAA WAA WHAAAAAA

POP POP POP

PROFESSOR PIG GRABBED THE VILLAIN AND SPUN HIM AROUND.

SEE **HERE**, YOU **BRUTE**!

AND IT WAS THEN THAT HE SAW A FACE OF **PURE EVIL**.

GASP!

IT WAS ALL PROFESSOR PIG COULD DO TO GASP IN ASTONISHMENT AS THE VILLAIN MADE HIS ESCAPE.

GASP!

HAR HAR HAR. **ESCAPE** !!!

THAT EVENING, PROFESSOR PIG PONDERED THE **SAVAGENESS** HE'D WITNESSED, AND HE HOPED THAT HE WOULD **NEVER AGAIN** ENCOUNTER THE MAN, OR **TEA** FOR THAT MATTER, FOR HE WAS FOOLISHLY DRINKING ANOTHER CUP.

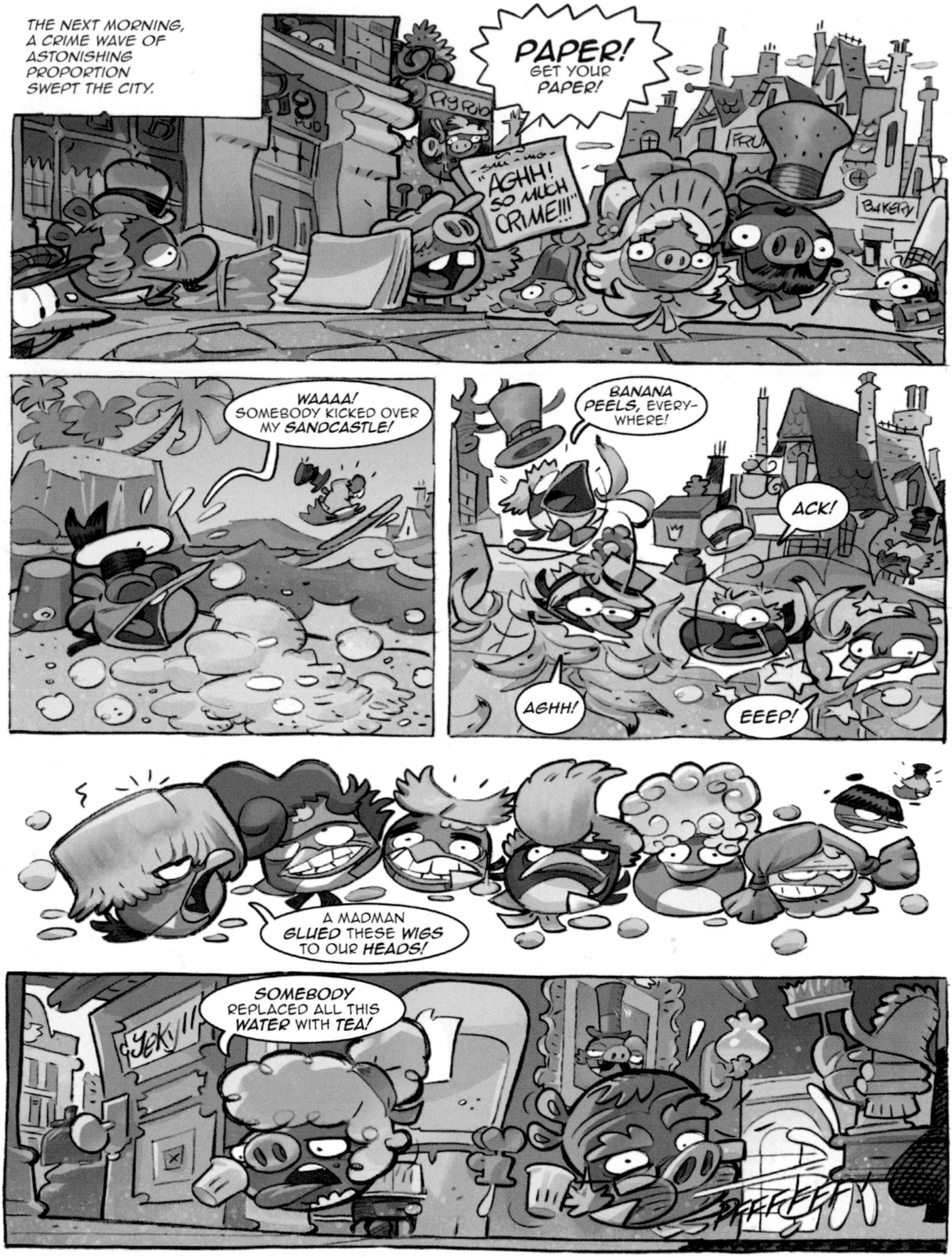
THE NEXT MORNING, A CRIME WAVE OF ASTONISHING PROPORTION SWEPT THE CITY.
PAPER! GET YOUR PAPER!
"AGHH! SO MUCH CRIME!!!"
BAKERY
WAAAA! SOMEBODY KICKED OVER MY SANDCASTLE!
BANANA PEELS, EVERY-WHERE!
ACK!
AGHH!
EEEP!
A MADMAN GLUED THESE WIGS TO OUR HEADS!
SOMEBODY REPLACED ALL THIS WATER WITH TEA!

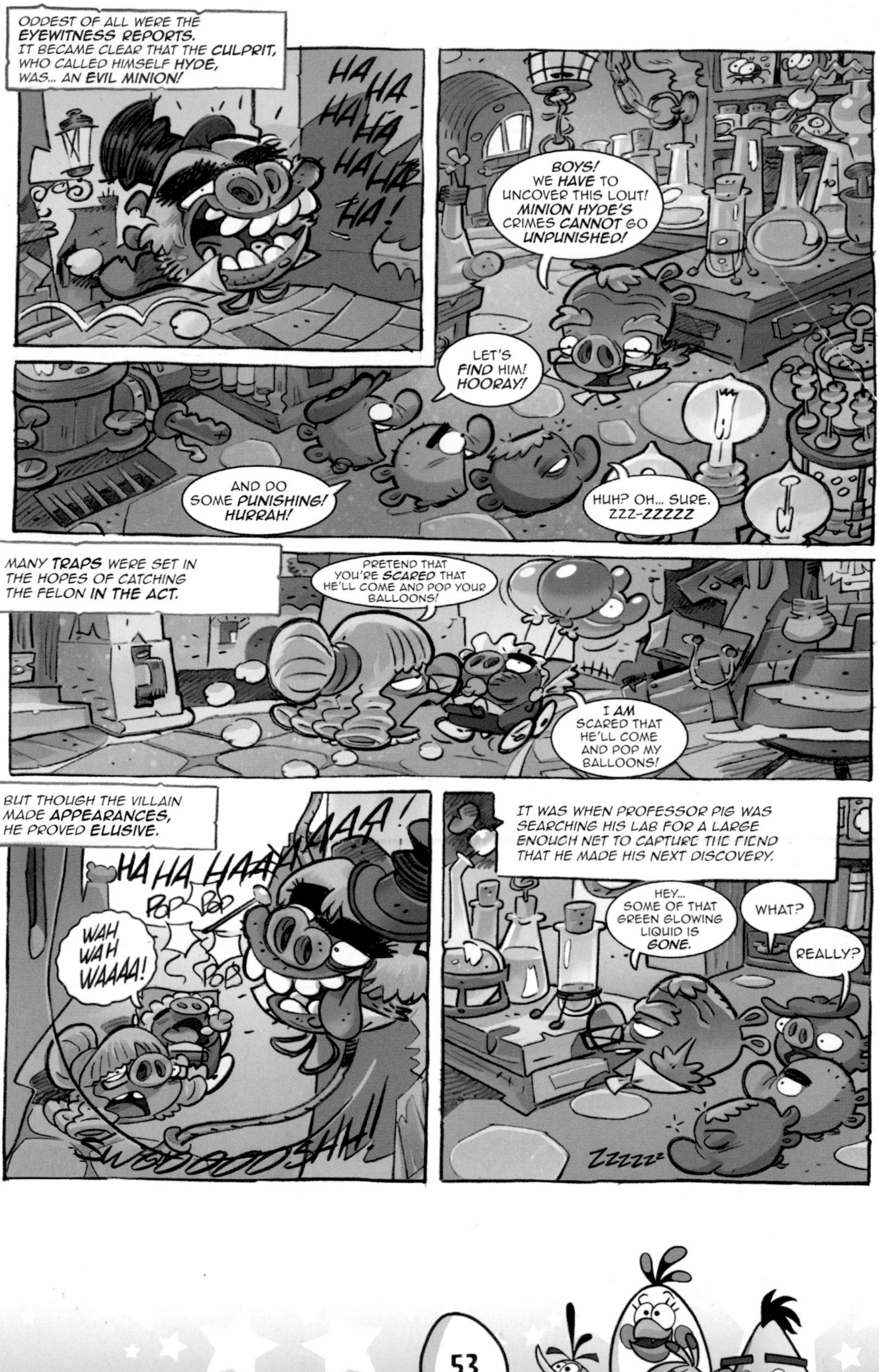
ODDEST OF ALL WERE THE EYEWITNESS REPORTS. IT BECAME CLEAR THAT THE CULPRIT, WHO CALLED HIMSELF HYDE, WAS... AN EVIL MINION!
HA HA HA HA HA HA HA!
BOYS! WE HAVE TO UNCOVER THIS LOUT! MINION HYDE'S CRIMES CANNOT GO UNPUNISHED!
LET'S FIND HIM! HOORAY!
AND DO SOME PUNISHING! HURRAH!
HUH? OH... SURE. ZZZ-ZZZZZ
MANY TRAPS WERE SET IN THE HOPES OF CATCHING THE FELON IN THE ACT.
PRETEND THAT YOU'RE SCARED THAT HE'LL COME AND POP YOUR BALLOONS!
I AM SCARED THAT HE'LL COME AND POP MY BALLOONS!
BUT THOUGH THE VILLAIN MADE APPEARANCES, HE PROVED ELUSIVE.
HA HA HAAAAAAA!
POP POP
WAH WAH WAAAA!
POP
SWOOOOOOSHH!
IT WAS WHEN PROFESSOR PIG WAS SEARCHING HIS LAB FOR A LARGE ENOUGH NET TO CAPTURE THE FIEND THAT HE MADE HIS NEXT DISCOVERY.
HEY... SOME OF THAT GREEN GLOWING LIQUID IS GONE.
WHAT?
REALLY?
ZZZZZZ

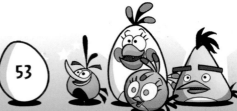

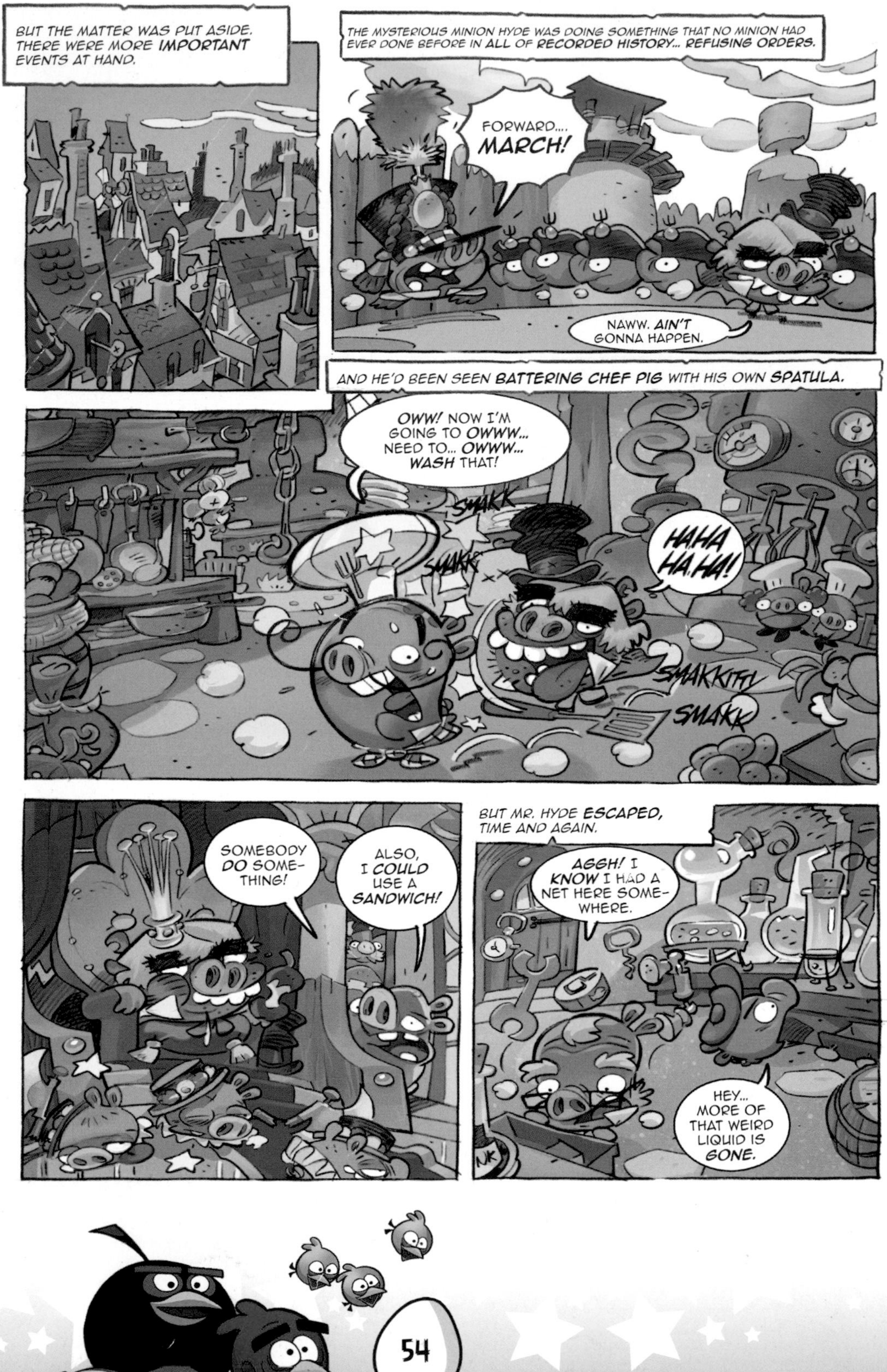
BUT THE MATTER WAS PUT ASIDE. THERE WERE MORE IMPORTANT EVENTS AT HAND.
THE MYSTERIOUS MINION HYDE WAS DOING SOMETHING THAT NO MINION HAD EVER DONE BEFORE IN ALL OF RECORDED HISTORY... REFUSING ORDERS.
FORWARD.... MARCH!
NAWW. AIN'T GONNA HAPPEN.
AND HE'D BEEN SEEN BATTERING CHEF PIG WITH HIS OWN SPATULA.
OWW! NOW I'M GOING TO OWWW... NEED TO... OWWW... WASH THAT!
SMAKK
SMAKK
HAHA HA HA!
SMAKKITY
SMAKK
SOMEBODY DO SOME-THING!
ALSO, I COULD USE A SANDWICH!
BUT MR. HYDE ESCAPED, TIME AND AGAIN.
AGGH! I KNOW I HAD A NET HERE SOME-WHERE.
HEY... MORE OF THAT WEIRD LIQUID IS GONE.

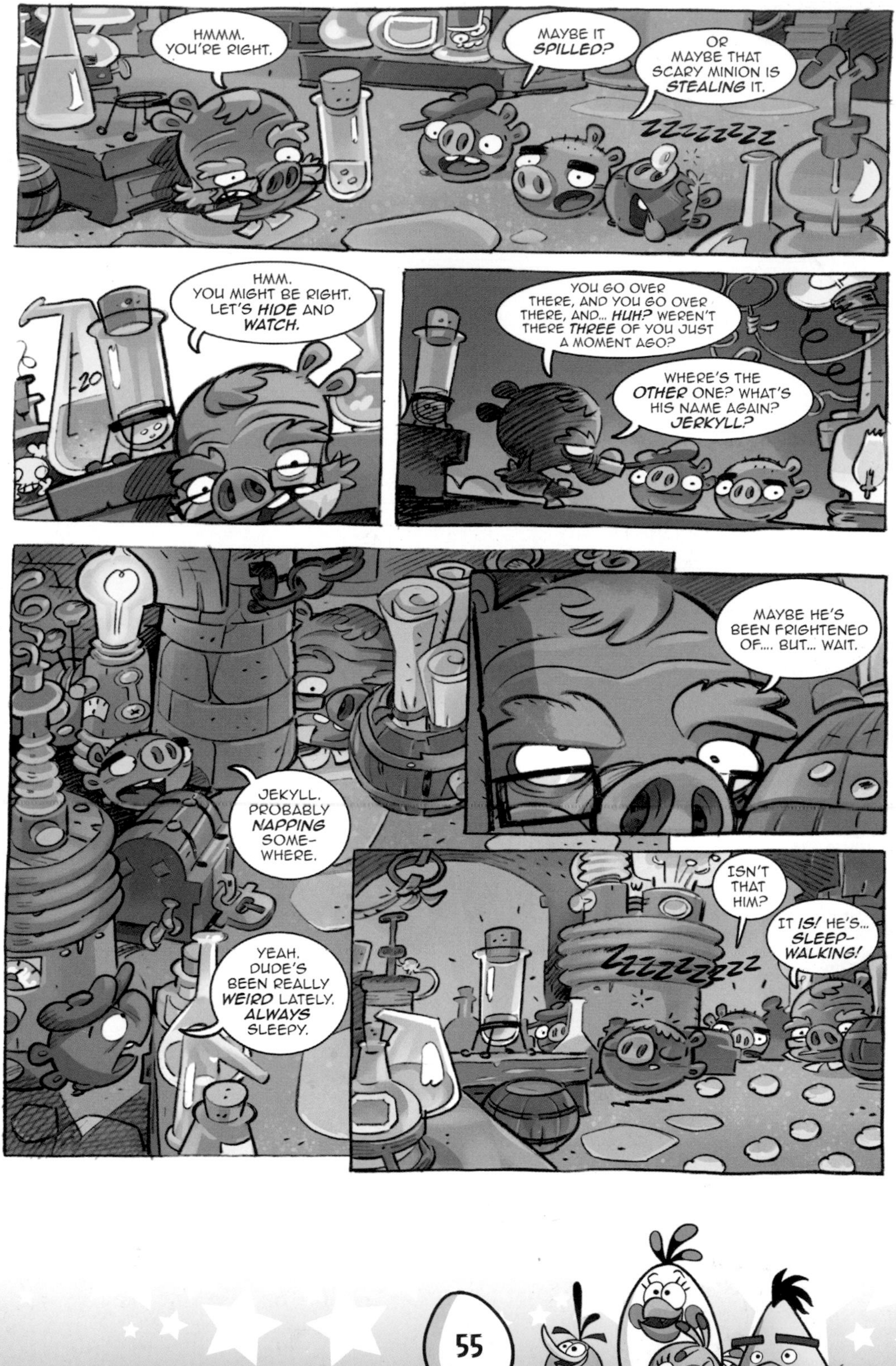
HMMM. YOU'RE RIGHT.
MAYBE IT SPILLED?
OR MAYBE THAT SCARY MINION IS STEALING IT.
ZZZZZZZZZ
HMM. YOU MIGHT BE RIGHT. LET'S HIDE AND WATCH.
YOU GO OVER THERE, AND YOU GO OVER THERE, AND... HUH? WEREN'T THERE THREE OF YOU JUST A MOMENT AGO?
WHERE'S THE OTHER ONE? WHAT'S HIS NAME AGAIN? JERKYLL?
JEKYLL. PROBABLY NAPPING SOMEWHERE.
MAYBE HE'S BEEN FRIGHTENED OF.... BUT... WAIT.
YEAH. DUDE'S BEEN REALLY WEIRD LATELY. ALWAYS SLEEPY.
ISN'T THAT HIM?
IT IS! HE'S... SLEEP-WALKING!
ZZZZZZZZZ

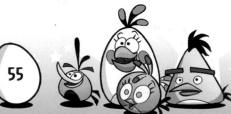

GUZZLE GUZZLE
GUZZLE
YUM! PEPPERMINT.
GUHHH!
POIK
POIK
POIK
POIK
POIK
GRR-RAAARRRRRR!!!
HA HA HA HA HA!
WAIT... HE'S THE EVIL MENACING MINION?

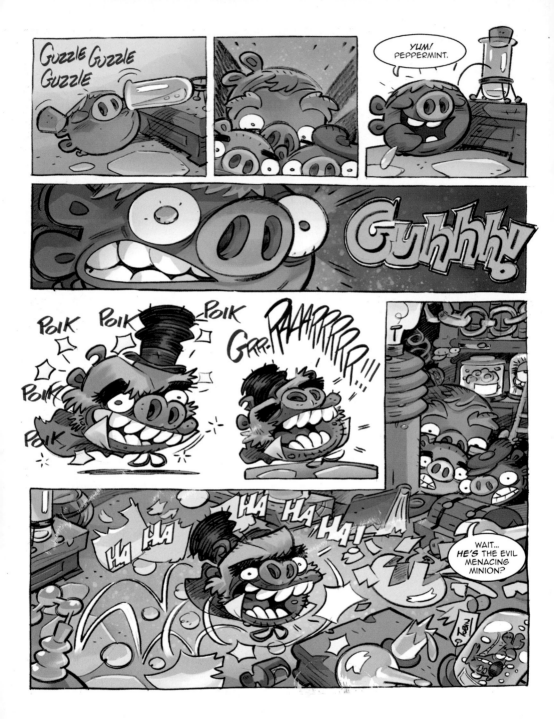

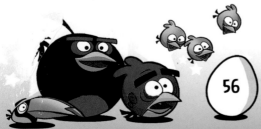

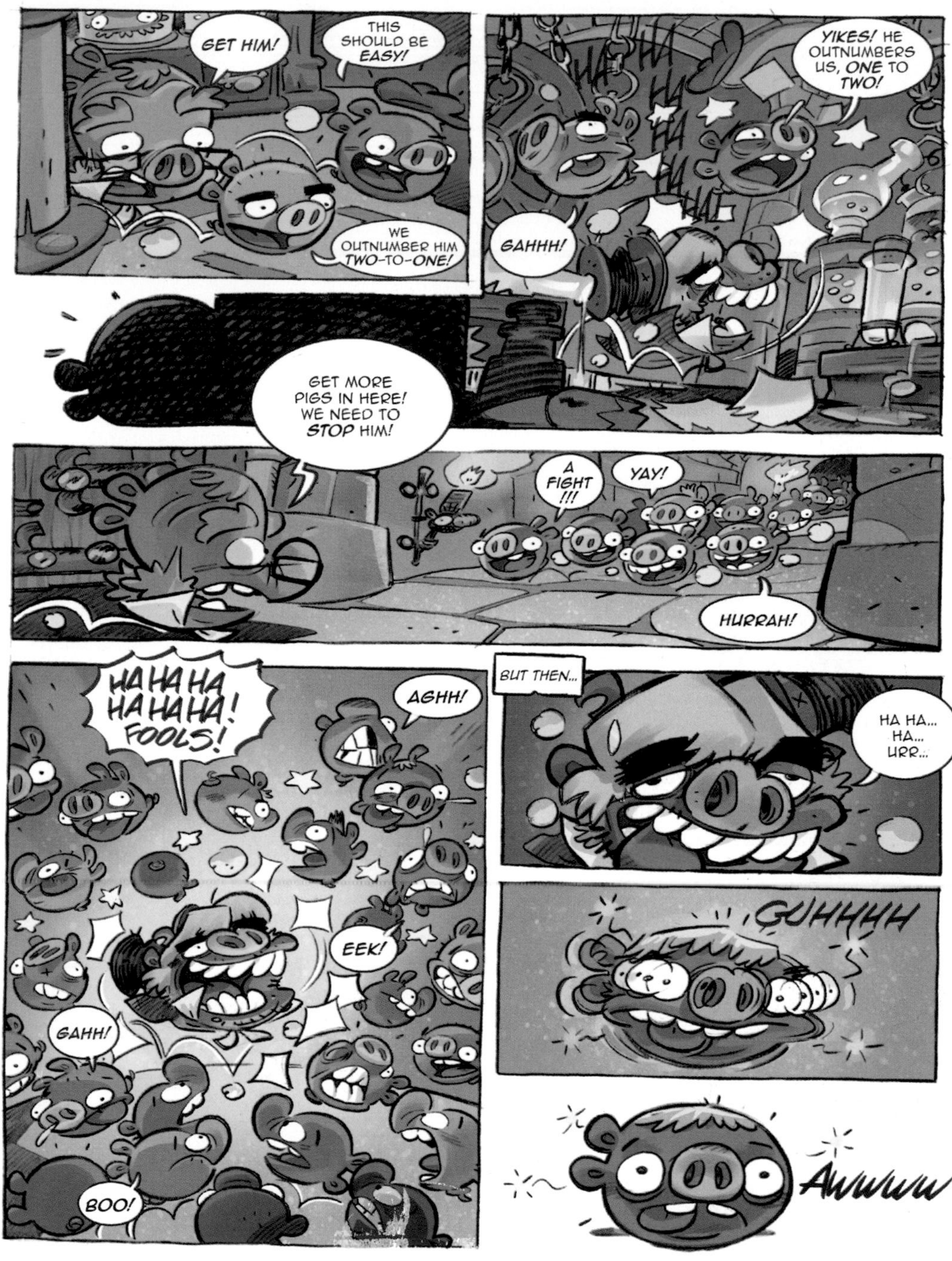
GET HIM!
THIS SHOULD BE EASY!
WE OUTNUMBER HIM TWO-TO-ONE!
HA HA HA HA HA HA!
YIKES! HE OUTNUMBERS US, ONE TO TWO!
GAHHH!
GET MORE PIGS IN HERE! WE NEED TO STOP HIM!
A FIGHT !!!
YAY!
HURRAH!
HA HA HA HA HA HA! FOOLS!
AGHH!
EEK!
GAHH!
BOO!
BUT THEN...
HA HA... HA... URR...
GUHHHH
AWWWW

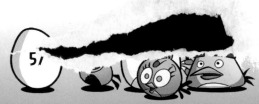

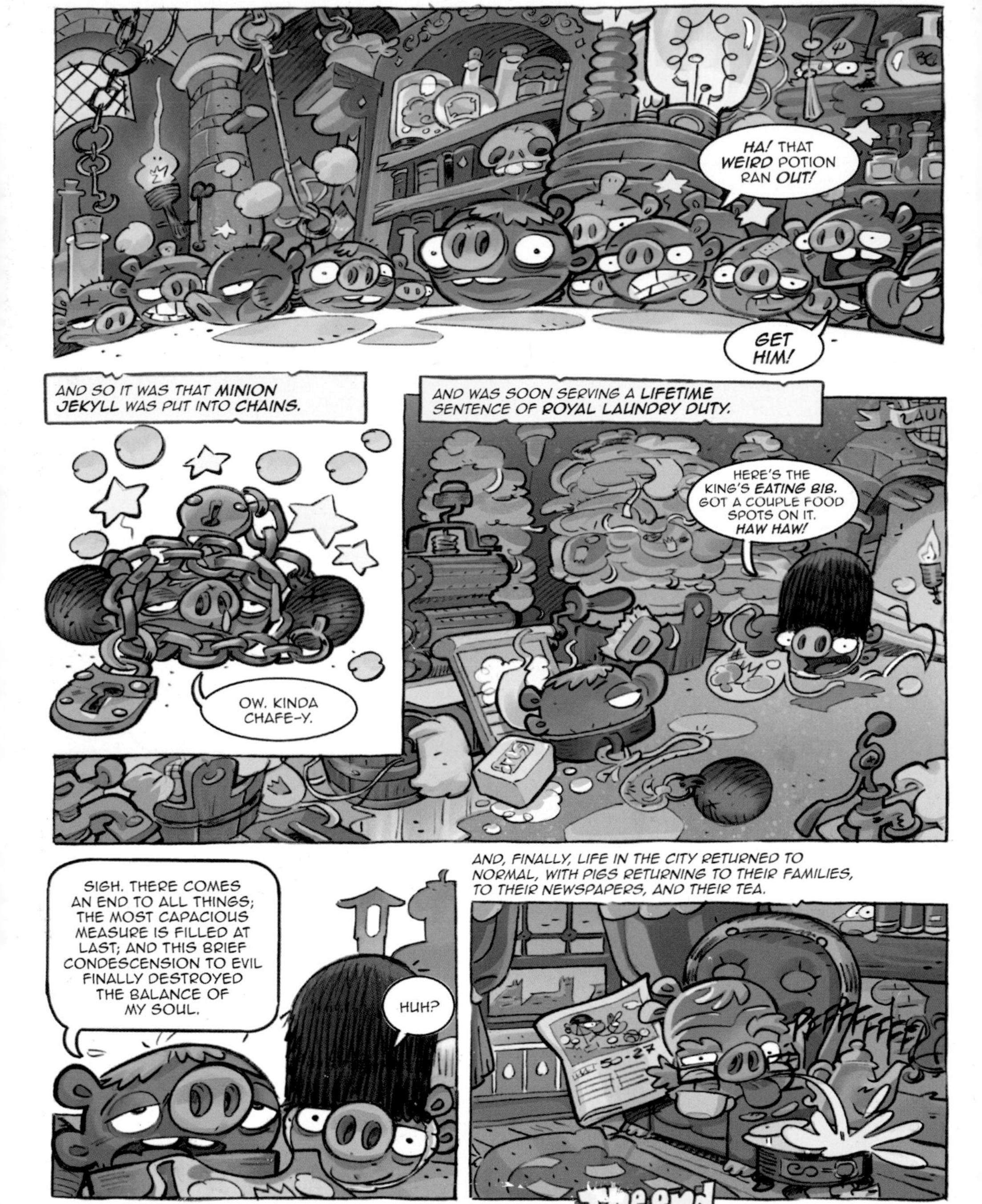
HA! THAT WEIRD POTION RAN OUT!
GET HIM!
AND SO IT WAS THAT MINION JEKYLL WAS PUT INTO CHAINS.
OW. KINDA CHAFE-Y.
AND WAS SOON SERVING A LIFETIME SENTENCE OF ROYAL LAUNDRY DUTY.
HERE'S THE KING'S EATING BIB. GOT A COUPLE FOOD SPOTS ON IT. HAW HAW!
SIGH. THERE COMES AN END TO ALL THINGS; THE MOST CAPACIOUS MEASURE IS FILLED AT LAST; AND THIS BRIEF CONDESCENSION TO EVIL FINALLY DESTROYED THE BALANCE OF MY SOUL.
HUH?
AND, FINALLY, LIFE IN THE CITY RETURNED TO NORMAL, WITH PIGS RETURNING TO THEIR FAMILIES, TO THEIR NEWSPAPERS, AND THEIR TEA.
50-27
The end

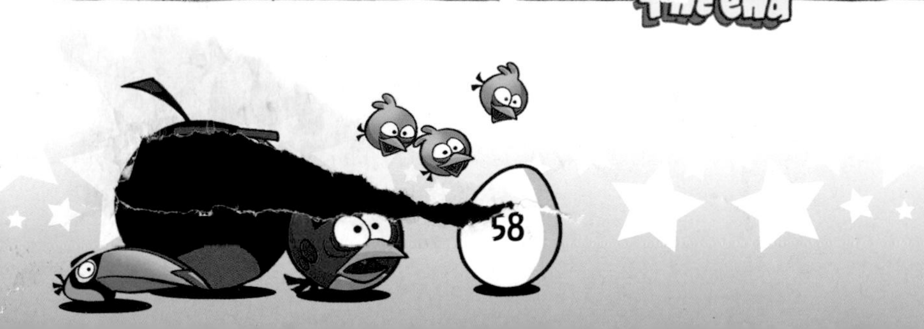

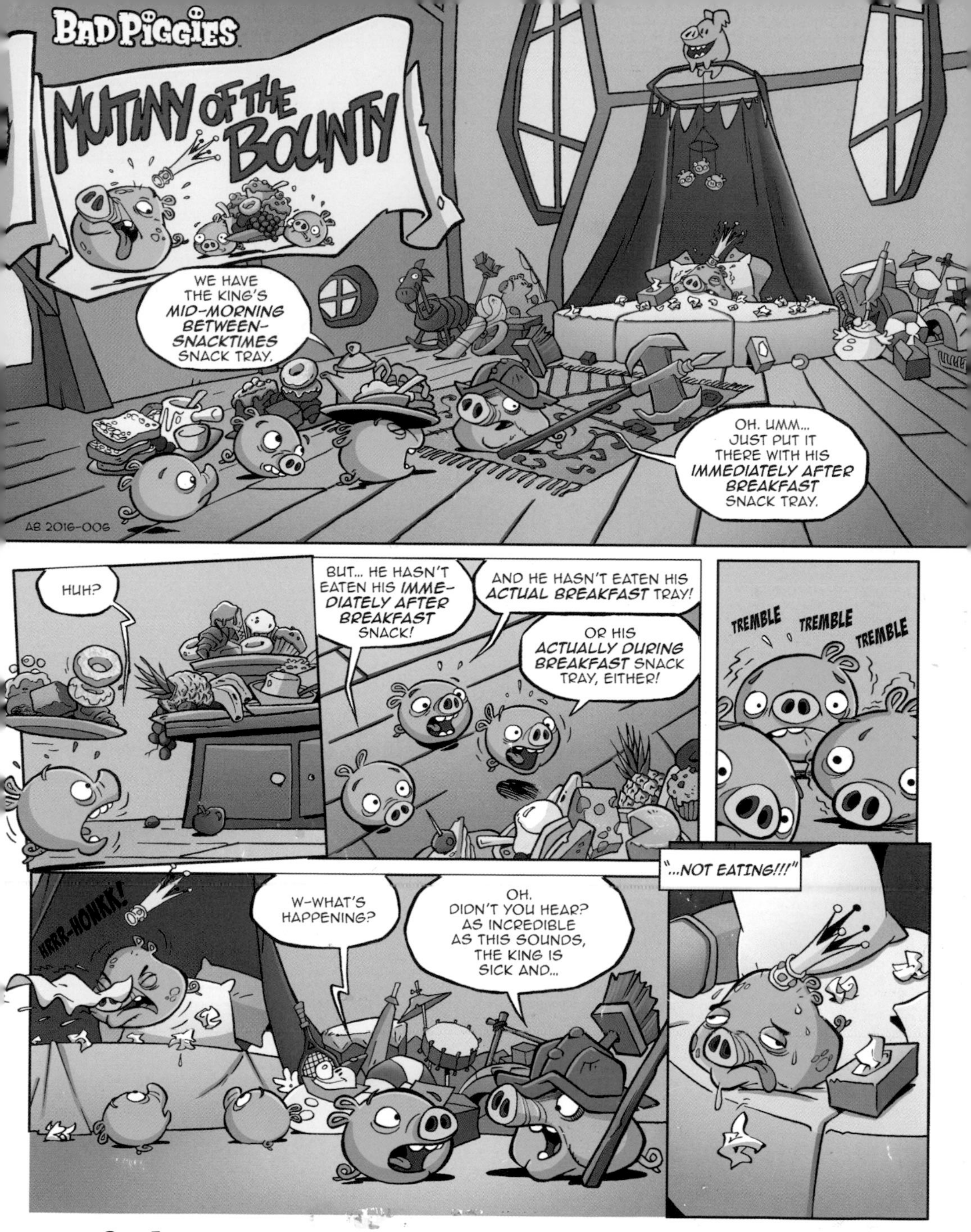
BAD PIGGIES
MUTINY OF THE BOUNTY
WE HAVE THE KING'S MID-MORNING BETWEEN-SNACKTIMES SNACK TRAY.
OH. UMM... JUST PUT IT THERE WITH HIS IMMEDIATELY AFTER BREAKFAST SNACK TRAY.
AB 2016-006
HUH?
BUT... HE HASN'T EATEN HIS IMMEDIATELY AFTER BREAKFAST SNACK!
AND HE HASN'T EATEN HIS ACTUAL BREAKFAST TRAY!
OR HIS ACTUALLY DURING BREAKFAST SNACK TRAY, EITHER!
TREMBLE
TREMBLE
TREMBLE
HRRR-HONKK!
W-WHAT'S HAPPENING?
OH. DIDN'T YOU HEAR? AS INCREDIBLE AS THIS SOUNDS, THE KING IS SICK AND...
"...NOT EATING!!!"

WRITTEN BY: PAUL TOBIN
ART BY: CÉSAR FERIOLI
COLORS BY: DIGIKORE
LETTERS BY: PISARA OY

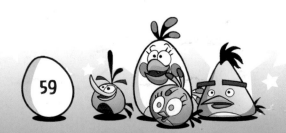

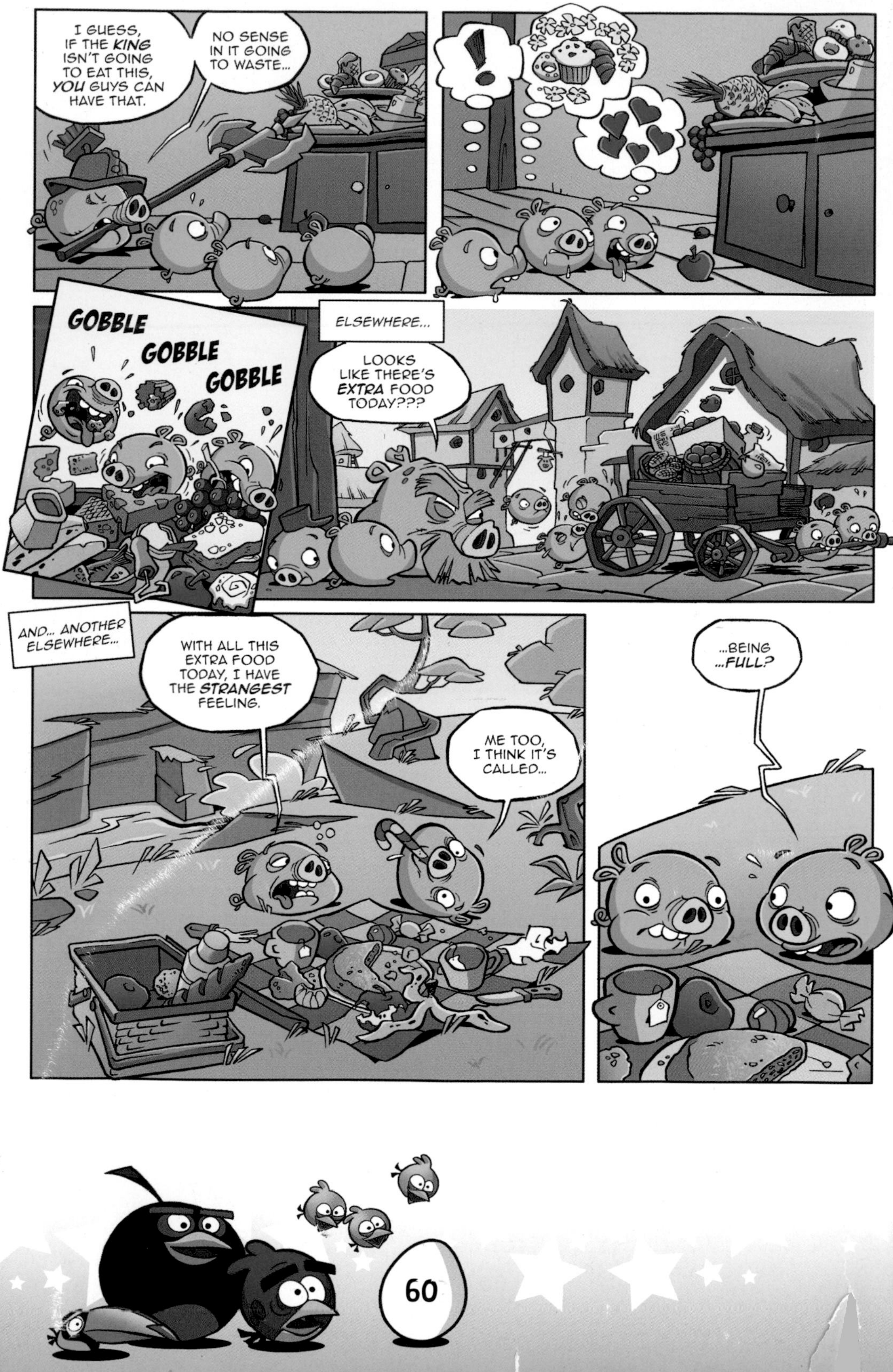
I GUESS, IF THE KING ISN'T GOING TO EAT THIS, YOU GUYS CAN HAVE THAT.
NO SENSE IN IT GOING TO WASTE...
!
GOBBLE
GOBBLE
GOBBLE
ELSEWHERE...
LOOKS LIKE THERE'S EXTRA FOOD TODAY???
AND... ANOTHER ELSEWHERE...
WITH ALL THIS EXTRA FOOD TODAY, I HAVE THE STRANGEST FEELING.
ME TOO, I THINK IT'S CALLED...
...BEING ...FULL?

MONDAY.
EAT ALL YOU WANT, GUYS. THE KING IS STILL TOO SICK TO EAT.
GOBBLE
GOBBLE
GOBBLE
GOBBLE
GOBBLE
GOBBLE
GOBBLE
TUESDAY.
GOBBLE
GOBBLE
ANOTHER PLATE, IF ANYONE'S STILL HUNGRY!
WEDNESDAY.
WAVE YOUR FLAGS IF YOU WANT EXTRA PIE!
WAVE
WAVE
WAVE
WAVE
WAVE
WAVE
WAVE
WAVE
WAVE
THURSDAY.
MUNCH
MUNCH
MUNCH
FRIDAY.
MUNCH
MUNCH
SATURDAY.
MUNCH

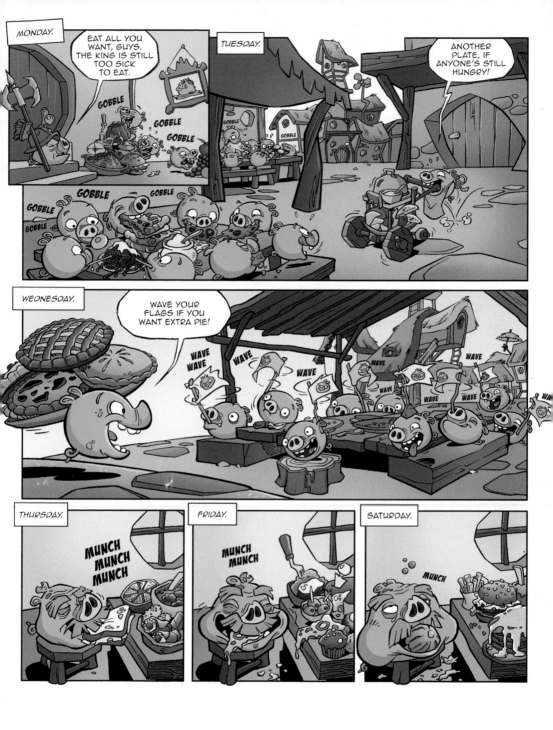

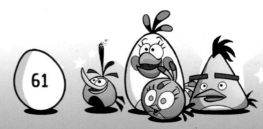

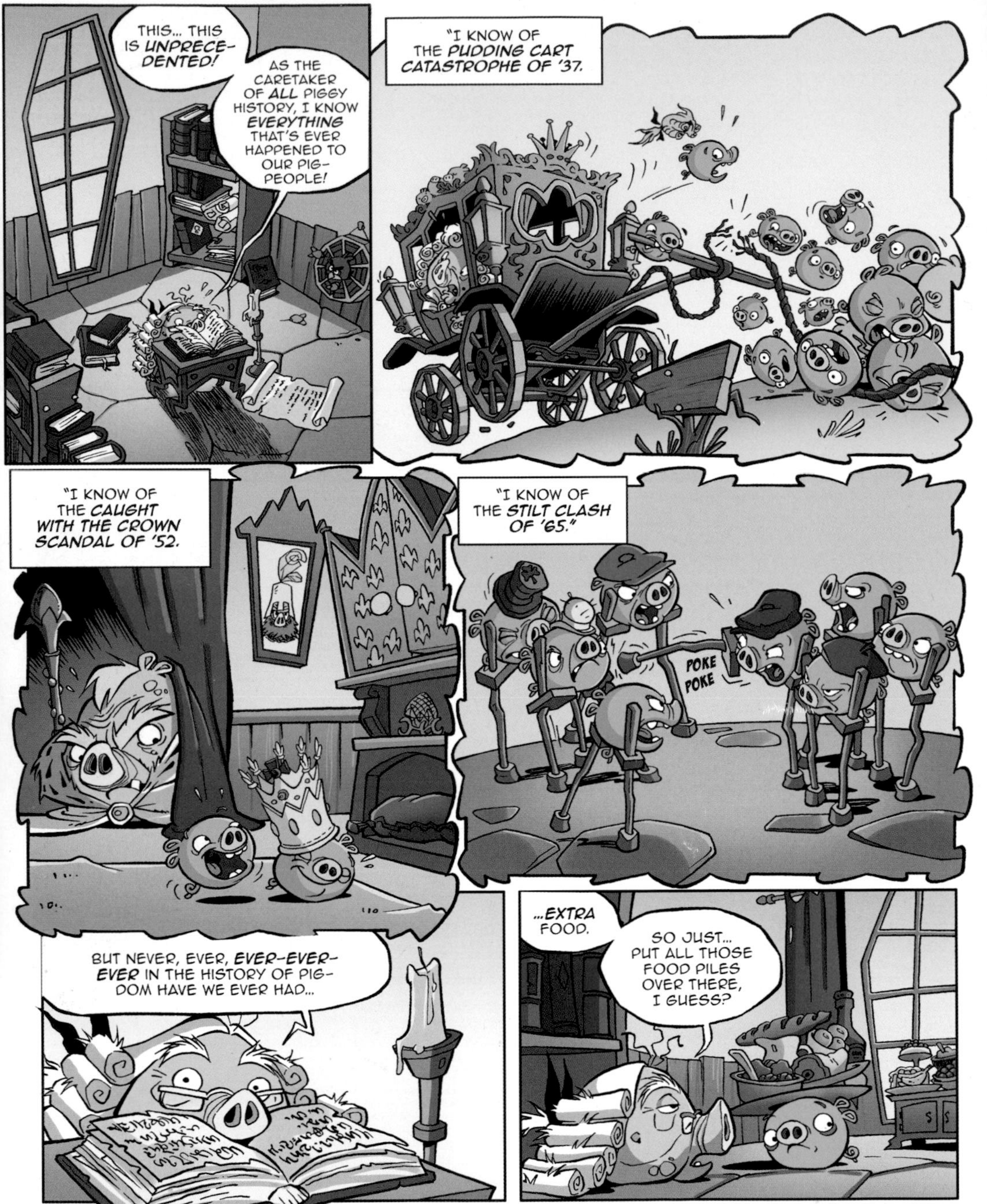
THIS... THIS IS UNPRECE-DENTED!
AS THE CARETAKER OF ALL PIGGY HISTORY, I KNOW EVERYTHING THAT'S EVER HAPPENED TO OUR PIG-PEOPLE!
"I KNOW OF THE PUDDING CART CATASTROPHE OF '37.
"I KNOW OF THE CAUGHT WITH THE CROWN SCANDAL OF '52.
"I KNOW OF THE STILT CLASH OF '65."
POKE POKE
BUT NEVER, EVER, EVER-EVER-EVER IN THE HISTORY OF PIG-DOM HAVE WE EVER HAD...
...EXTRA FOOD.
SO JUST... PUT ALL THOSE FOOD PILES OVER THERE, I GUESS?

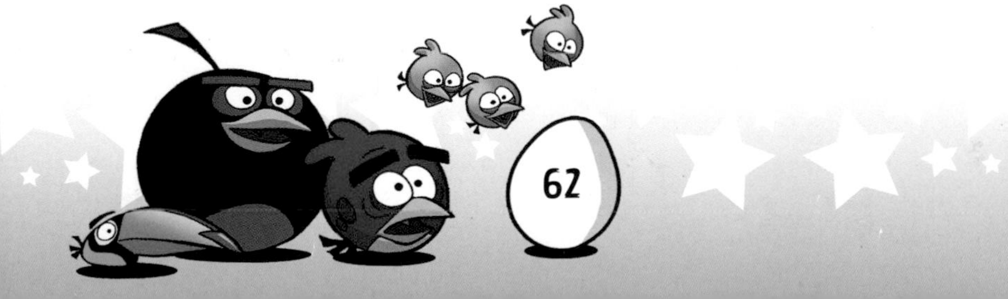

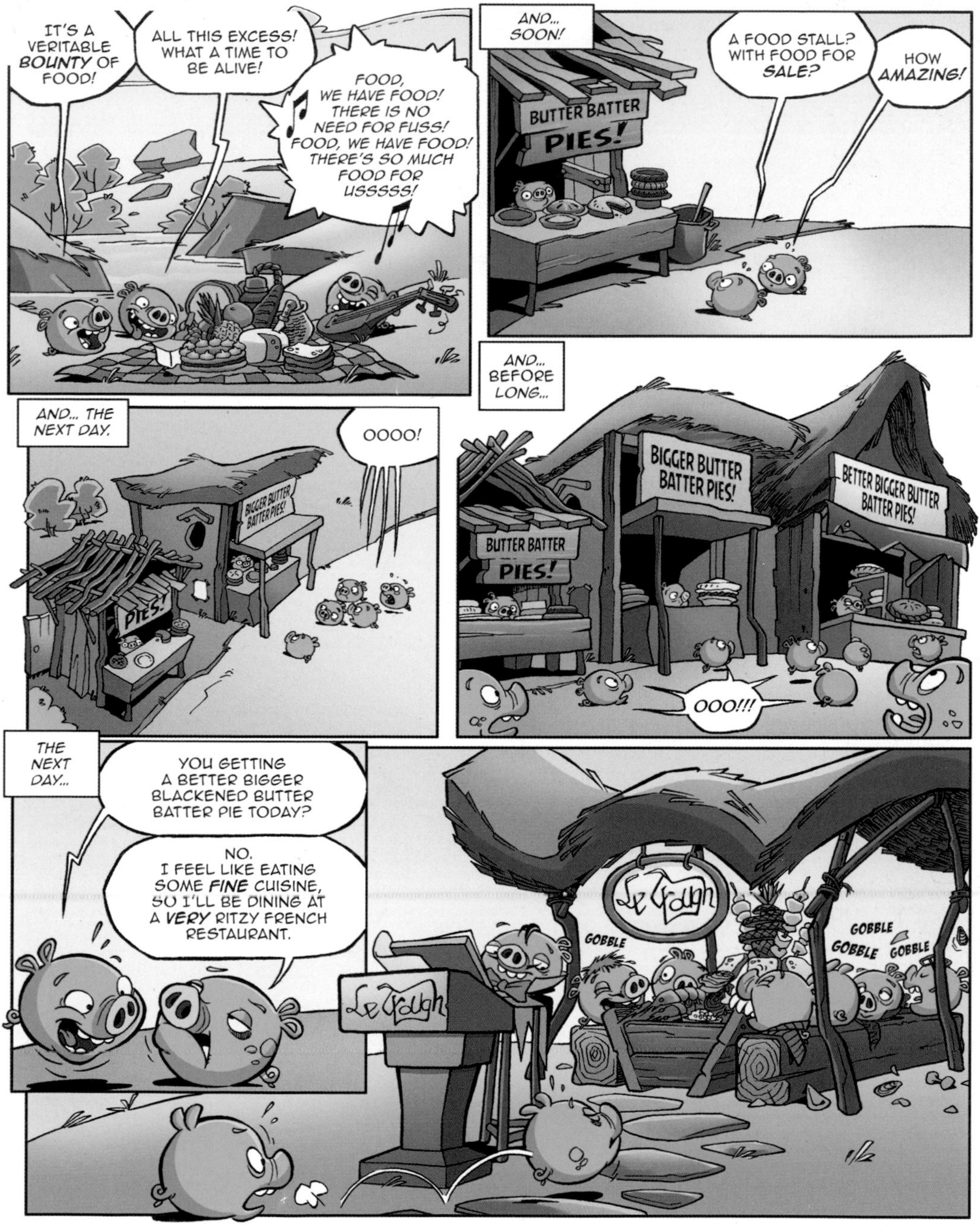
IT'S A VERITABLE BOUNTY OF FOOD!
ALL THIS EXCESS! WHAT A TIME TO BE ALIVE!
FOOD, WE HAVE FOOD! THERE IS NO NEED FOR FUSS! FOOD, WE HAVE FOOD! THERE'S SO MUCH FOOD FOR USSSSS!
AND... SOON!
BUTTER BATTER PIES!
A FOOD STALL? WITH FOOD FOR SALE?
HOW AMAZING!
AND... THE NEXT DAY.
BIGGER BUTTER BATTER PIES!
PIES!
OOOO!
AND... BEFORE LONG...
BUTTER BATTER PIES!
BIGGER BUTTER BATTER PIES!
BETTER BIGGER BUTTER BATTER PIES!
OOO!!!
THE NEXT DAY...
YOU GETTING A BETTER BIGGER BLACKENED BUTTER BATTER PIE TODAY?
NO. I FEEL LIKE EATING SOME FINE CUISINE, SO I'LL BE DINING AT A VERY RITZY FRENCH RESTAURANT.
Le Trough
Le Trough
GOBBLE
GOBBLE
GOBBLE
GOBBLE

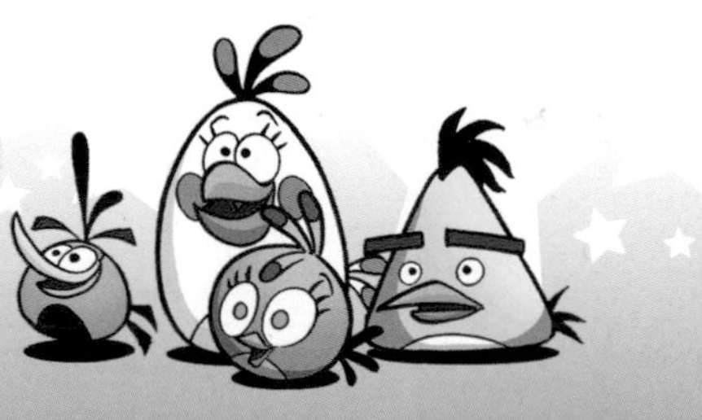

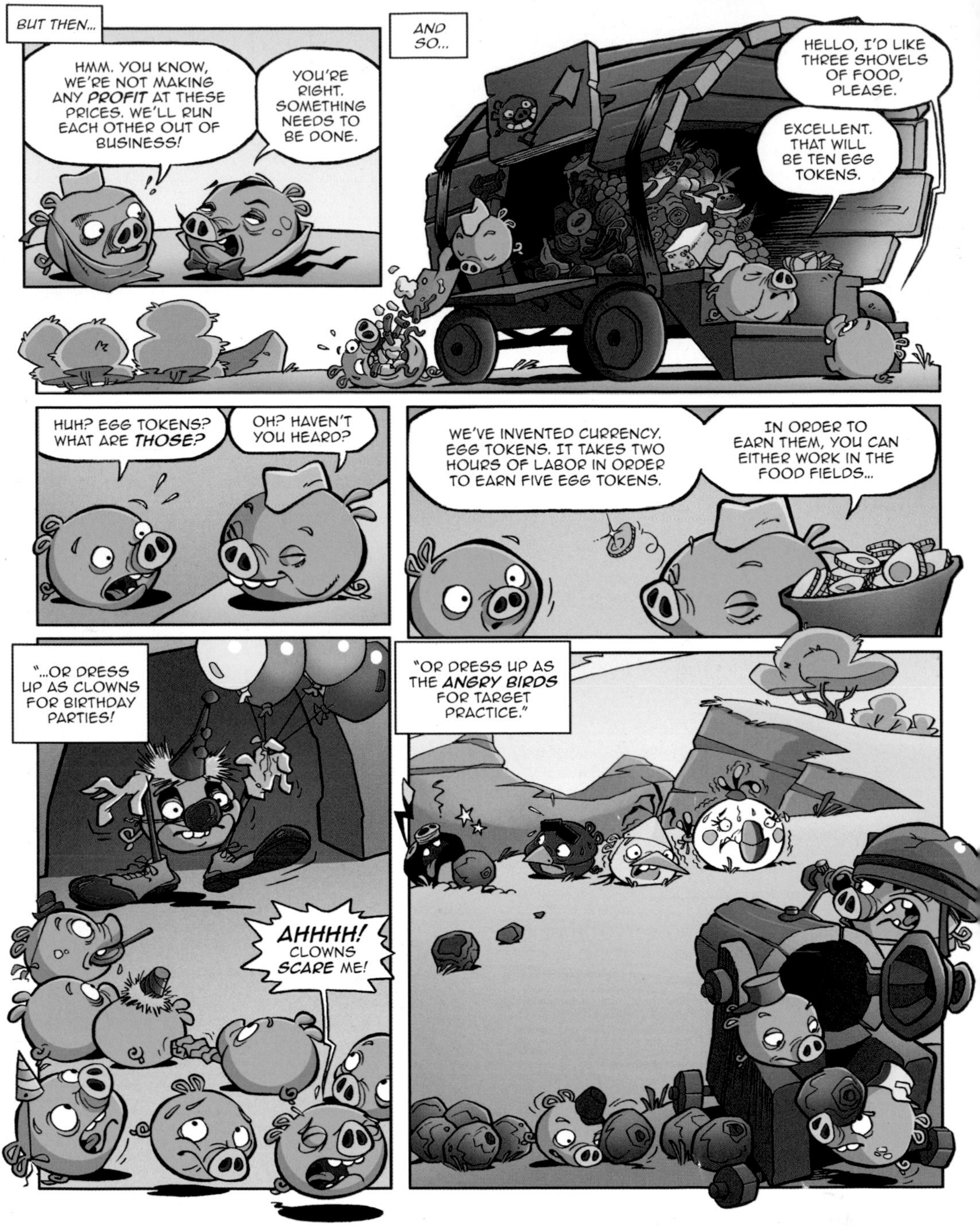

BUT THEN...
HMM. YOU KNOW, WE'RE NOT MAKING ANY PROFIT AT THESE PRICES. WE'LL RUN EACH OTHER OUT OF BUSINESS!
YOU'RE RIGHT. SOMETHING NEEDS TO BE DONE.
AND SO...
HELLO, I'D LIKE THREE SHOVELS OF FOOD, PLEASE.
EXCELLENT. THAT WILL BE TEN EGG TOKENS.
HUH? EGG TOKENS? WHAT ARE THOSE?
OH? HAVEN'T YOU HEARD?
WE'VE INVENTED CURRENCY. EGG TOKENS. IT TAKES TWO HOURS OF LABOR IN ORDER TO EARN FIVE EGG TOKENS.
IN ORDER TO EARN THEM, YOU CAN EITHER WORK IN THE FOOD FIELDS...
"...OR DRESS UP AS CLOWNS FOR BIRTHDAY PARTIES!
AHHHH! CLOWNS SCARE ME!
"OR DRESS UP AS THE ANGRY BIRDS FOR TARGET PRACTICE."

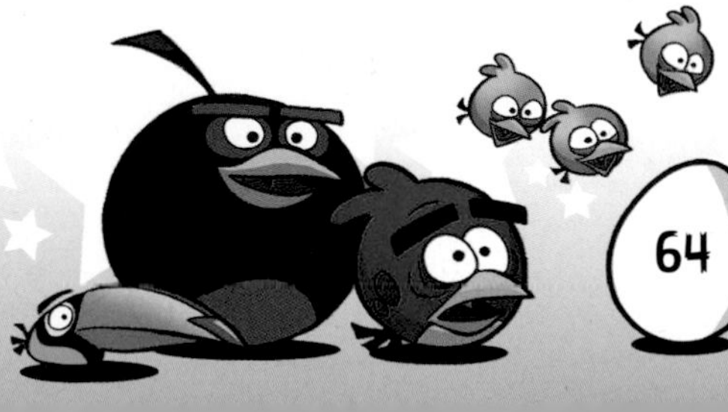

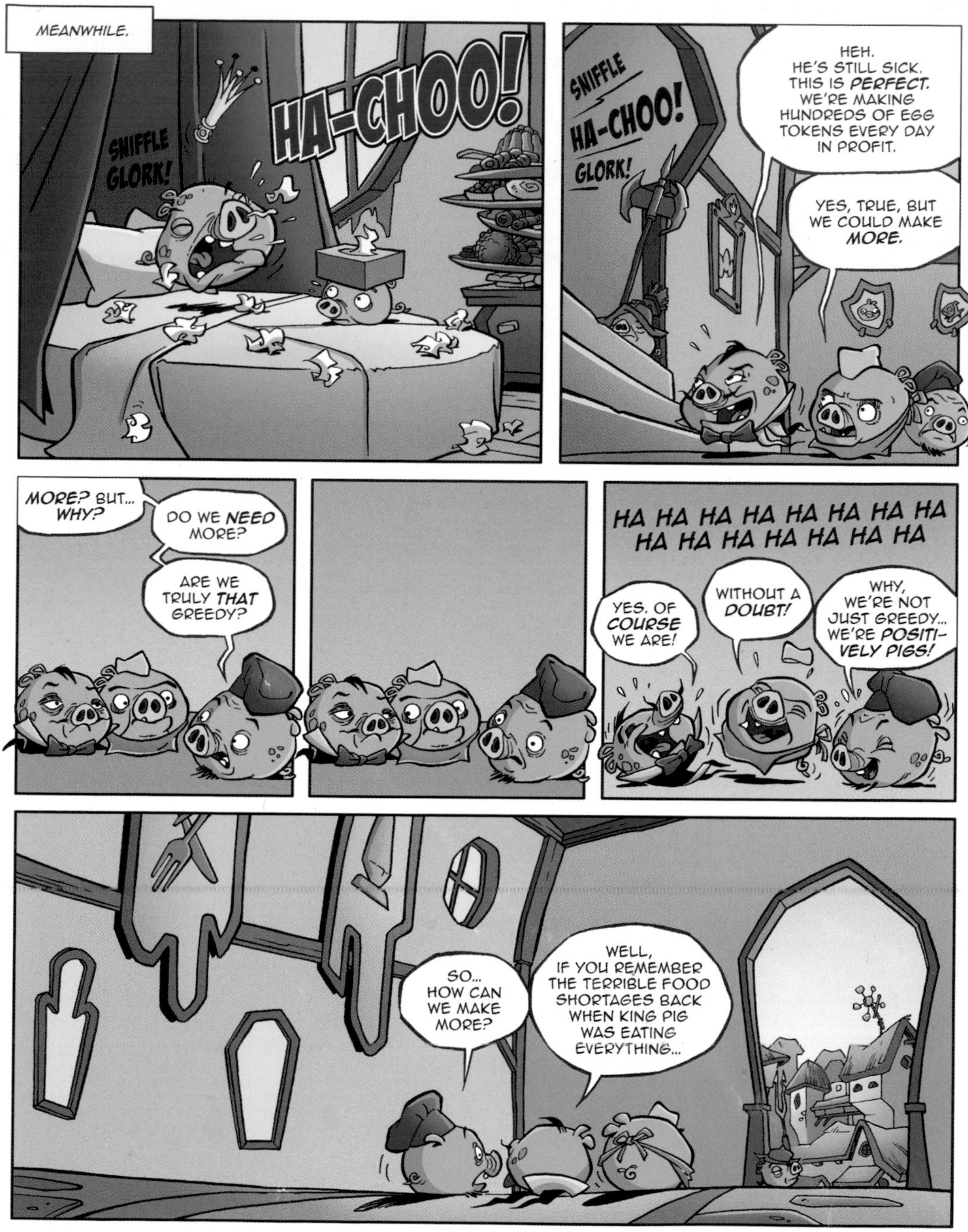
MEANWHILE.
SNIFFLE
GLORK!
HA-CHOO!
SNIFFLE
HA-CHOO!
GLORK!
HEH. HE'S STILL SICK. THIS IS PERFECT. WE'RE MAKING HUNDREDS OF EGG TOKENS EVERY DAY IN PROFIT.
YES, TRUE, BUT WE COULD MAKE MORE.
MORE? BUT... WHY?
DO WE NEED MORE?
ARE WE TRULY THAT GREEDY?
HA HA HA HA HA HA HA HA HA HA HA HA HA HA HA HA
YES. OF COURSE WE ARE!
WITHOUT A DOUBT!
WHY, WE'RE NOT JUST GREEDY... WE'RE POSITI-VELY PIGS!
SO... HOW CAN WE MAKE MORE?
WELL, IF YOU REMEMBER THE TERRIBLE FOOD SHORTAGES BACK WHEN KING PIG WAS EATING EVERYTHING...

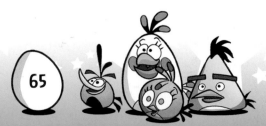

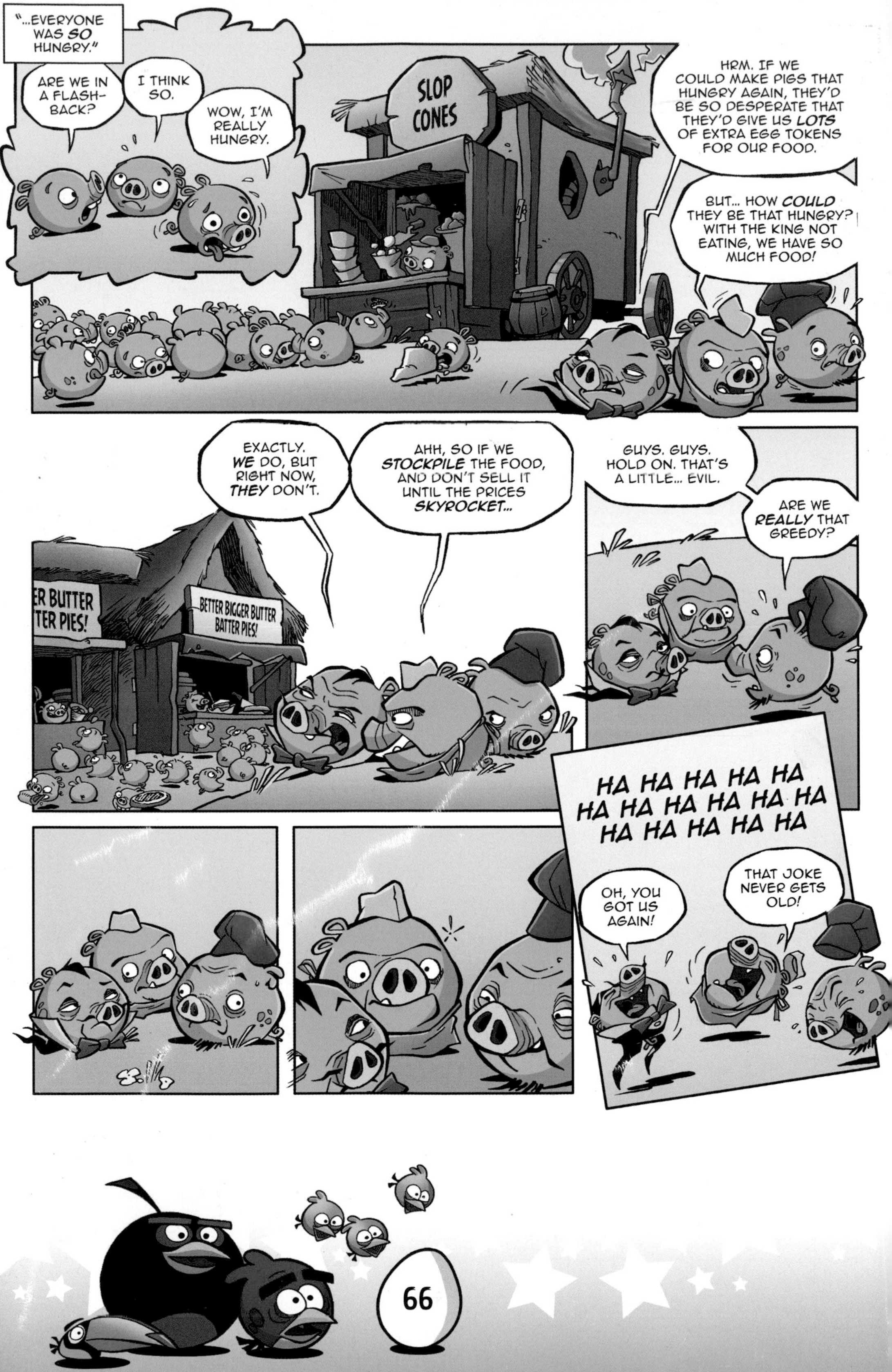
"...EVERYONE WAS SO HUNGRY."
ARE WE IN A FLASH-BACK?
I THINK SO.
WOW, I'M REALLY HUNGRY.
SLOP CONES
HRM. IF WE COULD MAKE PIGS THAT HUNGRY AGAIN, THEY'D BE SO DESPERATE THAT THEY'D GIVE US LOTS OF EXTRA EGG TOKENS FOR OUR FOOD.
BUT... HOW COULD THEY BE THAT HUNGRY? WITH THE KING NOT EATING, WE HAVE SO MUCH FOOD!
EXACTLY. WE DO, BUT RIGHT NOW, THEY DON'T.
AHH, SO IF WE STOCKPILE THE FOOD, AND DON'T SELL IT UNTIL THE PRICES SKYROCKET...
BETTER BIGGER BUTTER BATTER PIES!
GUYS. GUYS. HOLD ON. THAT'S A LITTLE... EVIL.
ARE WE REALLY THAT GREEDY?
HA HA HA HA HA HA HA HA HA HA HA HA HA HA HA HA
OH, YOU GOT US AGAIN!
THAT JOKE NEVER GETS OLD!

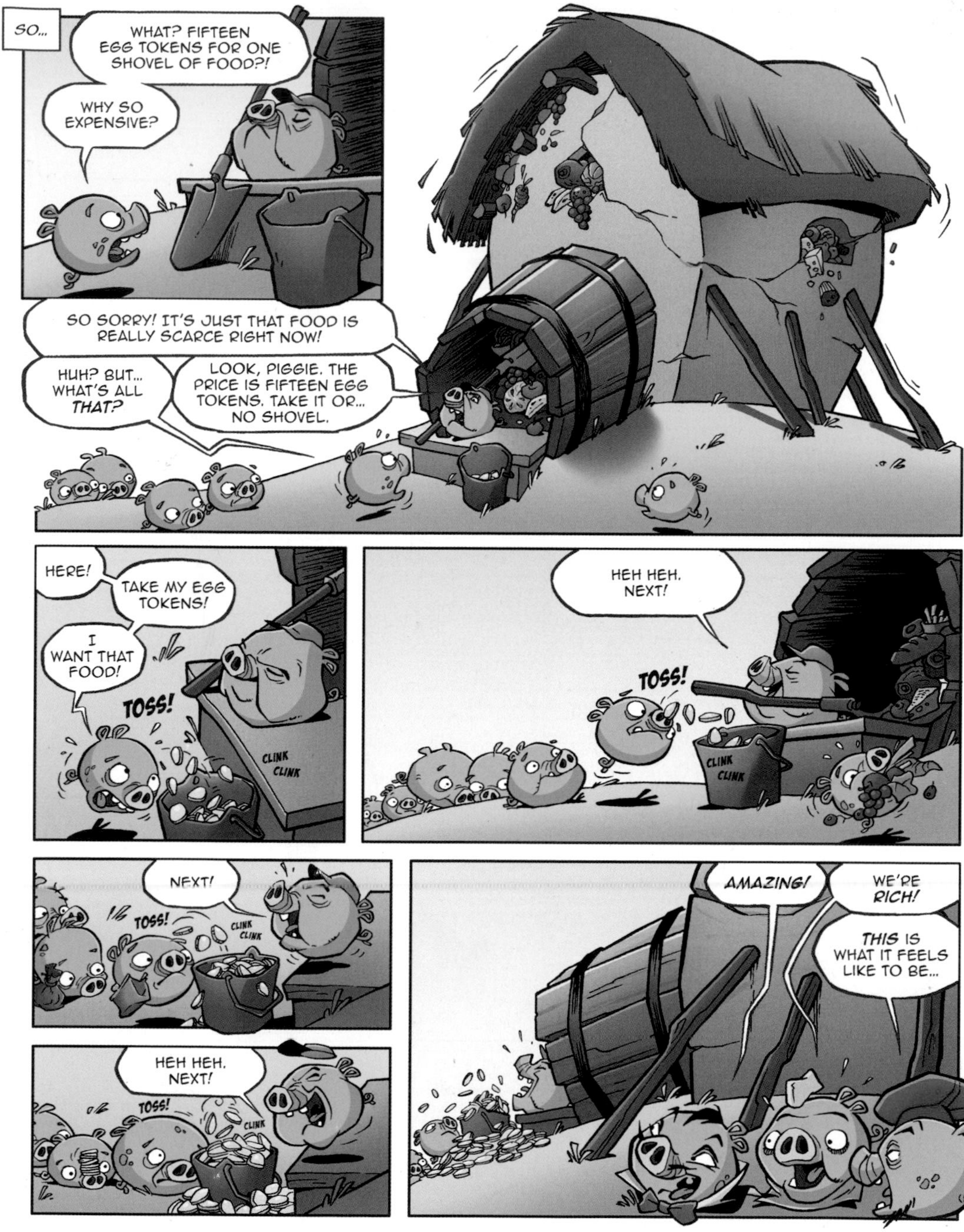
SO...
WHAT? FIFTEEN EGG TOKENS FOR ONE SHOVEL OF FOOD?!
WHY SO EXPENSIVE?
SO SORRY! IT'S JUST THAT FOOD IS REALLY SCARCE RIGHT NOW!
HUH? BUT... WHAT'S ALL *THAT?*
LOOK, PIGGIE. THE PRICE IS FIFTEEN EGG TOKENS. TAKE IT OR... NO SHOVEL.
HERE!
TAKE MY EGG TOKENS!
I WANT THAT FOOD!
TOSS!
CLINK CLINK
HEH HEH. NEXT!
TOSS!
CLINK CLINK
NEXT!
TOSS!
CLINK CLINK
HEH HEH. NEXT!
TOSS!
CLINK
AMAZING!
WE'RE *RICH!*
THIS IS WHAT IT FEELS LIKE TO BE...

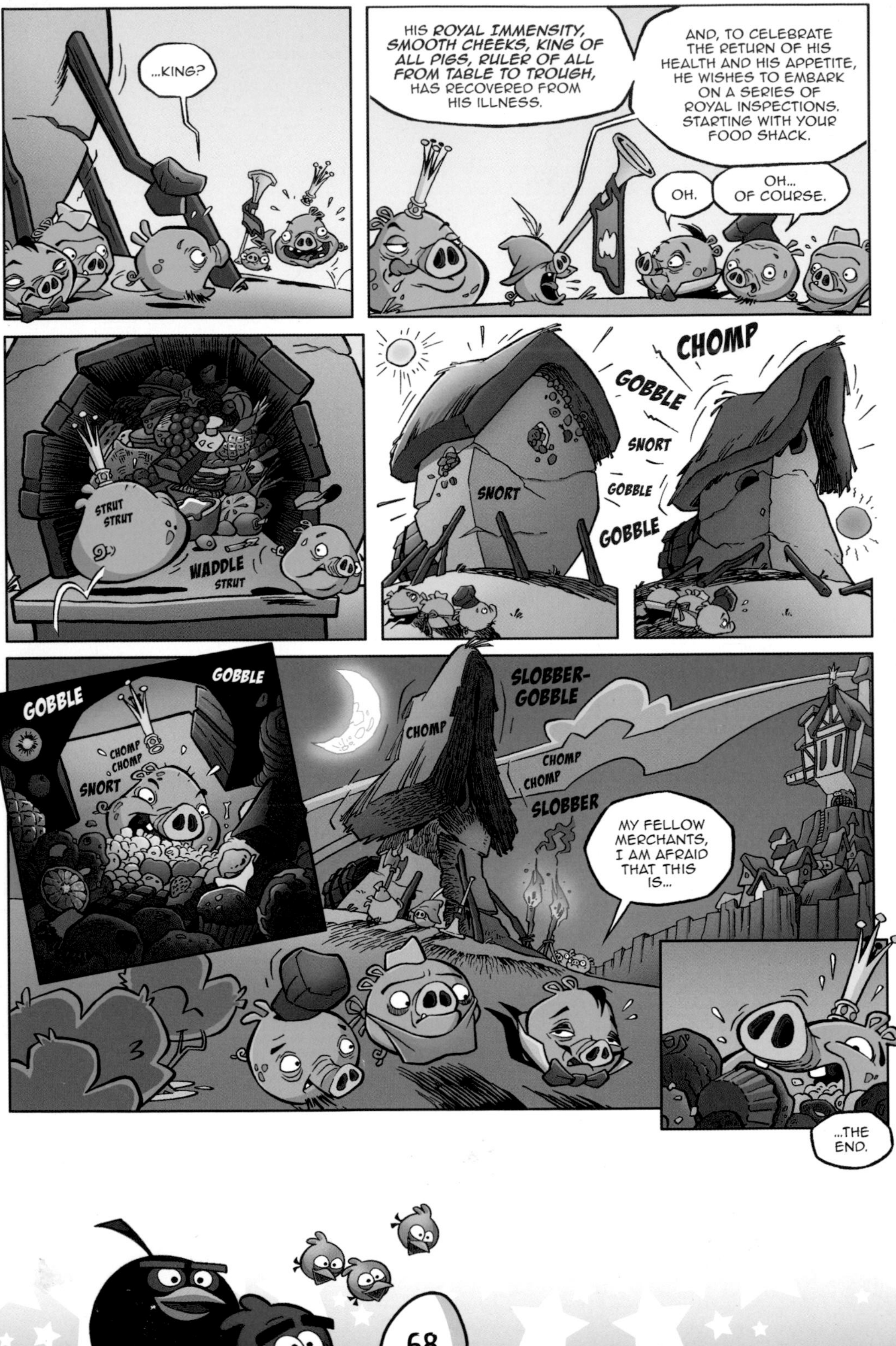
...KING?
HIS ROYAL IMMENSITY, SMOOTH CHEEKS, KING OF ALL PIGS, RULER OF ALL FROM TABLE TO TROUGH, HAS RECOVERED FROM HIS ILLNESS.
AND, TO CELEBRATE THE RETURN OF HIS HEALTH AND HIS APPETITE, HE WISHES TO EMBARK ON A SERIES OF ROYAL INSPECTIONS. STARTING WITH YOUR FOOD SHACK.
OH.
OH... OF COURSE.
STRUT
STRUT
WADDLE
STRUT
SNORT
CHOMP
GOBBLE
SNORT
GOBBLE
GOBBLE
GOBBLE
GOBBLE
CHOMP
CHOMP
SNORT
CHOMP
SLOBBER-GOBBLE
CHOMP
CHOMP
SLOBBER
MY FELLOW MERCHANTS, I AM AFRAID THAT THIS IS...
...THE END.

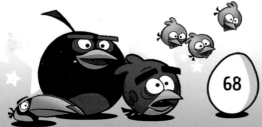

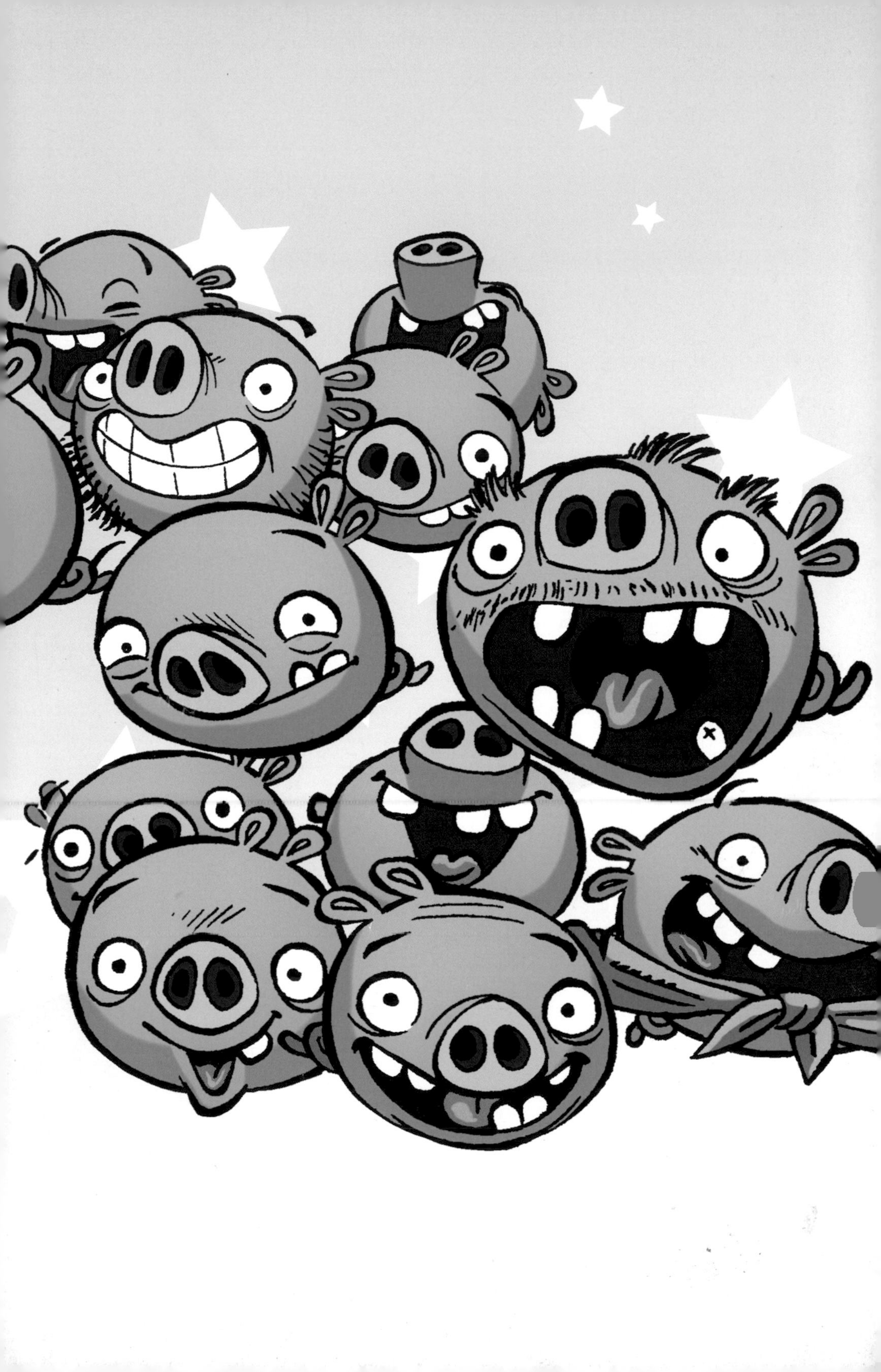

ARTWORK BY CIRO CANGIALOSI

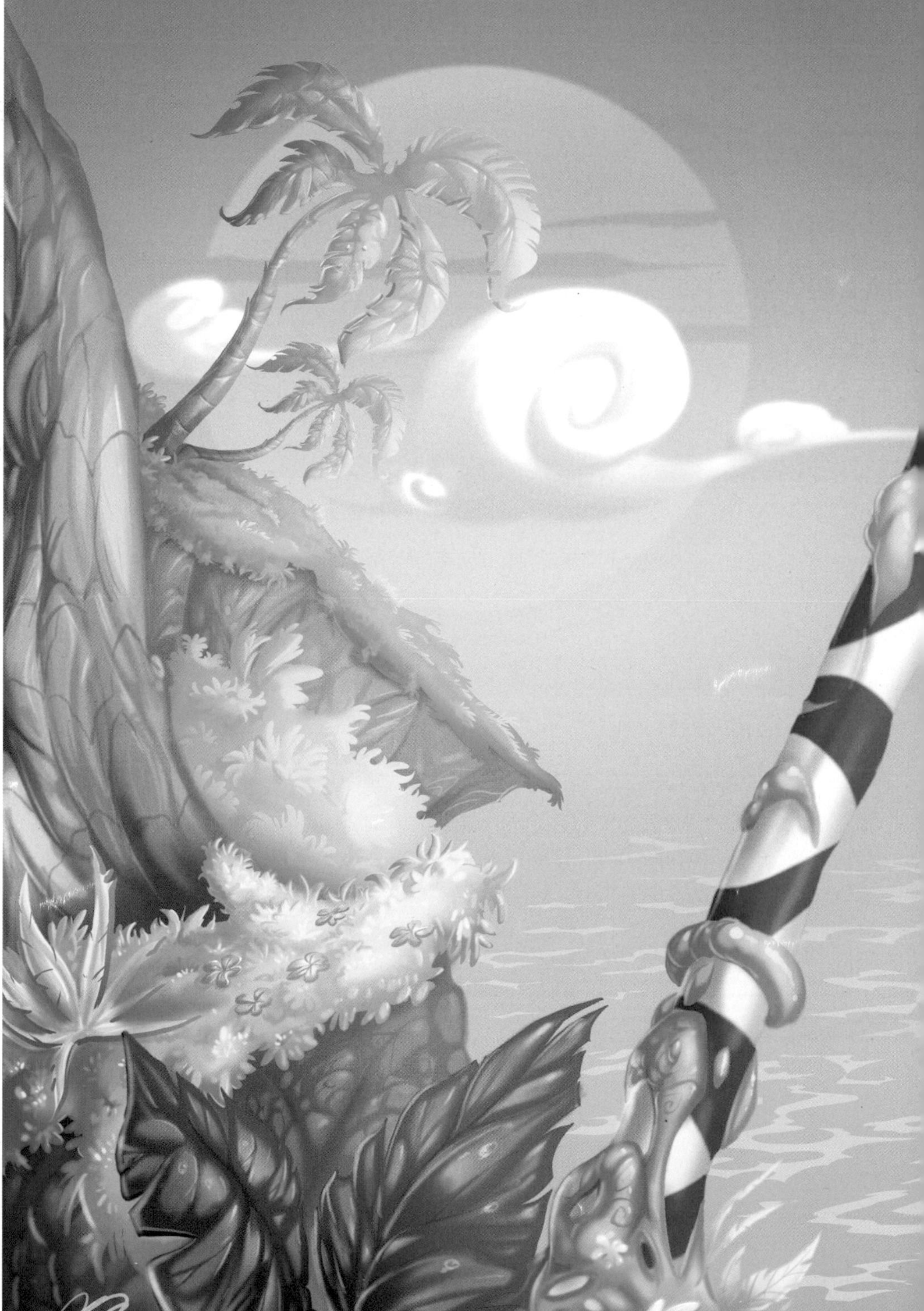

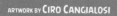

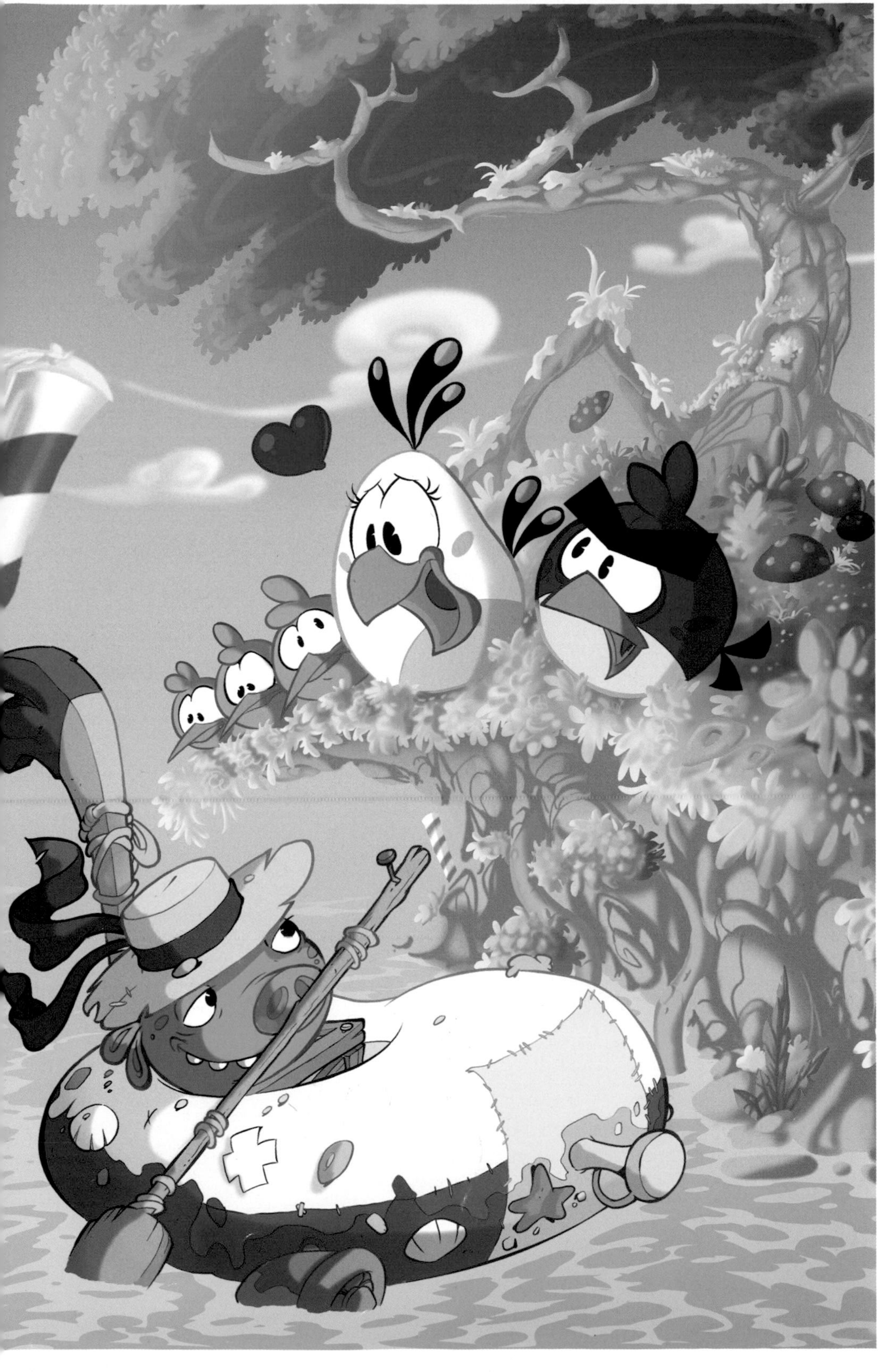

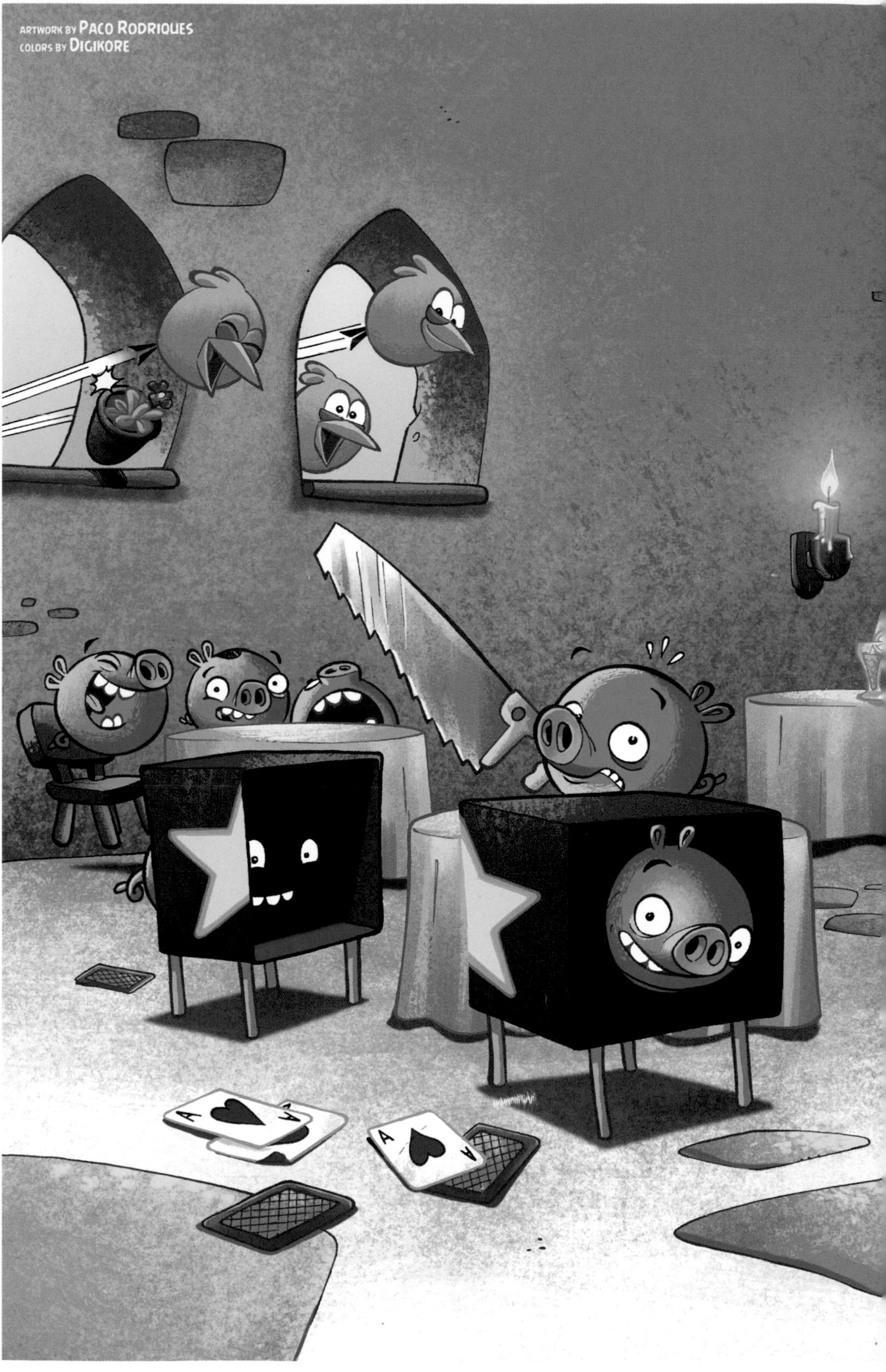
ARTWORK BY PACO RODRIQUES
COLORS BY DIGIKORE

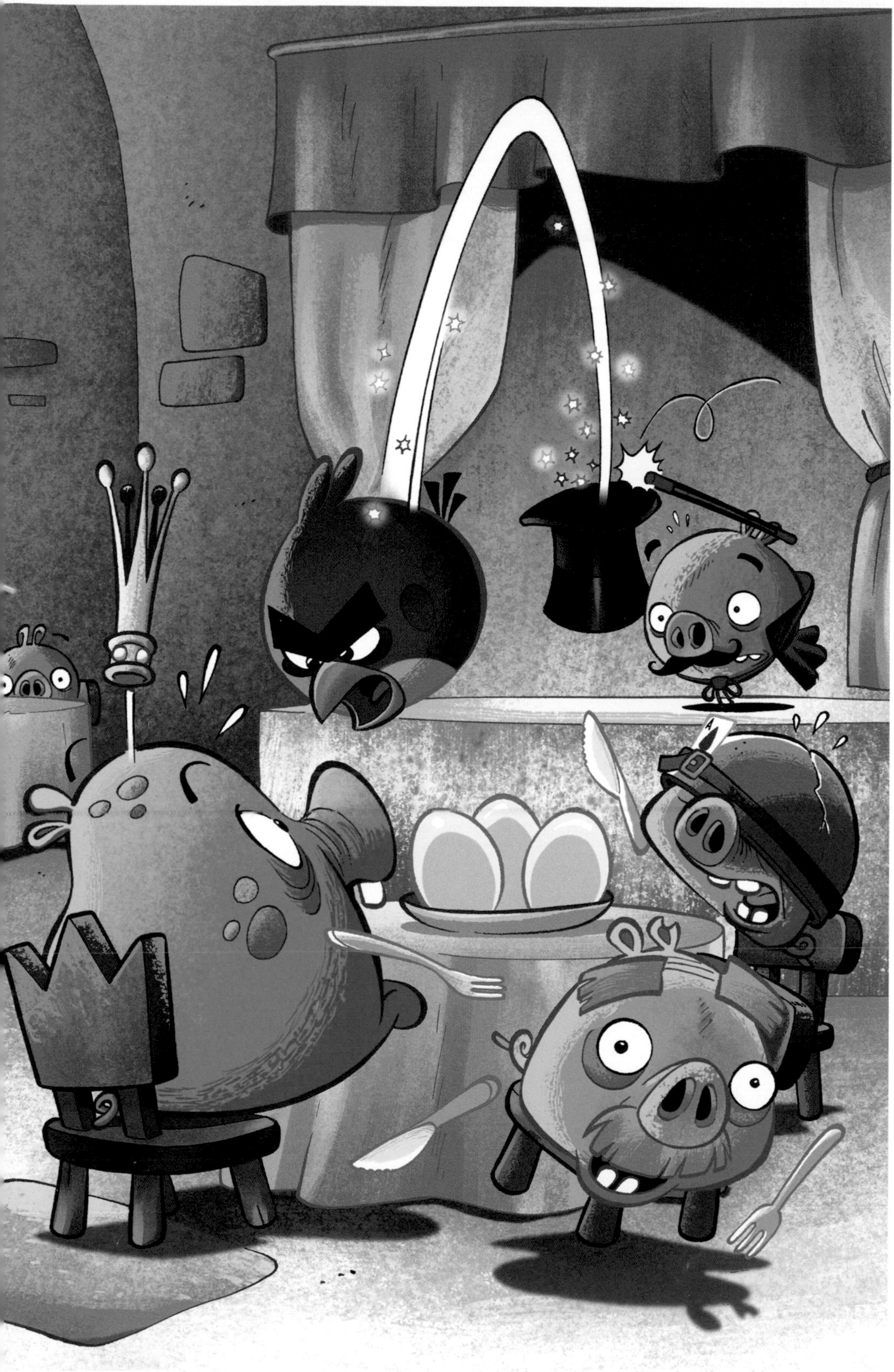

ARTWORK BY CIRO CANGIALOSI

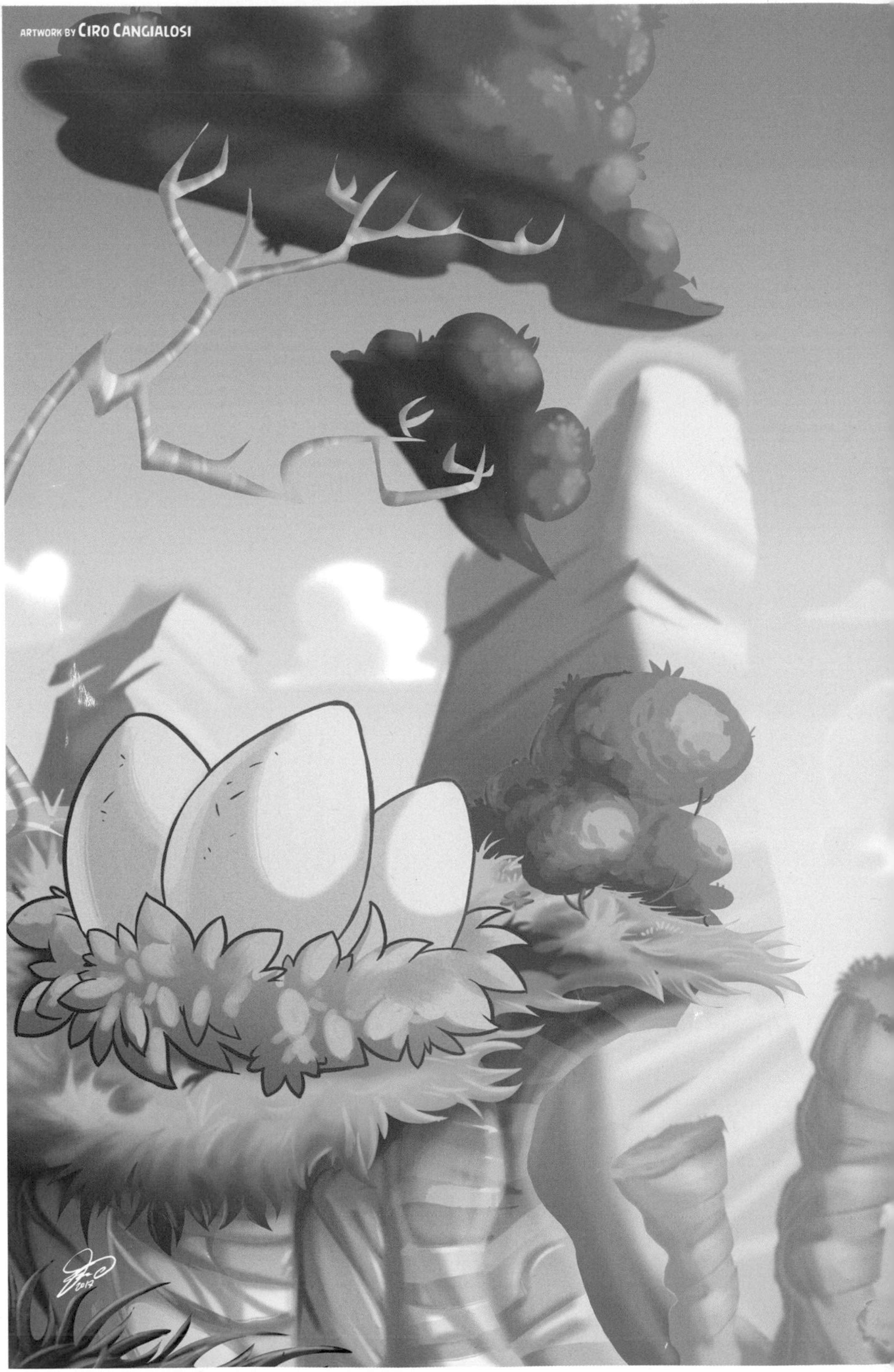

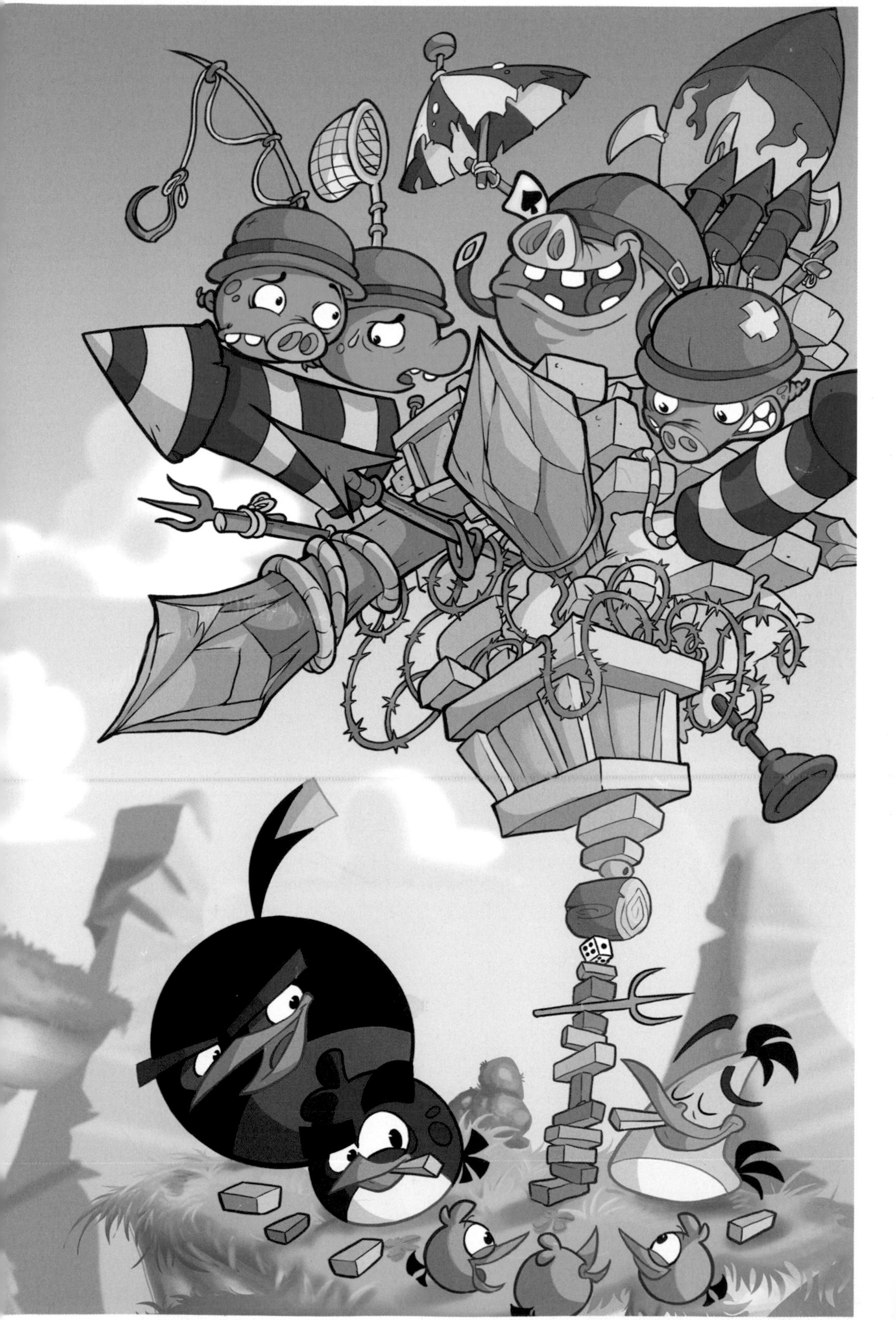

ARTWORK BY CIRO CANGIALOSI

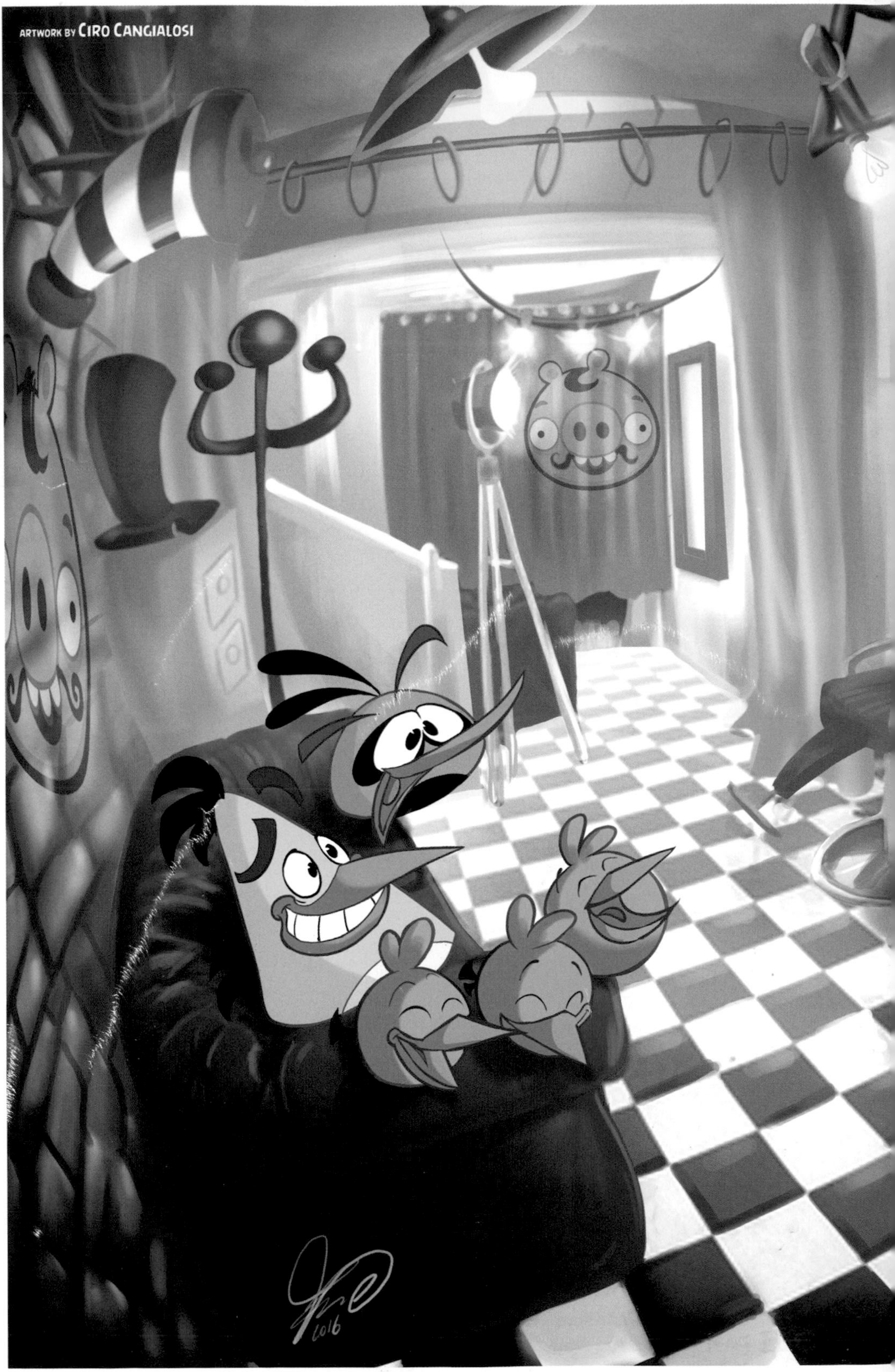

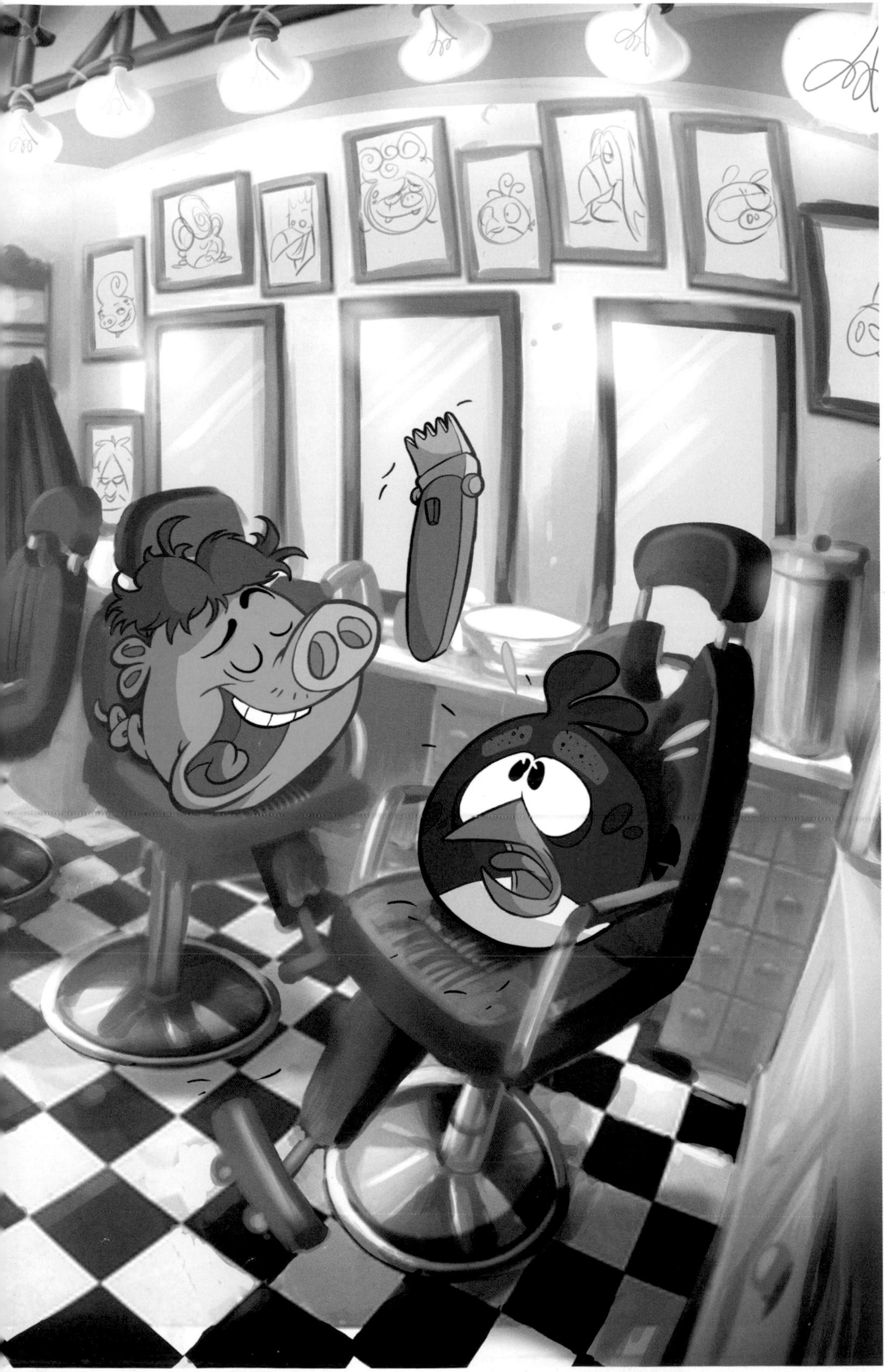

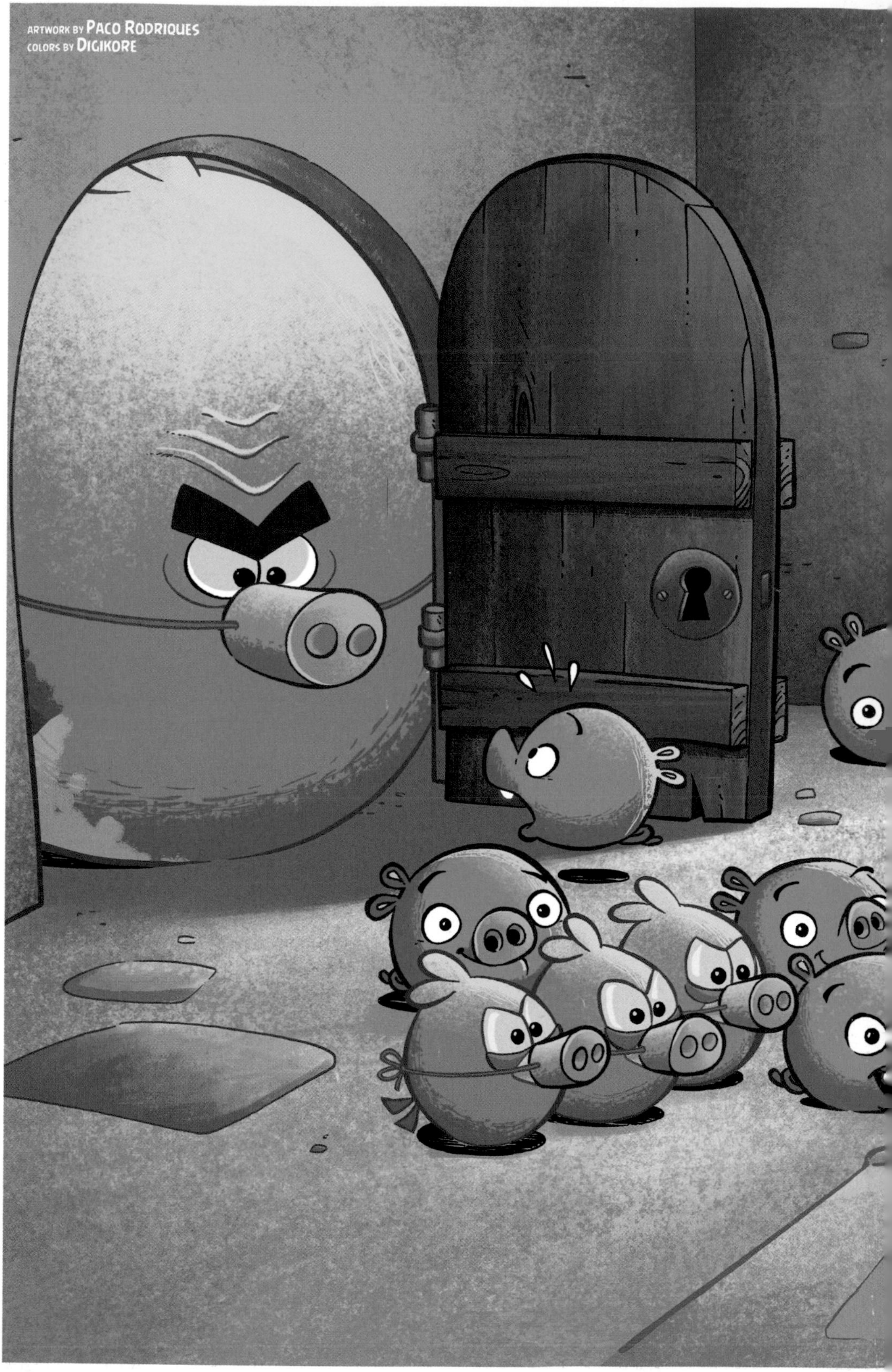
ARTWORK BY PACO RODRIQUES
COLORS BY DIGIKORE

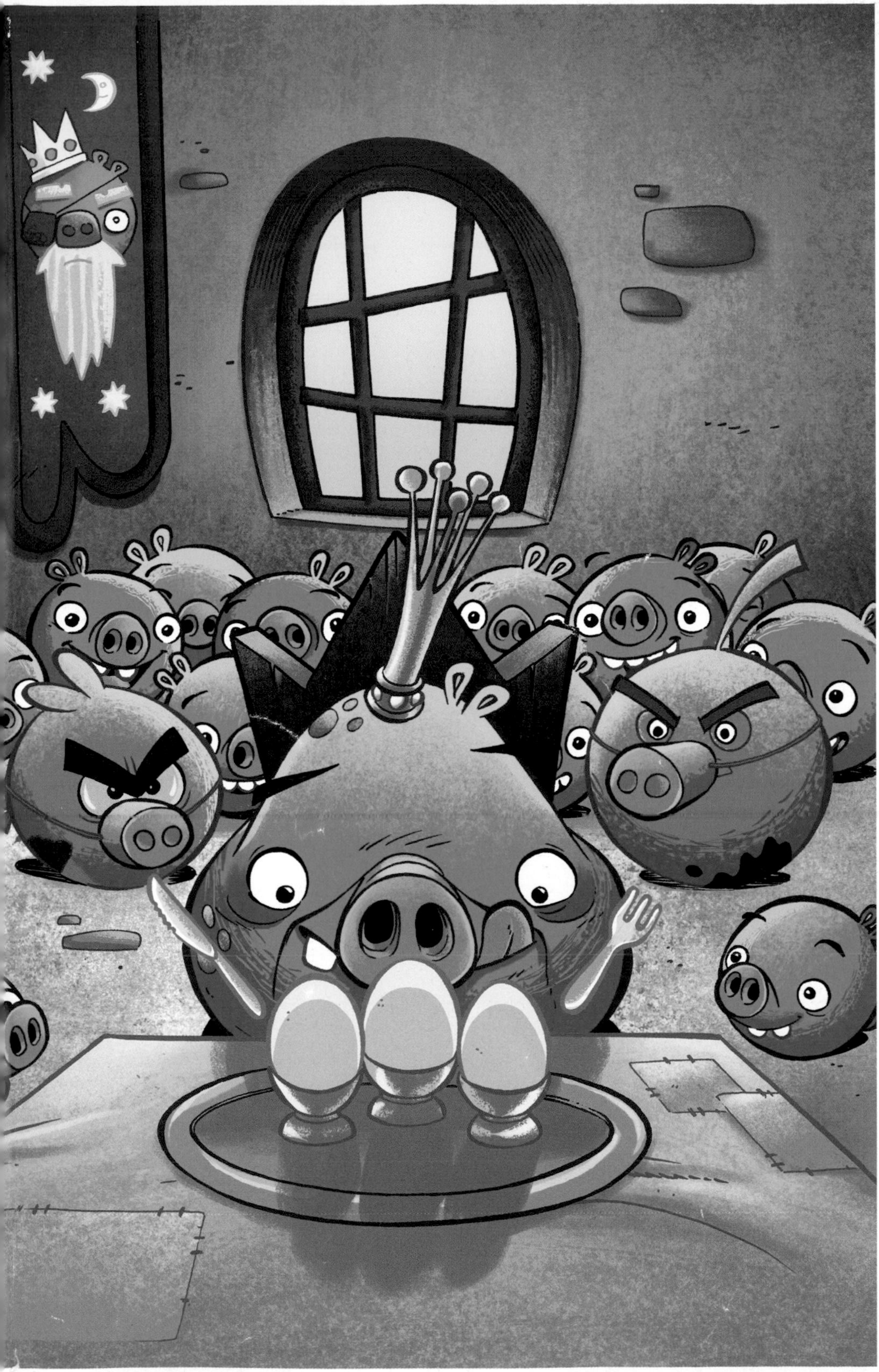

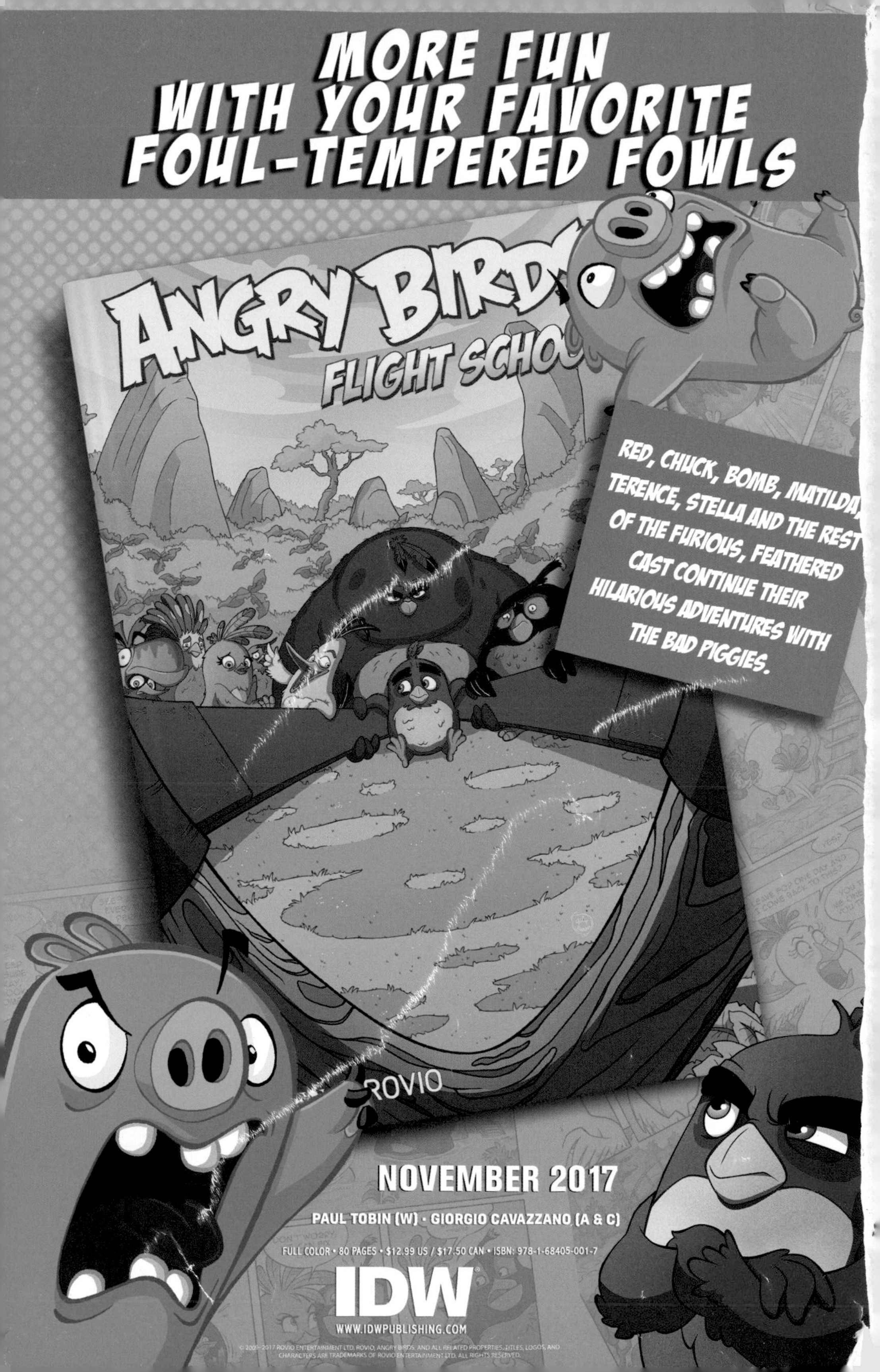
MORE FUN
WITH YOUR FAVORITE
FOUL-TEMPERED FOWLS
ANGRY BIRDS
FLIGHT SCHOOL
ROVIO
RED, CHUCK, BOMB, MATILDA, TERENCE, STELLA AND THE REST OF THE FURIOUS, FEATHERED CAST CONTINUE THEIR HILARIOUS ADVENTURES WITH THE BAD PIGGIES.
NOVEMBER 2017
PAUL TOBIN (W) · GIORGIO CAVAZZANO (A & C)
FULL COLOR • 80 PAGES • $12.99 US / $17.50 CAN • ISBN: 978-1-68405-001-7
IDW
WWW.IDWPUBLISHING.COM
© 2009–2017 ROVIO ENTERTAINMENT LTD. ROVIO, ANGRY BIRDS, AND ALL RELATED PROPERTIES, TITLES, LOGOS, AND CHARACTERS ARE TRADEMARKS OF ROVIO ENTERTAINMENT LTD. ALL RIGHTS RESERVED.